Tarl Cabot, sometime Assistant Professor of History at a small American college, once again finds himself transported to Counter-Earth, the planet Gor, from which he was snatched at the whim of the Priest Kings. He welcomes this return to the planet and to the woman he has grown to love and falls easily into his role of proud Warrior.

But he finds he can no longer be proud. His name, and the name of his City, and the names of all those he loved, have become anathema on Gor. He is an outcast and an outlaw.

Yet he knows the Priest Kings have not idly brought him back. What sinister purpose have they in mind this time?

By John Norman

THE CHRONICLES
OF COUNTER-EARTH

TARNSMAN OF GOR

OUTLAW OF GOR

PRIEST-KINGS OF GOR

NOMADS OF GOR

ASSASSIN OF GOR

RAIDERS OF GOR

CAPTIVE OF GOR

Available from Ballantine Books

This is an original publication—not a reprint.

OUTLAW
OF GOR

John Norman

BALLANTINE BOOKS • NEW YORK

SBN 345-22486-8-095

First U.S. Printing: December, 1967
Second U.S. Printing: January, 1970
Third U.S. Printing: December, 1971
Fourth U.S. Printing: December, 1972
Fifth U.S. Printing: March, 1973
Sixth U.S. Printing: December, 1973

First Canadian Printing: January, 1968
Second Canadian Printing: January, 1973

Printed in the United States of America

Cover Painting: Robert Foster

BALLANTINE BOOKS, INC.
201 East 50th Street, New York, N.Y. 10022

CONTENTS

	A Note on the Manuscript	vii
1	The Statement of Harrison Smith	9
2	Return to Gor	19
3	Zosk	25
4	The Sleen	33
5	The Valley of Ko-ro-ba	39
6	Vera	47
7	Thorn, Captain of Tharna	59
8	The City of Tharna	65
9	The Kal-Da Shop	73
10	The Palace of the Tatrix	83
11	Lara, Tatrix of Tharna	89
12	Andreas of the Caste of Poets	101
13	The Amusements of Tharna	109
14	The Black Tarn	117
15	A Bargain is Struck	129
16	The Pillar of Exchanges	141
17	The Mines of Tharna	147
18	We Are of the Same Chain	155
19	Revolt in the Mines	165
20	The Invisible Barrier	175
21	I Buy a Girl	185
22	Yellow Cords	199
23	Return to Tharna	211
24	The Barricade	223
25	The Roof of the Palace	237
26	A Letter from Tarl Cabot	245
	A Concluding Note on the Manuscript	255

A NOTE ON THE MANUSCRIPT

MY FRIEND, HARRISON SMITH, A young lawyer of the city, has recently given me a second manuscript, purportedly by the individual Tarl Cabot. It was his desire that I bring this second document, as I did the first, to the attention of a publisher. This time, however, because of the numerous claims and inquiries generated by the first manuscript *Tarnsman of Gor* (pertaining to various matters ranging from further alleged documentation for the existence of the Counter-Earth to disputes concerning the authorship of the manuscript), I have prevailed upon Smith to write something in the way of a preface to this second account, making clear his own role in these matters and telling us a bit more about Tarl Cabot, whom I have never had the good fortune to meet in person.

John Norman

1

THE STATEMENT OF
HARRISON SMITH

I FIRST MET TARL CABOT at a small liberal arts college in New Hampshire, where we had both accepted first year teaching appointments. He was an instructor in English history and I, intending to work for some three years to save money toward law school, had accepted an appointment as an instructor in physical education, a field which, to my annoyance, Cabot never convinced himself belonged in the curriculum of an educational institution.

We hiked a good deal, talked and fenced, and, I hoped, had become friends. I liked the young, gentle Englishman. He was quiet and pleasant, though sometimes he seemed remote, or lonely, somehow unwilling to break through that protective shield of formality behind which the educated Englishman, at heart perhaps as sentimental and hot-blooded as any man, attempts to conceal his feelings.

Young Cabot was rather tall, a good-sized man, well-built, with an animal ease in his walk that perhaps bespoke the docks of Bristol, his native city, rather than the cloisters of Oxford, at one of whose colleges he had obtained his later education. His eyes were clear, and blue, direct and honest. He was fairly complected. His hair, lamentably perhaps, though some of us loved him for it, was red, but not merely red—it was rather a tangled, blazing affront to the proprieties of the well-groomed academician. I doubt that he owned a comb, and I would be willing to swear that he would not have used one if he had. All in all, Tarl Cabot seemed to us a young, quiet, courteous Oxford gentleman, except for that hair. And then we weren't sure.

To my consternation and that of the college, Cabot disappeared shortly after the conclusion of the first semester. I am sure that this was not of his own intention. Cabot is a man who honors his commitments.

At the end of the semester, Cabot, like the rest of us, was weary of the academic routine, and was seeking some diversion. He decided to go camping—by himself—in the nearby White Mountains, which were very beautiful then, in the white, brittle splendor of a New Hampshire February.

I loaned him some of my camping gear and drove him into the mountains, dropping him off beside the highway. He asked me, and I am certain he was serious, to meet him at the same place in three days. I returned at the determined time, but he failed to keep the rendezvous. I waited several hours, and then returned at the same time the next day. Still he did not appear. Accordingly, then alarmed, I notified the authorities, and, by afternoon, a large-scale search was underway.

Eventually we found what we supposed to be the ashes of his fire, near a large flat rock some nine hours' climb from the highway. Our search, otherwise, was fruitless. Yet, several months later, I understand that Tarl Cabot stumbled out of these same mountains, alive and well, but apparently under the stress of some emotional shock which had culminated in amnesia—at least for that period during which he had been missing.

He never returned to teach at the college, to the relief of several of my elder colleagues who now confessed that they had thought that young Cabot had never really fitted in. Shortly thereafter I determined that I did not fit in either, and left the college. I did receive a check from Cabot to cover the cost of my camping equipment, which he had apparently lost. It was a thoughtful gesture but I wish instead that he had stopped to see me. I would have seized his hand and forced him to speak to me, to tell me what had happened.

Somehow, unlike my colleagues at the school, I had found the amnesia account too simple. It was not an adequate explanation; it couldn't be. How had he lived for those months, where had he been, what had he done?

It was almost seven years after I had known Tarl Cabot at the college when I saw him on the streets of Manhattan. By that time I had long ago saved the money I needed for law school and had not taught for three years. Indeed, I was then completing my studies at the school of law associated with one of New York's best known private universities.

He had changed very little, if at all. I rushed over to him and without thinking seized him by the shoulder. What happened next seemed almost too unbelievable to comprehend. He spun like a tiger with a sudden cry of rage in some strange tongue and I found myself seized in hands like steel and with great force hurled helplessly across his knee, my spine an inch from being splintered like kindling wood.

In an instant he released me, apologizing profusely even before recognizing me. In horror I realized that what he had done had been as much a reflex as the blinking of an eye or the jerking of a knee under a physician's hammer. It was the reflex of an animal whose instinct it is to destroy before it can be destroyed, or of a human being who has been tooled into such an animal, a human being who has been conditioned to kill swiftly, savagely, or be killed in the same fashion. I was covered with sweat. I knew that I had been an instant from death. Was this the gentle Cabot I had known?

"Harrison!" he cried. "Harrison Smith!" He lifted me easily to my feet, his words rapid and stumbling, trying to reassure me. "I'm sorry," he kept saying, "Forgive me! Forgive me, Old Man!"

We looked at one another.

He thrust out his hand impulsively, apologetically. I took it and we shook hands. I'm afraid my grip was a bit weak, and that my hand shook a little. "I'm really frightfully sorry," he said.

There was a knot of people who had gathered, standing a safe distance away on the sidewalk.

He smiled, the old ingenuous boyish smile I remembered from New Hampshire. "Would you like a drink?" he asked.

I smiled, too. "I could use one," I said.

In a small bar in midtown Manhattan, little more than a doorway and a corridor, Tarl Cabot and I renewed our friendship. We talked of dozens of things, but neither of us mentioned his abrupt response to my greeting, nor did we speak of those mysterious months in which he had disappeared in the mountains of New Hampshire.

In the ensuing months, my studies permitting, we saw one another fairly often. I seemed to answer a desperate need for human fellowship in that lonely man, and, for my part, I was more than happy to count myself his friend—unfortunately perhaps, his only friend.

I felt that the time would come when Cabot would speak to me of the mountains but that he himself would have to choose that time. I was not eager to intrude into his affairs, or his secrets as the case might be. It was enough to be once more his friend. I wondered upon occasion why Cabot did not speak to me more openly on certain matters, why he so jealously guarded the mystery of those months in which he had been absent from the college. I now know why he did not speak sooner. He feared I would have thought him mad.

It was late one night, in early February, and we were drinking once more at that small bar in which we had had our first drink that incredible sunny afternoon some months before. Outside there was a light snow falling, soft as colored felt in the lonely neon lights of the street. Cabot watched it, between swallows of Scotch. He seemed to be morose, moody. I recalled it was in February that he had departed from the college, years earlier.

"Perhaps we had better go home," I said.

Cabot continued to stare out the window, watching the neon snow drifting aimlessly down to the gray, trampled sidewalk.

"I love her," said Cabot, not really speaking to me.

"Who?" I asked.

He shook his head, and continued to watch the snow.

"Let's go home," I said. "It's late."

"Where is home?" asked Cabot, staring into the half-filled glass.

"Your apartment, a few blocks from here," I said, wanting him to leave, wanting to get him out of there. His mood was alien to anything I had seen in him before. Somehow I was frightened.

He would not be moved. He pulled his arm away from my hand. "It is late," he said, seeming to agree with me but intending perhaps more. "It must not be too late," he said, as though he had resolved on something, as though by the sheer force of his will he would stop the flow of time, the random track of events.

I leaned back in my chair. Cabot would leave when he was ready. Not before. I became aware of his silence, and the light subdued patter of conversation at the bar, the clink of glasses, the sounds of a foot scraping, of liquid swirling into a small, heavy glass.

Cabot lifted his Scotch again, holding it before him, not drinking. Then, ceremoniously, bitterly, he poured a bit of it out onto the table, where it splattered, partly soaking into a napkin. As he performed this gesture, he uttered some formula in that strange tongue I had heard but once before—when I had nearly perished at his hands. Somehow I had the feeling that he was becoming dangerous. I was uneasy.

"What are you doing?" I asked.

"I am offering a libation," he said. "Ta-Sardar-Gor."

"What does that mean?" I asked, my words fumbling a bit, blurred by the liquor, made unsteady by my fear.

"It means," laughed Cabot, a mirthless laugh, "—to the Priest-Kings of Gor!"

He rose unsteadily. He seemed tall, strange, almost of another world in that subdued light, in that quiet atmosphere of small, genial civilized noises.

Then without warning, with a bitter laugh, at once a

lament and a cry of rage, he hurled the glass violently to the wall. It shattered into a million sporadic gleaming fragments, shocking the place into a moment of supreme silence. And in that sudden instant of startled, awe-struck silence, I heard him clearly, intensely, repeat in a hoarse whisper that strange phrase, "Ta-Sardar-Gor!"

The bartender, a heavy, soft-faced man, waddled to the table. One of his fat hands nervously clutched a short leather truncheon, weighted with shot. The bartender jerked his thumb toward the door. He repeated the gesture. Cabot towering over him seemed not to comprehend. The bartender lifted the truncheon in a menacing gesture. Cabot simply took the weapon, seeming to draw it easily from the startled grip of the fat man. He looked down into the sweating, frightened fat face.

"You have lifted a weapon against me," he said. "My codes permit me to kill you."

The bartender and I watched with terror as Cabot's large firm hands twisted the truncheon apart, splitting the stitching, much as I might have twisted apart a roll of cardboard. Some of the shot dropped to the floor and rolled under the tables.

"He's drunk," I said to the bartender. I took Cabot firmly by the arm. He didn't seem to be angry any longer, and I could see that he intended no one any harm. My touch seemed to snap him out of his strange mood. He handed the ruined truncheon meekly back to the bartender.

"I'm sorry," said Cabot. "Really." He reached into his wallet and pressed a bill into the bartender's hands. It was a hundred dollar bill.

We put on our coats and went out into the February evening, into the light snow.

Outside the bar we stood in the snow, not speaking. Cabot, still half-drunk, looked about himself, at the brutal electric geometry of that great city, at the dark, lonely shapes that moved through the light snow, at the pale glimmering headlights of the cars.

"This is a great city," said Cabot, "and yet it is not

loved. How many are there here who would die for this city? How many who would defend to the death its perimeters? How many who would submit to torture on its behalf?"

"You're drunk," I said, smiling.

"This city is not loved," he said. "Or it would not be used as it is, kept as it is."

He walked sadly away.

Somehow I knew that this was the night on which I would learn the secret of Tarl Cabot.

"Wait!" I cried to him suddenly.

He turned and I sensed that he was glad that I had called to him, that my company on that night meant a great deal to him.

I joined him and together we went to his apartment. First he brewed a pot of strong coffee, an act for which my swirling senses were more than grateful. Then without speaking he went into his closet and emerged carrying a strongbox. He unlocked this with a key which he carried on his own person, and removed a manuscript, written in his own clear, decisive hand and bound with twine. He placed the manuscript in my hands.

It was a document pertaining to what Cabot called the Counter-Earth, the story of a warrior, of the siege of a city, and of the love of a girl. You perhaps know it as *Tarnsman of Gor*.

When, shortly after dawn, I had finished the account, I looked at Cabot, who, all the time, had been sitting at the window, his chin on his hands, watching the snow, lost in what thoughts I could scarce conjecture.

He turned and faced me.

"It's true," he said, "but you need not believe it."

I didn't know what to say. It could not, of course, be true, yet I felt Cabot to be one of the most honest men I had ever known.

Then I noticed his ring, almost for the first time, though I had seen it a thousand times. It had been mentioned in the account, that simple ring of red metal, bearing the crest of Cabot.

"Yes," said Cabot, extending his hand, "this is the ring."

I gestured to the manuscript. "Why have you shown me this?" I asked.

"I want someone to know of these things," said Cabot simply.

I arose, now conscious for the first time of a lost night of sleep, the effects of the drinking, and of the several cups of bitter coffee. I smiled wryly. "I think," I said, "I'd better go."

"Of course," said Cabot, helping me on with my coat. At the doorway he held out his hand. "Good-bye," he said.

"I'll see you tomorrow," I said.

"No," he said. "I am going again to the mountains."

It was in February, at this time, that he had disappeared seven years before.

I was shocked into clear consciousness. "Don't go," I said.

"I am going," he said.

"Let me come with you," I said.

"No," he said, "I may not come back."

We shook hands, and I had the strange feeling that I might never see Tarl Cabot again. My hand was clenched firmly on his, and his on mine. I had meant something to him, and he to me, and now as simply as this it seemed that friends might part forever, never to see or talk to one another again.

I found myself in the bleak white hallway outside his apartment, blinking at the exposed bulb in the ceiling. I walked for some hours, in spite of my fatigue, thinking, puzzling about these strange things of which I had heard.

Then suddenly I turned and, literally, ran back to his apartment. I had left him, my friend. To what I had no idea. I rushed to the door of the apartment and pounded on it with my fists. There was no answer. I kicked in the door, splintering the lock from the jamb. I entered the apartment. Tarl Cabot was gone!

On the table in that small furnished apartment was the

manuscript I had read through the long night—with an envelope fastened under the twine. The envelope bore my name and address. Inside was the simple note: "For Harrison Smith, should he care to have it." Dismal, I left the apartment, carrying the manuscript which was subsequently published as *Tarnsman of Gor*. That and memory were all that I retained of my friend, Tarl Cabot.

My examinations came and were successfully completed. Later, following more examinations, I was admitted to the bar in New York State, and I entered one of the immense law offices in the city, hoping to obtain eventually enough experience and capital to open a small practice of my own. In the rush of working, in the interminable, demanding jungle of detail required in my trade, the memory of Cabot was forced from my mind. There is perhaps little more to say here, other than the fact that I have not seen him again. Though I have reason to believe he lives.

Late one afternoon, after work, I returned to my apartment. There—in spite of the locked doors and windows—on a coffee table before the settee, was a second manuscript, that which now follows. There was no note, no explanation.

Perhaps, as Tarl Cabot once remarked, "The agents of the Priest-Kings are among us."

2

RETURN TO GOR

ONCE AGAIN, I, TARL CABOT, strode the green fields of Gor.

I awakened naked in the wind-swept grass, beneath that blazing star that is the common sun of my two worlds, my home planet, Earth, and its secret sister, the Counter-Earth, Gor.

I rose slowly to my feet, my fibers alive in the wind, my hair torn by its blasts, my muscles each aching and rejoicing in their first movements in perhaps weeks, for I had again entered that silver disk in the White Mountains which was the ship of the Priest-Kings, used for the Voyages of Acquisition, and, in entering, had fallen unconscious. In that state, as once long before, I had come to this world.

I stood so for some minutes, to let each sense and nerve drink in the wonder of my return.

I was aware again of the somewhat lesser gravity of the planet, but this awareness would pass as my system accommodated itself naturally to the new environment. Given the lesser gravity, feats of prowess which might seem superhuman on earth were commonplace on Gor. The sun, as I remembered it, seemed a bit larger than it did when viewed from the earth, but as before it was difficult to be altogether sure of this.

In the distance I could see some patches of yellow, the Ka-la-na groves that dot the fields of Gor. Far to my left I saw a splendid field of Sa-Tarna, bending beautifully in the wind, that tall yellow grain that forms a staple in the Gorean diet. To the right, in the far distance, I saw the smudge of mountains. From their extent and height, as far as I could judge, I guessed them to be the mountains of Thentis. From them, if this were true, I could gather my bearings for Ko-ro-ba, that city of cylinders to which, years ago, I had pledged my sword.

So standing, the sun upon me, without thinking I raised my arms as in pagan prayer to acknowledge the power of the Priest-Kings, which had once again brought me from Earth to this world, the power which once before had torn me from Gor when they were finished with me, taking me from my adopted city, my father and my friends, and from the girl I loved, dark-haired beautiful Talena, daughter of Marlenus, who had once been the Ubar of Ar, the greatest city of all known Gor.

There was no love in my heart for the Priest-Kings, those mysterious denizens of the Sardar Mountains, whoever or whatever they might be, but there was gratitude in my heart, either to them or to the strange forces that moved them.

That I had been returned to Gor to seek out once more my city and my love was, I was sure, not the spontaneous gesture of generosity, or of justice, that it might seem. The Priest-Kings, Keepers of the Holy Place in the Sardar Mountains, seeming knowers of all that occurred on Gor, masters of the hideous Flame Death that could with consuming fire destroy whatever they wished, whenever they might please, were not so crudely motivated as men, were not susceptible to the imperatives of decency and respect that can upon occasion sway human action. Their concern was with their own remote and mysterious ends; to achieve these ends, human creatures were treated as subservient instruments. It was rumored they used men as one might use pieces in a game, and when the piece had played its role it might be discarded, or perhaps, as in my case, removed from the board until it pleased the Priest-Kings to try yet another game.

I noticed, a few feet from me, lying on the grass, a

helmet, shield and spear, and a bundle of folded leather. I knelt to examine the articles.

The helmet was bronze, worked in the Greek fashion, with a unitary opening somewhat in the shape of a Y. It bore no insignia and its crest plate was empty.

The round shield, concentric overlapping layers of hardened leather riveted together and bound with hoops of brass, fitted with the double sling for carrying on the left arm, was similarly unmarked. Normally the Gorean shield is painted boldly and has infixed in it some device for identifying the bearer's city. If this shield were intended for me, and I had little doubt it was, it should have carried the sign of Ko-ro-ba, my city.

The spear was a typical Gorean spear, about seven feet in height, heavy, stout, with a tapering bronze head some eighteen inches in length. It is a terrible weapon and, abetted by the somewhat lighter gravity of Gor, when cast with considerable force, can pierce a shield at close quarters or bury its head a foot deep in solid wood. With this weapon groups of men hunt even the larl in its native haunts in the Voltai Range, that incredible pantherlike carnivore which may stand six to eight feet high at the shoulder.

Indeed, the Gorean spear is such that many warriors scorn lesser missile weapons, such as the longbow or crossbow, both of which are not uncommonly found on Gor. I regretted, however, that no bow was among the weapons at my disposal, as I had, in my previous sojourn on Gor, developed a skill with such weapons, and admittedly a fondness for them, a liking which had scandalized my former master-at-arms.

I recalled him with affection, the Older Tarl. Tarl is a common name on Gor. I looked forward eagerly to seeing him again, that rough, Viking giant of a man, that proud, bearded, affectionately belligerent swordsman who had taught me the craft of arms as practiced by the warriors of Gor.

I opened the leather bundle. In it I found the scarlet tunic, sandals and cloak which constitute the normal garb of a member of the Caste of Warriors. This was as it should be, as I was of that caste, and had been since that morning, some seven years ago, when in the Chamber of the Council of High Castes I had accepted weapons from the hands of my father, Matthew Cabot, Administrator of Ko-ro-ba, and had taken the Home Stone of that city as my own.

For the Gorean, though he seldom speaks of these things, a city is more than brick and marble, cylinders and bridges. It is not simply a place, a geographical location in which men have seen fit to build their dwellings, a collection of structures where they may most conveniently conduct their affairs.

The Gorean senses, or believes, that a city cannot be simply identified with its material elements, which undergo their transformations even as do the cells of a human body.

For them a city is almost a living thing, or more than a living thing. It is an entity with a history, as stones and rivers do not have history; it is an entity with a tradition, a heritage, customs, practices, character, intentions, hopes. When a Gorean says, for example, that he is *of* Ar, or Ko-ro-ba, he is doing a great deal more than informing you of his place of residence.

The Goreans generally, though there are exceptions, particularly the Caste of Initiates, do not believe in immortality. Accordingly, to be *of* a city is, in a sense, to have been a part of something less perishable than oneself, something divine in the sense of undying. Of course, as every Gorean knows, cities too are mortal, for cities can be destroyed as well as men. And this perhaps makes them love their cities the more, for they know that their city, like themselves, is subject to mortal termination.

This love of their city tends to become invested in a stone which is known as the Home Stone, and which is normally kept in the highest cylinder in a city. In the Home Stone—sometimes little more than a crude piece of carved rock, dating back perhaps several hundred generations to when the city was only a cluster of huts by the bank of a river, sometimes a magnificent and impressively wrought, jewel-incrusted cube of marble or granite—the city finds its symbol. Yet to speak of a symbol is to fall short of the mark. It is almost as if the city itself were identified with the Home Stone, as if it were to the city what life is to a man. The myths of these matters have it that while the Home Stone survives, so, too, must the city.

But not only is it the case that each city has its Home Stone. The simplest and humblest village, and even the most primitive hut in that village, perhaps only a cone of straw, will contain its own Home Stone, as will the fantastically appointed chambers of the Administrator of so great a city as Ar.

My Home Stone was the Home Stone of Ko-ro-ba, that city to which I had seven years ago pledged my sword. I was now eager to return to my city.

In the bundle, wrapped inside the tunic and cloak I found the shoulder belt, sheath and short sword of the Goreans. I took the blade from its sheath. It was well balanced, vicious, double-edged and about twenty to twenty-two inches in length. I knew the handle, and I could recognize certain marks on the blade. It was the weapon I had carried at the siege of Ar. It felt strange to hold it again in my hand, to feel its weight, the familiar grasp of the hilt. This blade had fought its way up the stairs of the Central Cylinder of Ar, when I had rescued Marlenus, embattled Ubar of that city. It had crossed with that of Pa-Kur, master assassin, on the roof of Ar's Cylinder of Justice, when I had fought for my love, Talena. And now again I held it in my hand. I wondered why, and knew only that the Priest-Kings had intended it so.

There were two items I had hoped to find in the bundle which were not there, a tarn-goad and a tarn-whistle. The tarn-goad is a rodlike instrument, about twenty inches long. It has a switch in the handle, much like an ordinary flashlight. When the goad is switched to the on-position and it strikes an object, it emits a violent shock and scatters a shower of yellow sparks. It is used for controlling tarns, the gigantic hawklike saddle-birds of Gor. Indeed, the birds are conditioned to respond to the goad, almost from the egg.

The tarn-whistle, as one might expect, is used to summon the bird. Usually, the most highly trained tarns will respond to only one note, that sounded by the whistle of their master. There is nothing surprising in this inasmuch as each bird is trained, by the Caste of Tarn Keepers, to respond to a different note. When the tarn is presented to a warrior, or sold to one, the whistle accompanies the bird. Needless to say, the whistle is important and carefully guarded, for, should it be lost or fall into the hands of an enemy, the warrior has, for all practical purposes, lost his mount.

I now dressed myself in the scarlet garb of a warrior of Gor. I was puzzled that the garb, like the helmet and shield, bore no insignia. This was contrary to the ways of Gor, for normally only the habiliments of outlaws and exiles, men without a city, lack the identifying devices of which the Gorean is so proud.

I donned the helmet, and slung the shield and sword over my left shoulder. I picked up the massive spear lightly in my right hand. Judging by the sun, and knowing that Ko-ro-ba lay northwest of the mountains, I strode in the direction of my city.

My step was light, my heart was happy. I was home, for where my love waited for me was home. Where my father had met me after more than twenty years of separation, where my warrior comrades and I had drunk and laughed together, where I had met and learned from my little friend, Torm, the Scribe, there was home.

I found myself thinking in Gorean, as fluently as though I had not been gone for seven years. I became aware that I was singing as I walked through the grass, a warrior song.

I had returned to Gor.

3

ZOSK

I HAD WALKED FOR SOME hours in the direction of Ko-ro-ba when I was delighted to come on one of the narrow roads to the city. I recognized it, and even had I not, the cylindrical pasang stones that marked its length were each inscribed with the sign of the city and the appropriate pasang count to its walls. A Gorean pasang is approximately .7 of a mile.

The road, like most Gorean roads, was built like a wall in the earth and was intended to last a hundred generations. The Gorean, having little idea of progress in our sense, takes great care in his building and workmanship. What he builds he expects men to use until the storms of time have worn it to dust. Yet this road, for all the loving craft of the Caste of Builders which had been lavished upon it, was only an unpretentious, subsidiary road, hardly wide enough for two carts to pass. Indeed, even the main roads to Ko-ro-ba were a far cry from the great highways that led to and from a metropolis like Ar.

Surprisingly, though the pasang stones told me I was close to Ko-ro-ba, stubborn tufts of grass were growing between the stones, and occasional vines were inching out, tendril by tendril, across the great stone blocks.

It was late afternoon and, judging by the pasang stones, I was still some hours from the city. Though it was still bright, many of the colorfully plumed birds had already sought their nests. Here and there swarms of night insects began to stir, lifting themselves under the leaves of bushes by the road. The shadows of the pasang stones had grown long, and, judging by the angle of these shadows (for the stones are set in such a way as to serve also as sundials) it was past the fourteenth Gorean Ahn, or hour. The Gorean day is divided into twenty Ahn, which are numbered consecutively. The tenth Ahn is noon, the twentieth, midnight. Each Ahn consists of forty Ehn, or minutes, and each Ehn of eighty Ihn, or seconds.

I wondered if it would be practical to continue my journey. The sun would soon be down, and the Gorean night is not without its dangers, particularly to a man on foot.

It is at night that the sleen hunts, that six-legged, long-bodied mammalian carnivore, almost as much a snake as an animal. I had never seen one, but had seen the tracks of one seven years before.

Also, at night, crossing the bright disks of Gor's three moons might occasionally be seen the silent, predatory shadow of the ul, a giant pterodactyl ranging far from its native swamps in the delta of the Vosk.

Perhaps most I dreaded those nights filled with the shrieks of the vart pack, a blind, batlike swarm of flying rodents, each the size of a small dog. They could strip a carcass in a matter of minutes, each carrying back some fluttering ribbon of flesh to the recesses of whatever dark cave the swarm had chosen for its home. Moreover, some vart packs were rabid.

One obvious danger lay in the road itself, and the fact that I had no light. After dark, various serpents seek out the road for its warmth, its stones retaining the sun's heat longer than the surrounding countryside. One such serpent was the huge, many-banded Gorean python, the hith. One to be feared even more perhaps was the tiny ost, a venomous, brilliantly orange reptile little more than a foot in length, whose bite spelled an excruciating death within seconds.

Accordingly, in spite of my eagerness to return to Ko-ro-ba, I decided that I would withdraw from the road, wrap myself in my cloak and spend the night in the shelter of some rocks, or perhaps crawl into the tangle of some thorn bushes, where one might sleep in relative security. Now that I was considering discontinuing my journey, I suddenly became acutely aware that I was both hungry and thirsty. No rations or water flask had been in the leather package found with the weapons.

I had scarcely stepped from the stones of the road when, coming down the road, each step carefully measured and solid, I saw a wide, hunched figure, bending under a gigantic bundle of sticks, strapped to his back by two cords which he held twisted in his fists in front of his body. His stature and burden proclaimed him a member of the Caste of Carriers of Wood, or Woodsmen, that Gorean caste which, with the Caste of Charcoal Makers, provides most of the common fuel for the Gorean cities.

The weight the man was carrying was prodigious, and would have staggered men of most castes, even that of the Warriors. The bundle reared itself at least a man's height above his bent back, and extended perhaps some four feet in width. I knew the support of that weight depended partly on the skillful use of the cords and back, but sheer strength was only too obviously necessary, and this man, and his caste brothers, over the generations, had been shaped to their task. Lesser men had turned outlaw or died. In rare cases, one might have been permitted by the Council of High Castes to raise caste. None of course would accept a lower caste, and there were lower castes, the Caste of Peasants, for example, the most basic caste of all Gor.

The man approached more closely. His eyes were almost covered with a white, shaggy, inverted bowl of hair, matted with twigs and leaves. The whiskers had been scraped from his face, probably by the blade of the broad, double-headed wood ax bound on top of the bundle. He wore the short, tattered sleeveless robe of his trade, with its leather back and shoulders. His feet were bare, and black to the ankles.

I stepped into the road before him.

"Tal," I said, lifting my right arm, palm inward, in a common Gorean greeting.

The shaggy creature, broad, powerful, monstrous in the proud deformation of his craft, stood before me, his feet planted firmly on the road. His head lifted. Its wide, narrow eyes, pale like water, regarded me through the brush of hair that almost concealed them.

In spite of his slow reaction to my presence, his deliberate and patient movements, I gathered that he was surprised. He had apparently not expected to meet anyone on this road. That puzzled me.

"Tal," he said, his voice thick, almost less than human.

I sensed that he was considering how quickly he could get to the ax bound across the bundle.

"I mean you no harm," I said.

"What do you want?" asked the carrier of wood, who must now have noticed that my shield and accouterments bore no insignia, and would have concluded that I was an outlaw.

"I am not an outlaw," I said.

He obviously did not believe me.

"I am hungry," I said. "I have had nothing to eat in many hours."

"I, too, am hungry," he said, "and have had nothing to eat in many hours."

"Is your hut near?" I asked. I knew it would be from the time of day at which I had encountered him. The sun regulates the schedule of most Gorean crafts and the woodsman would now be returning with his day's cutting.

"No," he said.

"I mean you and your Home Stone no harm," I said. "I have no money and cannot pay you, but I am hungry."

"A warrior takes what he wishes," said the man.

"I do not wish to take anything from you," I said.

He regarded me, and I thought the trace of a smile cracked through the stubbled leather of his broad face.

"I have no daughter," he said. "I have no silver, and no goods."

"Then I wish you prosperity," I laughed, "and will be on my way." I passed him and continued down the road.

I had moved but a few steps when his voice arrested me. It was hard to understand the words, for those of the lonely Caste of Woodsmen do not often speak.

"I have peas and turnips, garlic and onions in my hut," said the man, his bundle like a giant's hump on his back.

"The Priest-Kings themselves," I said, "could not ask for more."

"Then, Warrior," said the man, issuing Gor's blunt invitation to a low caste dinner, "share my kettle."

"I am honored," I said, and I was.

Whereas I was of high caste and he of low, yet in his own hut he would be, by the laws of Gor, a prince and sovereign, for then he would be in the place of his own Home Stone. Indeed, a cringing whelp of a man, who would never think of lifting his eyes from the ground in the presence of a member of one of the high castes, a crushed and spiritless churl, an untrustworthy villain or coward, an avaricious and obsequious pedlar often becomes, in the place of his own Home Stone, a veritable lion among his fellows, proud and splendid, generous and bestowing, a king be it only in his own den.

Indeed, frequent enough were the stories where even a warrior was overcome by an angry peasant into whose hut he had intruded himself, for in the vicinity of their Home Stones men fight with all the courage, savagery and resourcefulness of the mountain larl. More than one are the peasant fields of Gor which have been freshened with the blood of foolish warriors.

The broad-chested carrier of wood was grinning from ear to ear. He would have a guest tonight. He would speak little himself, being unskilled in speech, and being too proud to form sentences which he knew would most likely be stumbling and ungrammatical, but would sit by the fire until dawn refusing to let me sleep, wanting me to to talk to him, to tell him stories, to recount adventures, to give him news of faraway places. What I said, I knew, would be less important than the fact that something was said, that he had not been alone again.

"I am Zosk," he said.

I wondered if it were a use-name, or his real name. Members of low castes often call themselves by a use-name, reserving the real name for intimates and friends, to protect it against capture by a sorcerer or worker of spells who might use it to do them harm. Somehow I sensed that Zosk was his real name.

"Zosk of what city?" I asked.

The low-slung, broad frame seemed to stiffen. The muscles in his legs seemed suddenly to bulge like cable. The rapport I had felt with him seemed suddenly gone, like a sparrow flown or a leaf suddenly torn from a branch.

"Zosk . . . " he said.

"Of what city?" I asked.

"Of no city," he said.

"Surely," I said, "you are of Ko-ro-ba."

The squat, misformed giant of a man seemed almost to recoil as if struck, and to tremble. I sensed that this simple, unaffected primate of a man was suddenly afraid. Zosk, I felt, would have faced a larl armed only with his ax, but yet, here, he seemed frightened. The great fists holding the cords of the bundle of wood turned white; the sticks rattled in the bundle.

"I am Tarl Cabot," I said. "Tarl of Ko-ro-ba."

Zosk uttered an inarticulate cry, and began to stumble backwards. His hands fumbled on the cords and the great bundle of wood loosened and clattered to the stone flooring of the road. Turning to run his foot slipped on one of the sticks and he fell. He fell almost on top of the ax which lay on the road. Impulsively, as though it were a life-giving plank in the maelstrom of his fear, he seized the ax.

With the ax in his hands, suddenly he seemed to remember his caste, and he crouched in the road, there in the dusk, a few feet from me, like a gorilla clutching the broad-headed ax, breathing deeply, sucking in the air, mastering his fear.

His eyes glared at me through the grizzled, matted locks of his hair. I could not understand his fear, but I was proud to see him master it, for fear is the great common enemy of all living things, and his victory I felt somehow was also mine. I remembered once when I had feared thus in the mountains of New Hampshire, and how shamefully I had yielded to my fear and had run, a slave to the only degrading passion of man.

Zosk straightened as much as his giant bow of a backbone would allow him.

He was no longer afraid.

He spoke slowly. His voice was thick, but it was fully under his control.

"Say you are not Tarl Cabot of Ko-ro-ba," he said.

"But I am," I said.

"I ask your favor," said Zosk, his voice thick with emotion. He was pleading. "Say you are not Tarl Cabot of Ko-ro-ba."

"I am Tarl Cabot of Ko-ro-ba," I repeated firmly.

Zosk lifted his ax.

It seemed light in his massive grip. I felt it could have felled a small tree with a single blow. Step by step, he approached me, the ax held over his shoulder with both hands.

At last he stopped before me. I thought there were tears in his eyes. I made no move to defend myself. Somehow I knew Zosk would not strike. He struggled with himself, his simple wide face twisted in agony, his eyes tortured.

"May the Priest-Kings forgive me!" he cried.

He threw down the ax, which rang on the stones of the road to Ko-ro-ba. Zosk sank down and sat cross-legged in the road, his gigantic frame shaken with sobs, his massive head buried in his hands, his thick, guttural voice moaning with distress.

At such a time a man may not be spoken to, for according to the Gorean way of thinking pity humiliates both he who pities and he who is pitied. According to the Gorean way, one may love but one may not pity.

So I moved on.

I had forgotten my hunger. I no longer considered the dangers of the road.

I would make it to Ko-ro-ba by dawn.

4

THE SLEEN

IN THE DARKNESS I STUMBLED on toward the walls of Ko-ro-ba, striking the stones of the road with the butt of my spear, to keep on the road and to drive possible serpents from my path. It was a nightmarish journey, and a foolish one, trying to rush on through the night to find my city, bruising, falling, scraping myself in the darkness, yet driven on by such a torment of doubt and apprehension that I could allow myself no rest until I stood again on the lofty bridges of Ko-ro-ba.

Was I not Tarl of Ko-ro-ba? Was there not such a city? Each pasang stone proclaimed there was—at the end of this road. Yet why was the road untended? Why had it not been traveled? Why had Zosk of the Caste of Carriers of Wood acted as he had? Why did my shield, my helmet, my accouterments not bear the proud sign of Ko-ro-ba?

Once I shouted in pain. Two fangs had struck into my calf. An ost, I thought! But the fangs held fast, and I heard the popping, sucking sound of the bladderlike seed pods of a leech plant, as they expanded and contracted like small ugly lungs. I reached down and jerked the plant from the soil at the side of the road. It writhed in my hand like a snake, its pods gasping. I jerked the two fanglike thorns from my leg. The leech plant strikes like a cobra, and fastens two hollow thorns into its victim. The chemical responses of the bladderlike pods produce a mechanical pumping action, and the blood is sucked into the plant to nourish it. As I tore the thing from my leg,

33

glad that the sting had not been that of the venomous ost, the three hurtling moons of Gor broke from the dark cover of the clouds. I held the quivering plant up. Then I twisted it apart. Already my blood, black in the silvery night, mixed with the juices of the plant, stained the stem even to the roots. In a matter of perhaps two or three seconds, it had drawn perhaps a gill of liquid. With a shudder I hurled the loathsome plant away from the road. Normally such plants are cleared from the sides of the roads and from inhabited areas. They are primarily dangerous to children and small animals, but a grown man who might lose his footing among them would not be likely to survive.

I prepared to set forth on my journey again, grateful that now the three moons of Gor might guide my path on this perilous road. I asked myself, in a sane moment, if I should not seek shelter, and I knew that I should, but I could not—because questions burned within me that I could not dare to answer. Only the evidence of my eyes and ears could allay my fears, my bewilderment. I sought a truth I did not know, but knew I must discover—and it lay at the end of this road.

I caught a strange, unpleasant scent, much like a common weasel or ferret, only stronger. In that instant every sense was alert.

I froze, an almost animal response.

I was silent, not moving, seeking the shelter of stillness and immobility. My head turned imperceptibly as I scanned the rocks and bushes about the road. I thought I heard a slight sniffling, a grunt, a small doglike whine. Then nothing.

It too had frozen, probably sensing my presence. Most likely it was a sleen, hopefully a young one. I guessed it had not been hunting me or I would not have been likely to have smelled it. It would have approached from upwind. Perhaps I stood thus for six or seven minutes. Then I saw it, on its six short legs, undulate across the road, like a furred lizard, its pointed, whiskered snout swaying from side to side testing the wind.

I breathed a sigh of relief.

It was indeed a young sleen, not more than eight feet long, and it lacked the patience of an older animal. Its attack, if it should detect my presence, would be noisy, a whistling rush, a clumsy squealing charge. It glided away into the darkness, perhaps not fully convinced that it was not alone, a young animal ready to neglect and overlook those slight traces that can spell the difference between death and survival in Gor's brutal and predatory world.

I continued my journey.

Black, scudding clouds again obscured the three moons of Gor, and the wind began to rise. I could see the shadows of tall Ka-la-na trees bending against the darkness of the night, their leaves lifting and rustling on the long branches. I smelled rain in the air. In the far distance there was a sudden flash of lightning, and the sound of remote thunder reached me some seconds later.

As I hurried on, I became more apprehensive. By now it seemed to me that I should be able to see the lights of the cylinder city of Ko-ro-ba. The wind gathered force, seeming to tear at the trees.

In a flash of light I spied a pasang stone and eagerly rushed to it. In the mounting wind and darkness I traced the numbering on the stone. It was true. I should now be able to see the lights of Ko-ro-ba. Yet I could see nothing. The city must be in darkness.

Why were the lanterns not hung on the lofty bridges? Why were the lamps of a hundred colors and flames not lit in the compartments of the city, telling in the lamp codes of Gor of talk, of drinking, of love? Why were the huge beacons on the wall not burning, not summoning Ko-ro-ba's far-roving tarnsmen back to the shelter of her walls?

I stood by the pasang stone, trying to understand. I was confused, uncertain. Now that I had not seen the lights of Ko-ro-ba, as I would have expected, it struck me more forcibly that I had not even seen the lights of peasant cooking fires glowing in the hills surrounding the city, or the torches of rash sportsmen who hunt the sleen by night.

Yes, and by now I should have been challenged a dozen times by Ko-ro-ba's night patrols!

A monstrous chain of lightning exploded in the night about me, deafening me with the shock and roar of its thunder, splitting the darkness in violent fragments, breaking it to pieces like a clay bowl struck with a hammer of fire, and with the lightning, the storm descended, fierce cold torrents of icy rain whipped by the wind.

In a moment I was drenched in the icy water. The wind tore at my tunic. I was blinded in the fury of the storm. I wiped the cold water from my eyes, and thrust my fingers in my hair to force it back. The blinding fury of the lightning like a whip of electricity struck again and again into the hills dazzling me for an instant of crashing agony, then vanishing again into the darkness.

A bolt of lightning shattered on the road not fifty yards before me. For an instant it seemed to stand like a gigantic crooked spear poised in my path, luminous, uncanny, forbidding, then vanished. It had fallen in my path. The thought crossed my mind that it was a sign from the Priest-Kings that I should turn back.

I continued forward and stood where it had struck. In spite of the icy wind and rain I could feel the heat of the stones through my sandals. I raised my eyes to the storm, and my spear and shield, and shouted into the storm, my voice drowned in the turbulence of nature, a defiant puff of wind hurled against the forces that seemed arrayed against me.

"I am going to Ko-ro-ba!" I cried.

I had hardly moved another step when, in a flash of lightning, I saw the sleen, this time a fully grown animal, some nineteen or twenty feet long, charging toward me, swiftly, noiselessly, its ears straight against its pointed head, its fur slick with rain, its fangs bared, its wide nocturnal eyes bright with the lust of the kill.

A strange sound escaped me, an incredible laugh. It was a thing I could see, could feel, could fight!

With an eagerness and a lust that matched that of the beast itself, I rushed forward in the darkness and when I judged its leap I lunged forward with the broad-headed spear of Gor. My arm felt wet and trapped, and was raked with fangs and I was spun as the animal squealed with rage and pain and rolled on the road. I withdrew my arm from the weak, aimlessly snapping jaws.

Another flash of lightning and I saw the sleen on its belly chewing on the shaft of the spear, its wide nocturnal eyes unfocused and glazed. My arm was bloody, but the blood was mostly that of the sleen. My arm had almost rammed itself down the throat of the animal following the spear I had flung into its mouth. I moved my arm and fingers. I was unhurt.

In the next flash of lightning I saw the sleen was dead.

A shudder involuntarily shook me, though I do not know if this was due to the cold and the rain or the sight of the long, furred lizardlike body that lay at my feet. I tried to extract the spear but it was wedged between the ribs of the animal.

Coldly I took out my sword and hacked away the head of the beast and jerked the weapon free. Then, as sleen hunters do, for luck, and because I was hungry, I took my sword and cut through the fur of the animal and ate the heart.

It is said that only the heart of the mountain larl brings more luck than that of the vicious and cunning sleen. The raw meat, hot with the blood of the animal, nourished me, and I crouched beside my kill on the road to Ko-ro-ba, another predator among predators.

I laughed. "Did you, Oh Dark Brother of the Night, think to keep me from Ko-ro-ba?"

How absurd it seemed to me that a mere sleen should have stood between me and my city. Irrationally I laughed, thinking how foolish the animal had been. But how could it have known? How could it have known that I was Tarl of Ko-ro-ba, and that I was returning to my city? There is a Gorean proverb that a man who is returning to his city is not to be detained. Was the sleen not familiar with that saying?

I shook my head, to clear it of the wild thoughts. I

sensed that I was irrational, perhaps a bit drunk after the kill and the first food I had had in several hours.

Then, soberly, though I acknowledged it as a superstition, I performed the Gorean ritual of looking into the blood. With my cupped hands I drank a mouthful of blood, and then, holding another in my hands, I waited for the next flash of lightning.

One looks into the blood in one's cupped hands. It is said that if one sees one's visage black and wasted one will die of disease, if one sees oneself torn and scarlet one will die in battle, if one sees oneself old and white haired, one will die in peace and leave children.

The lightning flashed again, and I stared into the blood. In that brief moment, in the tiny pool of blood I held, I saw not myself but a strange face, like a globe of gold with disklike eyes, a face like none I had ever seen, a face that struck an eerie terror into my heart.

The darkness returned, and in the next flash of lightning I examined the blood again, but it was only blood, the blood of a sleen I had killed on the road to Ko-ro-ba. I could not even see myself reflected in the surface. I drank the blood, completing the ritual.

I stood up, and wiped the spear as well as I could on the fur of the sleen. Its heart had given me strength.

"Thank you, Dark Brother of the Night," I said to the animal.

I saw that water had gathered in the concave side of the shield. Gratefully, I lifted it and drank from it.

5

THE VALLEY OF KO-RO-BA

I BEGAN TO CLIMB NOW.

The road was familiar, the long, relatively steep ascent
to the crest of that series of ridges beyond which lay
Ko-ro-ba, an ascent that was the bane of strap-masters of
caravans, of bearers of burdens like poor Zosk, the
woodsman, of all travelers afoot.

Ko-ro-ba lay in the midst of green and rolling hills,
some hundreds of feet above the level of the distant
Tamber Gulf and that mysterious body of water beyond
it, spoken of in Gorean simply as Thassa, the Sea. Ko-ro-
ba was not set as high and remote as for example was
Thentis in the mountains of Thentis, famed for its tarn
flocks, but it was not a city of the vast plains either, like
the luxurious metropolis of Ar, or of the shore, like the
cluttered, crowded, sensuous Port Kar on the Tamber
Gulf. Whereas Ar was glorious, a city of imposing grandeur, acknowledged even by its blood foes; whereas Thentis had the proud violence of the rude mountains of Thentis for its setting; whereas Port Kar could boast the broad
Tamber for its sister, and the gleaming, mysterious Thassa
beyond, I thought my city to be truly the most beautiful,
its variegated lofty cylinders rising so gently, so joyfully,
among the calm, green hills.

An ancient poet, who incredibly enough to the Gorean
mind had sung the glories of many of the cities of Gor,
had spoken of Ko-ro-ba as the Towers of the Morning,
and it is sometimes spoken of by that name. The actual

word Ko-ro-ba itself, more prosaically, is simply an expression in archaic Gorean referring to a village market.

The storm had not abated but I had ceased to mind it. Drenched, cold, I climbed on, holding my shield obliquely before me to deflect the wind and make the climb easier. At last on the crest I waited and wiped the cold water from my eyes, waited for the flash of lightning that after these long years would reveal my city.

I longed for my city, and for my father, the magnificent Matthew Cabot, once Ubar, now Administrator of Ko-ro-ba, and for my friends, the proud Older Tarl, my master-at-arms, and Torm, the cheerful, grumbling little scribe who regarded even sleep and food as part of a conspiracy to separate him from the study of his beloved scrolls; and mostly, I longed for Talena, she whom I had chosen for my companion, she for whom I had fought on Ar's Cylinder of Justice, she who loved me, and whom I loved, dark-haired, beautiful Talena, daughter of Marlenus, once Ubar of Ar.

"I love you, Talena!" I cried.

And as my cry parted from my lips there was a great flash of lightning and the valley between the hills stood stark and white and I saw the valley was empty.

Ko-ro-ba was gone!

The city had vanished!

The darkness followed the flash of lightning and the shock of the thunder shook me with horror.

Again and again the lightning flashed, the thunder pounded in on me, and the darkness engulfed me once more. And each time I saw what I had seen before. The valley empty. Ko-ro-ba was gone.

"You have been touched by the Priest-Kings," said a voice behind me.

I spun about. shield before me, spear ready.

In the next flash of lightning I saw the white robes of an Initiate, the shaven head and the sad eyes of one of the Blessed Caste, servants it is said of the Priest-Kings themselves. He stood with his arms in his robe, tall on the road, watching me.

Somehow this man seemed different to me than the other Initiates I had met on Gor. I could not place the difference, yet it seemed there was something in him, or about him, that set him apart from the other members of his caste. He might have been any other Initiate, yet he was not. There was nothing extraordinary about him, unless perhaps it was a brow somewhat more lofty than is common, eyes that might have looked on sights few men had seen.

The thought struck me that I, Tarl of Ko-ro-ba, a mortal, here in the night on this road, might be looking upon the face of a Priest-King.

As we faced one another, the storm ceased, the lightning no longer shattered the night, the thunder no longer roared in my ears. The wind was calm. The clouds had dissipated. In pools of cold water lying among the stones of the road I could see the three moons of Gor.

I turned and looked upon the valley in which Ko-ro-ba had lain.

"You are Tarl of Ko-ro-ba," said the man.

I was startled. "Yes," I said, "I am Tarl of Ko-ro-ba." I turned to face him.

"I have been waiting for you," he said.

"Are you," I asked, "a Priest-King?"

"No," he said.

I looked at this man, seeming to be a man among other men, yet more.

"Do you speak for the Priest-Kings?" I asked.

"Yes," he said.

I believed him.

It was common, of course, for Initiates to claim to speak for the Priest-Kings; indeed, it was presumably the calling of their caste to interpret the will of the Priest-Kings to men.

But this man I believed.

He was not as other Initiates, though he wore their robes.

"Are you truly of the Caste of Initiates?" I asked.

"I am one who conveys the will of the Priest-Kings to

mortals," said the man, not choosing to answer my question.

I was silent.

"Henceforth," said the man, "you are Tarl of no city."

"I am Tarl of Ko-ro-ba," I said proudly.

"Ko-ro-ba has been destroyed," said the man. "It is as if it had never been. Its stones and its people have been scattered to the corners of the world, and no two stones and no two men of Ko-ro-ba may stand again side by side."

"Why has Ko-ro-ba been destroyed?" I demanded.

"It was the will of the Priest-Kings," said the man.

"But why was it the will of the Priest-Kings?" I shouted.

"Because it was," said the man, "and there is nothing higher in virtue of which the will of the Priest-Kings may be determined or questioned."

"I do not accept their will," I said.

"Submit," said the man.

"I do not," I said.

"Then be it so," he said, "you are henceforth condemned to wander the world alone and friendless, with no city, with no walls to call your own, with no Home Stone to cherish. You are henceforth a man without a city, you are a warning to all not to scorn the will of the Priest-Kings—beyond this you are nothing."

"What of Talena?" I cried. "What of my father, my friends, the people of my city?"

"Scattered to the corners of the world," said the robed figure, "and not a stone may stand upon a stone."

"Did I not serve the Priest-Kings," I asked, "at the siege of Ar?"

"The Priest-Kings used you for their ends, as it pleased them to do so."

I lifted my spear, and felt that I could have slain the robed figure so calm and terrible before me.

"Kill me if you wish," said the man.

I lowered the spear. My eyes were filled with tears. I was bewildered. Was it on my account that a city had perished? Was it I who had brought disaster to its people, to my father, to my friends and Talena? Had I been too foolish to understand that I was nothing before the power of the Priest-Kings? Was I now to wander the forlorn roads and fields of Gor in guilt and agony, a wretched example of the fate which the Priest-Kings could mete out to the foolish and proud?

Then suddenly I ceased to pity myself, and I was shocked, for looking into the eyes of the robed figure I saw human warmth in them, tears for me. It was pity, the forbidden emotion, and yet he could not restrain himself. Somehow the power I had felt in his presence seemed to have vanished. I was now only in the presence of a man, a fellow human being even though he wore the sublime robes of the proud Caste of Initiates.

He seemed to be struggling with himself, as though he wanted to speak his own words and not those of the Priest-Kings. He seemed to shake with pain, his hands pressed against his head, trying to speak to me, trying to tell me something. One hand stretched out to me, and the words, his own, far from the ringing authority of his former tones, were hoarse and almost inaudible.

"Tarl of Ko-ro-ba," he said, "throw yourself upon your sword."

He seemed ready to fall, and I held him.

He looked into my eyes. "Throw yourself upon your sword," he begged.

"Would that not frustrate the will of the Priest-Kings?" I asked.

"Yes," said he.

"Why do you tell me to do this?" I demanded.

"I followed you at the siege of Ar," he said. "On the Cylinder of Justice I fought with you against Pa-Kur and his assassins."

"An Initiate?" I asked.

He shook his head. "No," he said, "I was one of the guards of Ar, and I fought to save my city."

"Ar the Glorious," I said, speaking gently.

He was dying.

"Ar the Glorious," he said, weak, but with pride. He looked at me again. "Die now, Tarl of Ko-ro-ba," he said, "Hero of Ar." His eyes seemed to begin to burn in his head. "Do not shame yourself."

Suddenly he howled like a tortured dog, and what happened then I cannot bring myself to describe in detail. It seemed as though the entire inside of his head began to burst and burn, to bubble like some horrid viscous lava inside the crater of his skull.

It was an ugly death—his for having tried to speak to me, for having tried to tell me what was in his heart.

It was becoming light now, and dawn was breaking across the gentle hills that had sheltered Ko-ro-ba. I removed the hated robes of the Initiates from the body of the man and carried the naked body far from the road.

As I began to cover it with rocks, I noted the remains of the skull, now little more than a handful of shards. The brain had been literally boiled away. The morning light flashed briefly on something golden among the white shards. I lifted it. It was a webbing of fine golden wire. I could make nothing of it, and threw it aside.

I piled rocks on the body, enough to mark the grave and keep predators away.

I placed a large flat rock near the head of the cairn and, with the tip of my spear, scratched this legend on it. "I am a man of Glorious Ar." It was all I knew about him.

I stood beside the grave, and drew my sword. He had told me to throw myself upon it, to avoid my shame, to frustrate for once the will of the mighty Priest-Kings of Gor.

"No, Friend," I said to the remains of the former warrior of Ar. "No, I shall not throw myself upon my sword. Nor shall I grovel to the Priest-Kings nor live the life of shame they have allotted to me."

I lifted the sword toward the valley where Ko-ro-ba had stood.

"Long ago," I said, "I pledged this sword to the service of Ko-ro-ba. It remains so pledged."

Like every man of Gor I knew the direction of the Sardar Mountains, home of the Priest-Kings, forbidden vastness into which no man below the mountains, no mortal, may penetrate. It was said that the Supreme Home Stone of all Gor lay within those mountains and was the source of the Priest-Kings' power. It was said no man had returned alive from those mountains, that no man had looked upon a Priest-King and lived.

I resheathed my sword, fastened my helmet over my shoulder, lifted my shield and spear and set out in the direction of the Sardar Mountains.

6

VERA

THE SARDAR MOUNTAINS, WHICH I had never seen, lay more than a thousand pasangs from Ko-ro-ba. Whereas the Men Below the Mountains, as the mortals are called, seldom enter the mountains, and do not return when they do, many often venture to their brink, if only to stand within the shadows of those cliffs that hide the secrets of the Priest-Kings. Indeed, at least once in his life every Gorean is expected to make this journey.

Four times a year, correlated with the solstices and equinoxes, there are fairs held in the plains below the mountains, presided over by committees of Initiates, fairs in which men of many cities mingle without bloodshed, times of truce, times of contests and games, of bargaining and marketing.

Torm, my friend of the Caste of Scribes, had been to such fairs to trade scrolls with scholars from other cities, men he would never have seen were it not for the fairs, men of hostile cities who yet loved ideas more than they hated their enemies, men like Torm who so loved learning that they would risk the perilous journey to the Sardar Mountains for the chance to dispute a text or haggle over a coveted scroll. Similarly men of such castes as the Physicians and Builders make use of the fairs to disseminate and exchange information pertaining to their respective crafts.

The fairs do much to unite intellectually the otherwise so isolated cities of Gor. And I speculate that the fairs likewise do their bit toward stabilizing the dialects of Gor, which might otherwise in a few generations have diverged to the point of being mutually unintelligible—for the Goreans do have this in common, their mother tongue in all its hundred permutations, which they simply refer to as the Language, and all who fail to speak it, regardless of their pedigree or background, of their standards or level of civilization, are regarded as almost beyond the pale of humanity. Unlike the men of Earth, the Gorean has little sensitivity to race, but much to language and city. Like ourselves, he finds his reasons for hating his fellow-men, but his reasons are different.

I would have given much for a tarn in my journey, though I knew no tarn would fly into the mountains. For some reason neither the fearless hawklike tarns, nor the slow-witted tharlarions, the draft and riding lizards of Gor, would enter the mountains. The tharlarions become unmanageable and though the tarn will essay the flight the bird almost immediately becomes disoriented, uncoordinated, and drops screaming back to the plains below.

Gor, sparsely inhabited by human beings, teems with animal life, and in the next weeks I had no difficulty in living by hunting. I supplemented my diet with fresh fruit picked from bushes and trees, and fish speared in Gor's cold, swift-flowing streams. Once I brought the carcass of a tabuk, one of Gor's single-horned, yellow antelopes, which I had felled in a Ka-la-na thicket, to the hut of a peasant and his wife. Asking no questions, as was suitable given the absence of insignia on my garments, they feasted me on my own kill, and gave me fiber, and flints and a skin of wine.

The peasant on Gor does not fear the outlaw, for he seldom has anything worth stealing, unless it be a daughter. Indeed, the peasant and outlaw on Gor live in an almost unspoken agreement, the peasant tending to protect the outlaw and the outlaw sharing in return some of his plunder and booty with the peasant. The peasant does not regard this as dishonest on his part, or as grasping. It is simply a way of life to which he is accustomed. It is a different matter, of course, if it is explicitly known that the outlaw is from a city other than one's own. In that case he is usually regarded as an enemy, to be reported to the patrols as soon as possible. He is, after all, not of one's city.

As was wise I avoided cities in my long journey, though I passed several, for to enter a city without permission or without satisfactory reason is tantamount to a capital crime, and the punishment is usually a swift and brutal impalement. Pikes on the walls of Gorean cities are often surmounted with the remains of unwelcome guests. The Gorean is suspicious of the stranger, particularly in the vicinity of his native walls. Indeed, in Gorean the same word is used for both stranger and enemy.

There was reputedly one exception to this generally prevalent attitude of hostility toward the stranger, the city of Tharna, which, according to rumor, was willing to engage in what on Gor might be accounted the adventure of hospitality. There were many things supposedly strange about Tharna, among them that she was reportedly ruled by a queen, or Tatrix, and, reasonably enough in the circumstances, that the position of women in that city, in contrast with common Gorean custom, was one of privilege and opportunity.

I rejoiced that in at least one city on Gor the free women were not expected to wear the Robes of Concealment, confine their activities largely to their own quarters, and speak only to their blood relatives and, eventually, the Free Companion.

I thought that much of the barbarity of Gor might perhaps be traced to this foolish suppression of the fair sex, whose gentleness and intelligence might have made such a contribution in softening her harsh ways. To be sure, in certain cities, as had been the case in Ko-ro-ba, women were permitted status within the caste system and had a relatively unrestricted existence.

Indeed, in Ko-ro-ba, a woman might even leave her quarters without first obtaining the permission of a male relative or the Free Companion, a freedom which was unusual on Gor. The women of Ko-ro-ba might even be found sitting unattended in the theater or at the reading of epics.

In the cities of Gor that I knew, with the possible exception of Tharna, women had been most free in Ko-ro-ba, but now Ko-ro-ba was no more.

I wondered if I might be able to secure a tarn in the intriguing city of Tharna. It would shorten the trip to the Sardar Mountains by weeks. I had no money with which to purchase a tarn but I reasoned my hiring price as a swordsman might be sufficient to purchase a mount. For that matter, though I did not seriously consider the possibility, being without a city, in effect an outlaw, I was entitled in the Gorean way of thinking to take the bird or its purchase price in any way I saw fit.

As I was pondering these matters, I observed, approaching me, but not seeing me, in the distance, moving across a green meadow, a dark figure, that of a woman. Though she was young she walked slowly, mournfully, heedlessly, aimlessly.

It is unusual to find a woman unescorted outside the walls of a city, even near the walls. I was startled to see her alone in this wild, deserted place, far from roads and cities.

I decided to wait for her to approach.

I was puzzled.

On Gor a woman normally travels only with a suitable retinue of armed guards. Women, on this barbaric world, are often regarded, unfortunately, as little more than love prizes, the fruits of conquest and seizure. Too often they are seen less as persons, human beings with rights, individuals worthy of concern and regard than as potential pleasure slaves, silken, bangled prisoners, possible adornments to the pleasure gardens of their captors. There is a saying on Gor that the laws of a city extend no further than its walls.

She had not yet seen me. I leaned on my spear and waited.

The harsh, exogamous institution of capture is woven

into the very fabric of Gorean life. It is regarded as meritorious to abduct one's women from a foreign, preferably hostile city. Perhaps this institution, which on the surface seems so deplorable, is profitable from the standpoint of the race, preventing the gradual inbreeding of otherwise largely isolated, self-sufficient cities. Few seem to object to the institution of capture, not even the women who might seem to be its victims. On the contrary, incredibly enough, their vanity is terribly outraged if they are not regarded as worth the risks, usually mutilation and impalement. One cruel courtesan in the great city of Ar, now little more than a toothless, wrinkled hag, boasted that more than four hundred men had died because of her beauty.

Why was the girl alone?

Had her protectors been killed? Was she perhaps an escaped slave, fleeing from a hated master? Could she be, like myself, an exile from Ko-ro-ba? Its peoples have been scattered, I said to myself, and no two stones and no two men of Ko-ro-ba may stand again side by side. I gritted my teeth. The thought ran through my head, no stone may stand upon another stone.

If she were of Ko-ro-ba, I knew that I could not, for her own welfare, stay with her or help her. It would be to invite the Flame Death of the Priest-Kings for one or the other, perhaps both of us. I had seen a man die the Flame Death, the High Initiate of Ar on the summit of Ar's Cylinder of Justice, consumed in the sudden burst of blue fire that bespoke the displeasure of the Priest-Kings. Slim though her chances might be to escape wild beasts or slavers, they would be greater than the chance of escaping the wrath of the Priest-Kings.

If she were a free woman and not unfortunate, to be alone in this place was unwise and foolish.

She must know this, yet she did not seem to care.

Something of the nature of the institution of capture, and the Gorean's attitude toward it becomes clear when it is understood that one of a young tarnsman's first missions is often the capture of a slave for his personal quarters.

When he brings home his captive, bound naked across the saddle of his tarn, he gives her over, rejoicing, to his sisters, to be bathed, perfumed and clothed in the brief slave livery of Gor.

That night, at a great feast, he displays the captive, now suitably attired by his sisters in the diaphanous, scarlet dancing silks of Gor. Bells have been strapped to her ankles, and she is bound in slave bracelets. Proudly, he presents her to his parents, his friends and warrior comrades.

Then, to the festive music of flutes and drums, the girl kneels. The young man approaches her, bearing a slave collar, its engraving proclaiming his name and city. The music grows more intense, mounting to an overpowering, barbaric crescendo, which stops suddenly, abruptly. The room is silent, absolutely silent, except for the decisive click of the collar lock.

It is a sound the girl will never forget.

As soon as the lock closes, there is a great shout, congratulating, saluting the young man. He returns to his place among the tables that line the low-ceilinged chamber, hung with glowing brass lamps. He sits in the midst of his family, his closest well-wishers, his sword comrades, cross-legged on the floor in the Gorean fashion behind the long, low wooden table, laden with food, which stands at the head of the room.

Now all eyes are on the girl.

The restraining slave bracelets are removed. She rises. Her feet are bare on the thick, ornately wrought rug that carpets the chamber. There is a slight sound from the bells strapped to her ankles. She is angry, defiant. Though she is clad only in the almost transparent scarlet dancing silks of Gor, her back is straight, her head high. She is determined not to be tamed, not to submit, and her proud carriage bespeaks this fact. The spectators seem amused. She glares at them. Angrily she looks from face to face. There is no one she knows, or could know, because she has been taken from a hostile city, she is a woman of the enemy. Fists clenched, she stands in the center of the room, alone, all eyes upon her, beautiful in the light of the hanging lamps.

She faces the young man, wearing his collar.

"You will never tame me!" she cries.

Her outburst provokes laughter, skeptical observations, some good-natured hooting.

"I will tame you at my pleasure," replies the young man, and signals to the musicians.

The music begins again. Perhaps the girl hesitates. There is a slave whip on the wall. Then, to the barbaric, intoxicating music of the flute and drums, she dances for her captor, the bells on her ankles marking each of her movements, the movements of a girl stolen from her home, who must now live to please the bold stranger whose binding fiber she had felt, whose collar she wore.

At the end of her dance, she is given a cup of wine, but she may not drink. She approaches the young man and kneels before him, her knees in the dictated position of the Pleasure Slave, and, head down, she proffers the wine to him. He drinks. There is another general shout of commendation and well wishing, and the feast begins, for none before the young man may touch food on such occasions. From that moment on, the young man's sisters never again serve him, for that is the girl's task. She is his slave.

As she serves him again and again throughout the long feast, she steals glances at him, and sees that he is even more handsome than she had thought. Of his courage and strength she has already had ample evidence. As he eats and drinks with gusto on this occasion of his triumph, she regards him furtively, with a strange mixture of fear and pleasure. "Only such a man," she tells herself, "could tame me."

Perhaps it should only be added that the Gorean master, though often strict, is seldom cruel. The girl knows, if she pleases him, her lot will be an easy one. She will almost never encounter sadism or wanton cruelty, for the psychological environment that tends to breed these diseases is largely absent from Gor. This does not mean that she will not expect to be beaten if she disobeys, or fails to please her master. On the other hand, it is not too unusual a set of compartments on Gor where the master, in effect, willingly wears the collar, and his lovely slave, by the practice of the delightful wiles of her sex, with scandalous success wheedles her way triumphantly from the satisfaction of one whim to the next.

I wondered if the girl approaching was beautiful.

I smiled to myself.

Paradoxically, the Gorean, who seems to think so little of women in some respects, celebrates them extravagantly in others. The Gorean is keenly susceptible to beauty; it gladdens his heart, and his songs and art are often paeans to its glory. Gorean women, whether slave or free, know that their simple presence brings joy to men, and I cannot but think that this pleases them.

I decided the girl was beautiful. Perhaps it was something in her carriage, something subtle and graceful, something which could not be concealed by the dejected cast of her shoulders, her slow gait and apparent exhaustion, no, not even by the coarse heavy robes she wore. Such a girl, I thought, would surely have a master or, I hoped for her sake, a protector and companion.

There is no marriage, as we know it, on Gor, but there is the institution of the Free Companionship, which is its nearest correspondent. Surprisingly enough, a woman who is bought from her parents, for tarns or gold, is regarded as a Free Companion, even though she may not have been consulted in the transaction. More commendably, a free woman may herself, of her own free will, agree to be such a companion. And it is not unusual for a master to free one of his slave girls in order that she may share the full privileges of a Free Companionship. One may have, at a given time, an indefinite number of slaves, but only one Free Companion. Such relationships are not entered into lightly, and they are normally sundered only by death. Occasionally the Gorean, like his brothers in our world, perhaps even more frequently, learns the meaning of love.

The girl was now quite close to me, and yet had not

seen me. Her head was down. She was clad in Robes of Concealment, but their texture and color were a far cry from the glorious vanities often expressed in such garments, the silken purples, yellows and scarlets that the Gorean maiden delighted in; the robes were of coarse brown cloth, tattered and caked with dirt. Everything about her bespoke misery and dejection.

"Tal," I said, quietly, that I might not startle her too much, lifting my arm in gentle salute.

She had not known of my presence, and yet she did not seem much surprised. This was a moment she had apparently expected for many days, and now it had come. Her head lifted and her eyes, fine gray eyes, dulled with sorrow and perhaps hunger, regarded me. She seemed to take no great interest in me, or her fate. I gathered that I might have been anyone.

We faced one another without speaking for a moment.

"Tal, Warrior," she said, softly, her voice emotionless.

Then, for a Gorean woman, she did an incredible thing. Without speaking, she slowly unwound the veil from her face and dropped it to her shoulders. She stood before me, as it is said, face-stripped, and that by her own hand. She looked at me, openly, directly, not brazenly, but without fear. Her hair was brown and fine, the splendid gray eyes seemed even more clear, and her face, I saw, was beautiful, even more beautiful than I had imagined.

"Do I please you?" she asked.

"Yes," I said. "You please me very much."

I knew that this might be the first time a man had looked upon her face, except perhaps a member of her own family, if she had such.

"Am I beautiful?" she asked.

"Yes," I said, "you are beautiful."

Deliberately, with both hands, she slipped her garment some inches down her shoulders, fully revealing her white throat. It was bare, not encircled by one of the slender, graceful slave collars of Gor. She was free.

"Do you wish me to kneel to be collared?" she asked.

"No," I said.

"Do you wish to see me fully?" she asked.

"No," I said.

"I have never been owned before," she said. "I do not know how to act, or what to do—save only that I know I must do whatever you wish."

"You were free before," I said, "and you are free now."

For the first time, she seemed startled. "Are you not one of them?" she asked.

"One of whom?" I asked, now alert, for if there were slavers on the trail of this girl it would mean trouble, perhaps bloodshed.

"The four men who have been following me, men from Tharna," she said.

"Tharna?" I asked, genuinely surprised. "I thought the men of Tharna revered women, alone perhaps of the men of Gor."

She laughed bitterly. "They are not in Tharna now," she said.

"They could not take you to Tharna as a slave," I said. "Would the Tatrix not free you?"

"They would not take me to Tharna," she responded. "They would use me and sell me, perhaps to some passing merchant, perhaps in the Street of Brands in Ar."

"What is your name?" I asked.

"Vera," she said.

"Of what city?" I asked.

Before she could respond, if respond she would have, her eyes suddenly widened in fear, and I turned. Approaching across the meadow, ankle deep in the wet grass, were four warriors, helmeted and carrying spears and shields. By their shield insignia and blue helmets I knew them to be men of Tharna.

"Run!" she cried, and turned to flee.

I held her arm.

She stiffened in hate. "I see!" she hissed. "You will hold me for them, you will claim right of capture and demand a portion of my price!" She spat in my face.

I was pleased at her spirit.

"Stand quiet," I said. "You would not get far."

"I have fled from those men for six days," wept the girl, "living on berries and insects, sleeping in ditches, hiding, running."

She could not have run if she had wished. Her legs seemed to quiver under her. I put my arm about her, lending her my support.

The warriors approached me professionally, fanning out. One, not their officer, approached me directly; another, a few feet behind the first and on his left, followed him. The first, if necessary would engage me, and the second drive in on my right with his spear. The officer was the third man in the formation, and the other warrior hung several yards in the rear. It was his business to observe the entire field, for I might not be alone, and to cover the retreat of his fellows with his spear should the need arise. I admired the simple maneuvre, executed without command, almost a matter of reflex, and sensed why Tharna, in spite of being ruled by a woman, had survived among the hostile cities of Gor.

"We want the woman," said the officer.

I gently disengaged myself from the girl, and shoved her behind me. The meaning of the action was not lost on the warriors.

The eyes of the officer were narrow in the Y-like opening of his helmet.

"I am Thorn," he said, "a Captain of Tharna."

"Why do you want the woman?" I taunted. "Do not the men of Tharna revere women?"

"This is not the soil of Tharna," said the officer, annoyed.

"Why should I yield her to you?" I asked.

"Because I am a Captain of Tharna," he said.

"But this is not the soil of Tharna," I reminded him.

From behind me the girl whispered, an abject whisper. "Warrior, do not die for my sake. In the end it will all be the same." Then, raising her voice, she spoke to the officer. "Do not kill him, Thorn of Tharna. I will go with you."

She stepped out from behind me, proud but resigned to her fate, ready to give herself over to these wretches to be collared and chained, stripped and sold in the markets of Gor.

I laughed.

"She is mine," I said, "and you may not have her."

The girl gave a gasp of astonishment and looked at me questioningly.

"Unless you pay her price," I added.

The girl closed her eyes, crushed.

"And her price?" asked Thorn.

"Her price is steel," I said.

A look of gratitude flashed in the girl's face.

"Kill him," said Thorn to his men.

7

THORN, CAPTAIN OF THARNA

WITH ONE SOUND THREE BLADES sprang from their sheaths, mine, that of the officer and that of the warrior who would first engage me. The man on the right would not draw his blade but wait until the first warrior had made his attack and would then strike from the side with the spear. The warrior in the rear only lifted his spear, ready to cast it should a clean opening present itself.

But it was I who attacked first.

I suddenly turned on the warrior on my right with the spear and with the swiftness of the mountain larl sprang at him, evaded his clumsy, startled thrust, and drove my blade between his ribs, jerking it free and turning just in time to meet the sword attack of his companion. Our blades had not crossed six times when he, too, lay at my feet, crowded into a knot of pain, clutching at the grass.

The officer had rushed forward but now stopped. He, like his men, had been taken aback. Though they were four and I was one I had carried the battle to them. The officer had been an instant too late. Now my sword stood between him and my body. The other warrior, behind him, his spear poised, had approached to within ten yards. At that distance he would not be likely to miss. Indeed, even if the missile struck and penetrated my shield, I would have to cast the shield away and would find myself at a serious disadvantage. Yet, the odds were more even now.

"Come, Thorn of Tharna," I said, beckoning to him. "Let us try our skill."

But Thorn backed away and signaled to the other warrior to lower his spear. He removed his helmet, and sat on his heels in the grass, the warrior behind him.

Thorn, Captain of Tharna, looked at me, and I at him.

He had a new respect for me now, which meant that he would be more dangerous. He had seen the swift engagement with his swordsmen and he was probably considering whether or not he could match my prowess. I felt that he would not cross blades with me unless he were convinced he could win, and that he was not altogether convinced, at least not yet.

"Let us talk," said Thorn of Tharna.

I squatted down on my heels, as he did.

"Let us talk," I agreed.

We resheathed our weapons.

Thorn was a large man, big boned, powerful, now tending to corpulence. His face was heavy and yellowish, but mottled with patches of purple where small veins had burst under the skin. He was not bearded, save for the trace of a tiny wisp of hair that marked each side of his chin, almost like a streak of dirt. His hair was long, and bound in a knot behind his head in Mongol fashion. His eyes, like those of an urt, one of the small horned rodents of Gor, were set obliquely in his skull. They were not clear, their redness and shadows testifying to long nights of indulgence and dissipation. It was obvious that Thorn, unlike my old enemy Pa-Kur, who presumably had perished at the siege of Ar, was not a man above sensual vices, not a man who could with fanatical purity and single-minded devotion sacrifice himself and entire peoples to the ends of his ambition and power. Thorn would never make a Ubar. He would always be a henchman.

"Give me my man," said Thorn, gesturing to the figure that lay in the grass, still moving.

I decided that Thorn, whatever he was or wasn't, was a good officer.

"Take him," I said.

The spearman beside Thorn went to the fallen man and examined his wound. The other warrior was clearly dead.

"He may live," said the spearman.

Thorn nodded. "Bind his wound."

Thorn turned to me again.

"I still want the woman," he said.

"You may not take her," I said.

"She is only one woman," said Thorn.

"Then give her up," I said.

"One of my men is dead," said Thorn. "You can have his share of her selling price."

"You are generous," I said.

"Then it is agreed?" he asked.

"No," I said.

"I think we can kill you," said Thorn, plucking a stalk of grass and meditatively chewing on it, regarding me all the while.

"Perhaps," I admitted.

"On the other hand," said Thorn, "I do not wish to lose another man."

"Then give up the woman," I said.

Thorn looked at me intently, puzzled, chewing on the piece of grass.

"Who are you?" he asked.

I was silent.

"You are an outlaw," he said. "That I can see by the lack of insignia on your shield and tunic."

I saw no reason to dispute his opinion.

"Outlaw," said he, "what is your name?"

"Tarl," I responded.

"Of what city?" he asked.

It was the inevitable question.

"Ko-ro-ba," I said.

The effect was electric. The girl, who had been standing behind us, stifled a scream. Thorn and his warrior sprang to their feet. My sword was free of its sheath.

"Returned from the Cities of Dust," gasped the warrior.

"No," I said, "I am a living man, as you."

"Better you had gone to the Cities of Dust," said Thorn. "You are cursed by the Priest-Kings."

I looked at the girl.

"Your name is the most hated on Gor," she said, her voice flat, her eyes not meeting mine.

We four stood together, not speaking. It seemed a long time. I felt the grass on my ankles, still wet from the morning dew. I heard a bird cry in the distance.

Thorn shrugged.

"I will need time," he said, "to bury my man."

"Granted," I said.

Silently, Thorn and the other warrior scooped out a narrow trench and buried their comrade. Then wrapping a cloak about two spears, and fastening it with binding fiber, they formed an improvised litter. On this, Thorn and his warrior placed their wounded companion.

Thorn looked at the girl and, to my astonishment, she approached him and extended her wrists. He snapped slave bracelets on them.

"You do not need to go with them," I told her.

"I would bring you no pleasure," she said bitterly.

"I will free you," I said.

"I accept nothing from the hands of Tarl of Ko-ro-ba," she said.

I reached out my hand to touch her, and she shuddered and drew back.

Thorn laughed mirthlessly. "Better to have gone to the Cities of Dust than to be Tarl of Ko-ro-ba," he said.

I looked at the girl, now after her long days of suffering and flight at last a captive, her slender wrists encircled at last by Thorn's hated bracelets, beautifully wrought bracelets, like many, of exquisite workmanship, bright with color, set even with jewels, but like all slave bracelets, of unyielding steel.

The bracelets contrasted with the meanness of her coarse brown garment. Thorn fingered the garment. "We will get rid of this," he told her. "Soon, when you have been properly prepared, you will be dressed in costly pleasure silk, given sandals perhaps, scarves, veils and jewels, garments to gladden the heart of a maiden."

"Of a slave," she said.

Thorn lifted her chin with his finger. "You have a beautiful throat," he said.

She looked at him angrily, sensing his meaning.

"It will soon wear a collar," he said.

"Whose?" she demanded haughtily.

Thorn looked at her carefully. The chase had apparently in his eyes been well worth it. "Mine," he said.

The girl almost swooned.

My fists were clenched.

"Well, Tarl of Ko-ro-ba," said Thorn, "it ends thus. I take this girl and leave you to the Priest-Kings."

"If you take her to Tharna," I said, "the Tatrix will free her."

"I will not take her to Tharna, but to my villa," said Thorn, "which lies outside the city." He laughed unpleasantly. "And there," he said, "as a good man of Tharna should, I will revere her to my heart's content."

I felt my hand clench on the hilt of my sword.

"Stay your hand, Warrior," said Thorn. He turned to the girl. "To whom do you belong?" he asked.

"I belong to Thorn, Captain of Tharna," she said.

I replaced the sword in my sheath, shattered, helpless. I could kill Thorn and his warrior perhaps, free her. But what then? Free her to the beasts of Gor, to another slaver? She would never accept my protection, and by her own actions she preferred Thorn and slavery to a favor from the man called Tarl of Ko-ro-ba.

I looked at her. "Are you of Ko-ro-ba?" I asked.

She stiffened, and looked at me with hatred. "I was," she said.

"I am sorry," I said.

She looked at me, tears of hatred burning in her eyes. "Why have you dared to survive your city?" she asked.

"To avenge it," I replied.

She looked into my eyes for a long time. And then, as Thorn and the warrior picked up the litter with their wounded companion and began to depart, she said to me, "Good-bye, Tarl of Ko-ro-ba."

"I wish you well, Vera of the Towers of the Morning,"
I said.

She turned quickly, following her master, and I remained standing alone in the field.

8

THE CITY OF THARNA

THE STREETS OF THARNA WERE crowded, yet strangely silent. The gate had been open and though I had been carefully scrutinized by its guards, tall spearmen in blue helmets, no one had objected to my entry. It must be as I had heard, that the streets of Tharna were open to all men who came in peace, whatever their city.

Curiously, I examined the crowds, all seemingly bent on their business, yet strangely tight lipped, subdued, much different from the normal, bustling throngs of a Gorean city. Most of the male citizens wore gray tunics, perhaps indicative of their superiority to pleasure, their determination to be serious and responsible, to be worthy scions of that industrious and sober city.

On the whole they seemed to me a pale and depressed lot, but I was confident they could accomplish what they set their minds to, that they might succeed in tasks which the average Gorean male, with his impatience and lightness of heart, would simply abandon as distasteful or not worth the effort, for the average Gorean male, it must be admitted, tends to regard the joys of life somewhat more highly than its duties.

On the shoulders of their gray tunics only a small band of color indicated caste. Normally the caste colors of Gor would be in abundant evidence, enlivening the streets and bridges of the city, a glorious spectacle in Gor's bright, clear air.

I wondered if men in this city were not proud of their

castes, as were, on the whole, other Goreans, even those of the so-called lower castes. Even men of a caste as low as that of the Tarn-Keepers were intolerably proud of their calling, for who else could raise and train those monstrous birds of prey? I supposed Zosk the Woodsman was proud in the knowledge that he with his great broad-headed ax could fell a tree in one blow, and that perhaps not even a Ubar could do as much. Even the Caste of Peasants regarded itself as the "Ox on which the Home Stone Rests" and could seldom be encouraged to leave their narrow strips of land, which they and their fathers before them had owned and made fruitful.

I missed in the crowd the presence of slave girls, common in other cities, usually lovely girls clad only in the brief, diagonally striped slave livery of Gor, a sleeveless, briefly skirted garment terminating some inches above the knee, a garment that contrasts violently with the heavy, cumbersome Robes of Concealment worn by free women. Indeed, it was known that some free women actually envied their lightly clad sisters in bondage, free, though wearing a collar, to come and go much as they pleased, to feel the wind on the high bridges, the arms of a master who celebrated their beauty and claimed them as his own. I remembered that in Tharna, ruled by its Tatrix, there would be few, if any, female slaves. Whether or not there were male slaves I could not well judge, for the collars would have been hidden by the gray robes. There is no distinctive garment for a male slave on Gor, since, as it is said, it is not well for them to discover how numerous they are.

The purpose, incidentally, of the brief garment of the female slave is not simply to mark out the girl in bondage but, in exposing her charms, to make her, rather than her free sister, the favored object of raids on the part of roving tarnsmen. Whereas there is status in the capture of a free woman, there is less risk in the capture of a slave; the pursuit is never pressed as determinedly in their cases, and one does not have to imperil one's life for a girl who might, once the Robes of Concealment have been cast off, turn out to have the face of an urt and the temper of a sleen.

Perhaps I was most startled on the silent streets of Tharna by the free women. They walked in this city unattended, with an imperious step, the men of Tharna moving to let them pass—in such a way that they never touched. Each of these women wore resplendent Robes of Concealment, rich in color and workmanship, standing out among the drab garments of the men, but instead of the veil common with such robes the features of each were hidden behind a mask of silver. The masks were of identical design, each formed in the semblance of a beautiful, but cold face. Some of these masks had turned to gaze upon me as I passed, my scarlet warrior's tunic having caught their eye. It made me uneasy to be the obect of their gaze, to be confronted by those passionless, glittering silver masks.

Wandering in the city I found myself in Tharna's marketplace. Though it was apparently a market day, judging from the numerous stalls of vegetables, the racks of meat under awnings, the tubs of salted fish, the cloths and trinkets spread out on carpets before the seated, cross-legged merchants, there was none of the noisy clamor that customarily attends the Gorean market. I missed the shrill, interminable calls of the vendors, each different; the good-natured banter of friends in the marketplace exchanging gossip and dinner invitations; the shouts of burly porters threading their way through the tumult; the cries of children escaped from their tutors and playing tag among the stalls; the laughter of veiled girls teasing and being teased by young men, girls purportedly on errands for their families, yet somehow finding the time to taunt the young swains of the city, if only by a flash of their dark eyes and a perhaps too casual adjustment of their veil.

Though on Gor the free maiden is by custom expected to see her future companion only after her parents have selected him, it is common knowledge that he is often a youth she has met in the marketplace. He who speaks for

her hand, especially if she is of low caste, is seldom
unknown to her, although the parents and the young
people as well solemnly act as though this were the case.
The same maiden whom her father must harshly order
into the presence of her suitor, the same shy girl who, her
parents approvingly note, finds herself delicately unable to
raise her eyes in his presence, is probably the same girl
who slapped him with a fish yesterday and hurled such a
stream of invective at him that his ears still smart, and all
because he had accidentally happened to be looking in her
direction when an unpredictable wind had, in spite of her
best efforts, temporarily disarranged the folds of her veil.

But this market was not like other markets I had
known on Gor. This was simply a drab place in which to
buy food and exchange goods. Even the bargaining that
went on, for there are no fixed prices in a Gorean
market, seemed dreary, grim, lacking the zest and rivalry
of other markets I had seen, the glorious expletives and
superlative insults traded between buyer and seller with
such incomparable style and gusto. Indeed, upon occasion, in other markets, a buyer who had succeeded in
winning the haggling would bestow five times as many
coins on the seller as he had agreed to pay, humiliating
him with a smug, "Because I wish to pay you what it is
worth." Then, if the seller is sufficiently outraged, he
might give back the buyer the coins, including most of
those he had agreed to pay, saying, with mock contrition,
"I do not wish to cheat you." Then another round of
insults occurs, and, eventually, both parties satisfied, some
compromise having been reached, the transaction is concluded. Buyer and seller part, each convinced that he has
had by far the best of the bargain.

In this market, on the other hand, a steward would
simply approach a vendor and point to some article, and
hold up a certain number of fingers. The vendor would
then hold up a higher number, sometimes bending his
fingers at the knuckle to indicate a fraction of the value
unit, which would be, presumably, the copper tarn disk.
The steward might then improve his offer, or prepare to

depart. The vendor would then either let him go or lower his price, by expressionlessly lifting fewer fingers than before. When either party called off the bargaining, his fists were closed. If a sale had been made, the steward would take a number of pierced coins, threaded on a string hung about his left shoulder, hand them to the vendor, pick up his article and depart. When words were exchanged, they were whispered and curt.

As I left the marketplace, I noted two men, furtive, round-shouldered in their nondescript gray robes, who followed me. Their faces were concealed in the folds of their garments, which had been drawn over their heads in the manner of a hood. Spies, I thought. It was an intelligent precaution for Tharna to take, to keep an eye on the stranger, lest her hospitality be abused. I made no effort to elude their surveillance, for that might perhaps have been interpreted as a breach of etiquette on my part, perhaps even a confession of villainous intention. Besides, as they did not know that I knew they followed me, this gave me a certain advantage in the matter. It was possible, of course, that they were merely curious. After all, how many scarlet-clad warriors appeared from day to day in the drab streets of Tharna?

I climbed one of the towers of Tharna, wanting to look out upon the city. I emerged on the highest bridge I could find. It was railed, as most Gorean bridges, high or low, are not. Slowly I let my eye wander the city, surely in its people and their customs one of the most unusual on Gor.

Tharna, though a city of cylinders, did not seem to my eye as beautiful as many other cities I had seen. This was perhaps because the cylinders were, on the whole, less lofty than those of other cities, and much broader, giving an impression of a set of squat, accumulated disks, so different from the lofty forests of sky-challenging towers and battlements distinguishing most Gorean cities. Moreover, in contrast to most cities, the cylinders of Tharna seemed excessively solemn, as if overcome by their own weight. They were scarcely distinguishable from one another, an aggregate of grays and browns, so different from the thousand gay colors that gleamed in most cities, where each cylinder in towering splendor lodged its claim to be the bravest and most beautiful of all.

Even the horizontal plains about Tharna, marked by their occasional outcroppings of weathered boulders, seemed to be gray, rather cold and gloomy, perhaps sad. Tharna was not a city to lift the heart of a man. Yet I knew that this city was, from my point of view, one of the most enlightened and civilized on Gor. In spite of this conviction, incomprehensibly, I found myself depressed by Tharna, and wondered if it, in its way, were not somehow, subtly, more barbaric, more harsh, less human than its ruder, less noble, more beautiful sisters. I determined that I should try to secure a tarn and proceed as quickly as possible to the Sardar Mountains, to keep my appointment with the Priest-Kings.

"Stranger," said a voice.

I turned.

One of the two nondescript men who had been following me had approached. His face was concealed in the folds of his robe. With one hand he held the folds together, lest the wind should lift the cloth and reveal his face, and with the other hand, he clutched the rail on the bridge, as if uncomfortable, uneasy at the height.

A slight rain had begun to fall.

"Tal," I said to the man, lifting my arm in the common Gorean greeting.

"Tal," he responded, not taking his arm from the rail. He approached me, more closely than I liked.

"You are a stranger in this city," he said.

"Yes," I said.

"Who are you, Stranger?"

"I am a man of no city," I said, "whose name is Tarl." I wanted no more of the havoc I had wreaked earlier by the mere mention of the name of Ko-ro-ba.

"What is your business in Tharna?" he asked.

"I should like to obtain a tarn," I said, "for a journey I have in mind." I had answered him rather directly. I assumed him to be a spy, charged with learning my reasons for visiting Tharna. I scorned to conceal this reason, though the object of my journey I reserved to myself. That I was determined to reach the Sardar Mountains he need not know. That I had business with the Priest-Kings was not his concern.

"A tarn is expensive," he said.

"I know," I said.

"Have you money?" he asked.

"No," I said.

"How then," he asked, "do you propose to obtain your tarn?"

"I am not an outlaw," I said, "though I wear no insignia on my tunic, or shield."

"Of course not," he said quickly. "There is no place in Tharna for an outlaw. We are a hard-working and honest folk."

I could see that he did not believe me, and somehow I did not believe him either. For no good reason I began to dislike him. With both hands I reached to his hood and jerked it from his face. He snatched at the cloth and replaced it quickly. I had caught a brief glimpse of a sallow face, with skin like a dried lemon and pale blue eyes. His comrade, who had been furtively peering about, started forward and then stopped. The sallow-faced man, clutching the folds of the hood about his face, twisted his head to the left and the right to see if anyone might be near, if anyone might have observed.

"I like to see to whom I speak," I said.

"Of course," said the man ingratiatingly, a bit unsteadily, drawing the hood even more closely about his features.

"I want to obtain a tarn," I said. "Can you help me?" If he could not, I had decided to terminate the interview.

"Yes," said the man.

I was interested.

"I can help you obtain not only a tarn," said the man, "but a thousand golden tarn disks and provisions for as lengthy a journey as you might wish."

"I am not an assassin," I said.

"Ah!" said the man.

Since the siege of Ar, when Pa-Kur, Master Assassin, had violated the limits of his caste and had presumed, in contradiction to the traditions of Gor, to lead a horde upon the city, intending to make himself Ubar, the Caste of Assassins had lived as hated, hunted men, no longer esteemed mercenaries whose services were sought by cities, and, as often by factions within cities. Now many assassins roamed Gor, fearing to wear the somber black tunic of their caste, disguised as members of other castes, not infrequently as warriors.

"I am not an assassin," I repeated.

"Of course not," said the man. "The Caste of Assassins no longer exists."

I doubted that.

"But are you not intrigued, Stranger," asked the man, his pale eyes squinting up at me through the folds of the gray robe, "by the offer of a tarn, gold and provisions?"

"What must I do to earn this?" I asked.

"You need kill no one," said the man.

"What then?" I asked.

"You are bold and strong," he said.

"What must I do?" I asked.

"You have undoubtedly had experience in affairs of this sort," suggested the man.

"What would you have me do?" I demanded.

"Carry off a woman," he said.

The light drizzle of rain, almost a gray mist matching the miserable solemnity of Tharna, had not abated, and had, by now, soaked through my garments. The wind, which I had not noticed before, now seemed cold.

"What woman?" I asked.

"Lara," said he.

"And who is Lara?" I asked.

"Tatrix of Tharna," he said.

9

THE KAL-DA SHOP

STANDING THERE ON THE BRIDGE, in the rain, facing the obsequious, hooded conspirator, I felt suddenly sad. Here even in the noble city of Tharna there was intrigue, political strife, ambition that would not brook confinement. I had been taken for an assassin, or an outlaw, been assessed as a likely instrument for the furtherance of the foul schemes of one of Tharna's dissatisfied factions.

"I refuse," I said.

The small lemon-faced man drew back as if slapped. "I represent a personage of power in this city," he said.

"I wish no harm to Lara, Tatrix of Tharna," I told him.

"What is she to you?" asked the man.

"Nothing," I said.

"And yet you refuse?"

"Yes," I said, "I refuse."

"You are afraid," he said.

"No," I said, "I am not afraid."

"You will never get your tarn," hissed the man. He turned on his heel and still clinging to the railing on the bridge scurried to the threshhold of the cylinder, his comrade before him. At the threshhold he called back. "You will never leave the walls of Tharna alive," he said.

"Be it so," I said, "I will not do your bidding."

The slight, gray-robed figure, almost as insubstantial as the mist itself, appeared ready to leave, but suddenly hesitated. He appeared to waver for a moment, then he briefly conferred with his companion. They seemed to reach some agreement. Cautiously, his companion remaining behind, he edged out onto the bridge again.

"I spoke hastily," he said. "No danger will come to you in Tharna. We are a hard-working and honest folk."

"I am pleased to hear that," I said.

Then to my surprise he pressed a small, heavy leather sack of coins into my hand. He smiled up at me, a twisted grin visible through the obscuring folds of the gray robe. "Welcome to Tharna!" he said, and fled across the bridge and into the cylinder.

"Come back!" I cried, holding the bag of coins out to him. "Come back!"

But he was gone.

At least this night, this rainy night, I would not sleep again in the fields, for thanks to the puzzling gift of the hooded conspirator, I had the means to purchase lodging. I left the bridge, and descended through the spiral stair-well of the cylinder, soon finding myself on the streets again.

Inns, as such, are not plentiful on Gor, the hostility of cities being what it is, but usually some can be found in each city. There must, after all, be provision made for entertaining merchants, delegations from other cities, authorized visitors of one sort or another, and to be frank the innkeeper is not always scrupulous about the credentials of his guests, asking few questions if he receives his handful of copper tarn disks. In Tharna, however, famed for its hospitality, I was confident that inns would be common. It was surprising then that I could locate none.

I decided, if worse came to worst, that I could always go to a simple Paga Tavern where, if those of Tharna resembled those of Ko-ro-ba and Ar, one might, curled in a rug behind the low tables, unobtrusively spend the night for the price of a pot of Paga, a strong, fermented drink brewed from the yellow grains of Gor's staple crop, Sa-Tarna, or Life-Daughter. The expression is related to

Sa-Tassna, the expression for meat, or for food in general, which means Life-Mother. Paga is a corruption of Pagar-Sa-Tarna, which means Pleasure of the Life-Daughter. It was customary to find diversions other than Paga in the Paga Taverns, as well, but in gray Tharna the cymbals, drums and flutes of the musicians, the clashing of bangles on the ankles of dancing girls would be unfamiliar sounds.

I stopped one of the anonymous, gray-robed figures hurrying through the wet, cold dusk.

"Man of Tharna," I asked, "where can I find an inn?"

"There are no inns in Tharna," said the man, looking at me closely. "You are a stranger," he said.

"A weary traveler who seeks lodging," I said.

"Flee, Stranger," said he.

"I am welcome in Tharna," I said.

"Leave while you have time," he said, looking about to see if anyone were listening.

"Is there no Paga Tavern near," I asked, "where I can find rest?"

"There are no Paga Taverns in Tharna," said the man, I thought with a trace of amusement.

"Where can I spend the night?" I asked.

"You can spend it beyond the walls in the fields," he said, "or you can spend it in the Palace of the Tatrix."

"It sounds to me as though the Palace of the Tatrix were the more comfortable," I said.

The man laughed bitterly. "How many hours, Warrior," asked he, "have you been within the walls of Tharna?"

"At the sixth hour I came to Tharna," I said.

"It is then too late," said the man, with a trace of sorrow, "for you have been within the walls for more than ten hours."

"What do you mean?" I asked.

"Welcome to Tharna," said the man, and hurried away into the dusk.

I had been disturbed by this conversation and without really intending it had begun to walk to the walls. I stood before the great gate of Tharna. The two giant beams that barred it were in place, beams that could only be moved by a team of broad tharlarions, draft lizards of Gor, or by a hundred slaves. The gates, bound with their bands of steel, studded with brass plates dull in the mist, the black wood looming over me in the dusk, were closed.

"Welcome to Tharna," said a guard, leaning on his spear in the shadows of the gate.

"Thank you, Warrior," I said, and turned back to the city.

Behind me I heard him laugh, much the same bitter laugh that I had heard from the citizen.

In wandering through the streets, I came at last to a squat portal in the wall of a cylinder. On each side of the door, in a small niche sheltered from the drizzle, there sputtered the yellow flame of a small tharlarion oil lamp. By this flickering light I could read the faded lettering on the door: KAL-DA SOLD HERE.

Kal-da is a hot drink, almost scalding, made of diluted Ka-la-na wine, mixed with citrus juices and stinging spices. I did not care much for this mouth-burning concoction, but it was popular with some of the lower castes, particularly those who performed strenuous manual labor. I expected its popularity was due more to its capacity to warm a man and stick to his ribs, and to its cheapness (a poor grade of Ka-la-na wine being used in its brewing) than to any gustatory excellence. But I reasoned on this night of all nights, this cold, depressing wet night, a cup of Kal-da might go well indeed. Moreover, where there was Kal-da there should be bread and meat. I thought of the yellow Gorean bread, baked in the shape of round, flat loaves, fresh and hot; my mouth watered for a tabuk steak or, perhaps, if I were lucky, a slice of roast tarsk, the formidable six-tusked wild boar of Gor's temperate forests. I smiled to myself, felt the sack of coins in my tunic, bent down and pushed the door open.

I decended three steps, and found myself in a warm, dimly lit, low-ceilinged room, cluttered with the low tables common on Gor, around which huddled groups of five or six of the gray-robed men of Tharna. The murmur of conversation ceased as I entered. The men regarded me. There seemed to be no warriors in the room. None of the men appeared to be armed.

I must have seemed strange to them, a scarlet-clad warrior, bearing weapons, suddenly entering, a man from another city unexpectedly in their midst.

"What is your business?" asked the proprietor of the place, a small, thin, bald-headed man wearing a short-sleeved gray tunic and slick black apron. He did not approach, but remained behind the wooden counter, slowly, deliberately wiping the puddles of spilled Kal-da from its stained surface.

"I am passing through Tharna," I said. "And I would like to purchase a tarn to continue my journey. Tonight I want food and lodging."

"This is not a place," said the man, "for one of High Caste."

I looked about, at the men in the room, into the dejected, haggard faces. In the light it was difficult to determine their caste for they all wore the gray robes of Tharna and only a band of color on the shoulder indicated their station in the social fabric. What struck me most about them had nothing to do with caste, but rather their lack of spirit. I did not know if they were weak, or if they merely thought poorly of themselves. They seemed to me to be without energy, without pride, to be flat, dry, crushed men, men without self-respect.

"You are of high caste, of the Caste of Warriors," said the proprietor. "It is not proper that you should remain here."

I did not much care for the prospect of emerging again into the cold, rainy night, of tramping once more through the streets, miserable, chilled to the bone, looking for a place to eat and sleep. I took a coin from the leather sack and threw it to the proprietor. He snatched it expertly from the air like a skeptical cormorant. He examined the coin. It was a silver tarn disk. He bit against the metal, the muscles on his jaw bulging in the lamplight. A trace of

avaricious pleasure appeared in his eyes. I knew he would
not care to return it.

"What caste is it?" I demanded.

The proprietor smiled. "Money has no caste," he said.

"Bring me food and drink," I said.

I went to an obscure, deserted table near the back of
the room, where I could face the door. I leaned my shield
and spear against the wall, set the helmet beside the table,
unslung the sword belt, laying the weapon across the table
before me, and prepared to wait.

I had hardly settled myself behind the table when the
proprietor had placed a large, fat pot of steaming Kal-da
before me. It almost burned my hands to lift the pot. I
took a long, burning swig of the brew and though, on
another occasion, I might have thought it foul, tonight it
sang through my body like the bubbling fire it was, a
sizzling, brutal irritant that tasted so bad and yet charmed
me so much I had to laugh.

And laugh I did.

The men of Tharna who were crowded in that place
looked upon me as though I might be mad. Disbelief, lack
of comprehension, was written on their features. This man
had laughed. I wondered if men laughed often in Tharna.

It was a dreary place, but the Kal-da had already made
it appear somewhat more promising.

"Talk, laugh!" I said to the men of Tharna, who had
said not a word since my entrance. I glared at them. I
took another long swig of Kal-da and shook my head to
throw the swirling fire from eyes and brain. I seized my
spear from the wall and pounded it on the table.

"If you cannot talk," I said, "if you cannot laugh, then
sing!"

They were convinced they were in the presence of one
demented. It was, I suppose, the Kal-da, but I like to
think, too, it was just impatience with the males of Tharna, the intemperate expression of my exasperation with
this gray, dismal place, its glum, solemn, listless inhabi-
tants. The men of Tharna refused to budge from their
silence.

"Do we not speak the Language?" I asked, referring to the beautiful mother tongue spoken in common by most of the Gorean cities. "Is the Language not yours?" I demanded.

"It is," mumbled one of the men.

"Then why do you not speak it?" I challenged.

The man was silent.

The proprietor arrived with hot bread, honey, salt and, to my delight, a huge, hot roasted chunk of tarsk. I crammed my mouth with food and washed it down with another thundering draught of Kal-da.

"Proprietor!" I cried, pounding on the table with my spear.

"Yes, Warrior," cried he.

"Where are the Pleasure Slaves?" I demanded.

The proprietor seemed stunned.

"I would see a woman dance," I said.

The men of Tharna seemed horrified. One whispered, "There are no Pleasure Slaves in Tharna."

"Alas!" I cried, "not a bangle in all Tharna!"

Two or three of the men laughed. At last I had touched them.

"Those creatures that float in the street behind masks of silver," I asked, "are they truly women?"

"Truly," said one of the men, restraining a laugh.

"I doubt it," I cried. "Shall I fetch one, to see if she will dance for us?"

The men laughed.

I had pretended to rise to my feet, and the proprietor, with horror, had shoved me back down, and rushed for more Kal-da. His strategy was to pour so much Kal-da down my throat that I would be unable to do anything but roll under the table and sleep. Some of the men crowded around the table now.

"Where are you from?" asked one eagerly.

"I have lived all my life in Tharna," I told them.

There was a great roar of laughter.

Soon, pounding the time on the table with the butt of my spear, I was leading a raucous round of songs, mostly wild drinking songs, warrior songs, songs of the encampment and march, but too I taught them songs I had learned in the caravan of Mintar the Merchant, so long ago, when I had first loved Talena, songs of love, of loneliness, of the beauties of one's cities, and of the fields of Gor.

The Kal-da flowed free that night and thrice the oil in the hanging tharlarion lamps needed to be renewed by the sweating, joyful proprietor of the Kal-da shop. Men from the streets, dumbfounded by the sounds which came from within, pressed through the squat door and soon had joined in. Some warriors entered, too, and instead of attempting to restore order had incredibly taken off their helmets, filled them with Kal-da and sat cross-legged with us, to sing and drink their fill.

The lights in the tharlarion lamps had finally flickered and gone out, and the chill light of dawn at last bleakly illuminated the room. Many of the men had left, more had perhaps fallen on the tables, or lay along the sides of the room. Even the proprietor slept, his head across his folded arms on the counter, behind which stood the great Kal-da brewing pots, at last empty and cold. I rubbed the sleep from my eyes. There was a hand on my shoulder.

"Wake up," demanded a voice.

"He's the one," said another voice, one I seemed to remember.

I struggled to my feet, and confronted the small, lemon-faced conspirator.

"We've been looking for you," said the other voice, which I now saw belonged to a burly guardsman of Tharna. Behind him in their blue helmets stood three others.

"He's the thief," said the lemon-faced man, pointing to me. His hand darted to the table where the bag of coins lay, half spilled out in the dried puddles of Kal-da.

"These are my coins," said the conspirator. "My name is stitched into the leather of the sack." He shoved the sack under the nose of the guardsman.

"Ost," read the guardsman. It was also the name of a

species of tiny, brightly orange reptile, the most venomous on Gor.

"I am not a thief," I said. "He gave me the coins."

"He is lying," said Ost.

"I am not," I said.

"You are under arrest," said the guardsman.

"In whose name?" I demanded.

"In the name of Lara," said the man, "Tatrix of Tharna."

10

THE PALACE OF THE TATRIX

RESISTANCE WOULD HAVE BEEN USELESS.

My weapons had been removed while I slept, foolish and trusting in the hospitality of Tharna. I faced the guards unarmed. Yet the officer must have read defiance in my eyes because he signaled his men, and three spears dropped to threaten my breast.

"I stole nothing," I said.

"You may plead your case before the Tatrix," said the guard.

"Shackle him," insisted Ost.

"Are you a warrior?" asked the guardsman.

"I am," I said.

"Have I your word that you will accompany me peaceably to the palace of the Tatrix?" asked the guardsman.

"Yes," I said.

The guardsman spoke to his men. "Shackles will not be necessary."

"I am innocent," I told the guardsman.

He looked at me, his gray eyes frank in the Y-slot in his somber blue helmet of Tharna. "It is for the Tatrix to decide," he said.

"You must shackle him!" wheezed Ost.

"Quiet, worm," said the guardsman, and the conspirator subsided into squirming silence.

I followed the guardsman, yet ringed with his men, to the palace of the Tatrix. Ost scurried along behind us, puffing and gasping, his short, bandy legs struggling to keep pace with the stride of warriors.

I felt that even had I chosen to forswear my pledge, which as a warrior of Gor I would not, my chances of escape would have been small indeed. In all likelihood three spears would have transfixed my body within my first few steps toward freedom. I respected the quiet, efficient guardsmen of Tharna, and I had already encountered her skilled warriors in a field far from the city. I wondered if Thorn were in the city, and if Vera now wore her pleasure silk in his villa.

I knew that if justice were done in Tharna I would be acquitted, yet I was uneasy—for how was I to know if my case would be fairly heard and decided? That I had been in possession of Ost's sack of coins would surely seem good prima-facie evidence of guilt, and this might well sway the decision of the Tatrix. How would my word, the word of a stranger, weigh against the words of Ost, a citizen of Tharna and perhaps one of significance?

Yet, incredibly perhaps, I looked forward to seeing the palace and the Tatrix, to meeting face to face the unusual woman who could rule, and rule well, a city of Gor. Had I not been arrested I guessed I might, of my own free will, have called upon the Tatrix of Tharna, and, as one citizen had expressed it, spent my night in her palace.

After we had walked for perhaps some twenty minutes through the drab, graveled, twisted streets of Tharna, its gray citizens parting to make way for us and to stare expressionlessly at the scarlet-clad prisoner, we came to a broad winding avenue, steep and paved with black cobblestones, still shiny from the rains of the night. On each side of the avenue was a gradually ascending brick wall, and as we trudged upward the walls on each side became higher and the avenue more narrow.

At last, a hundred yards ahead, cold in the morning light, I saw the palace, actually a rounded fortress of brick, black, heavy, unadorned, formidable. At the entrance to the palace the somber, wet avenue shrunk to a passage large enough only for a single man, and the walls at the same time rose to a height of perhaps thirty feet.

The entrance itself was nothing more than a small, simple iron door, perhaps eighteen inches in width, perhaps five feet in height. Only one man could come or go at a time from the palace of Tharna. It was a far cry from the broad-portaled central cylinders of many of the Gorean cities, through which a brace of golden-harnessed tharlarions might be driven with ease. I wondered if within this stern, brutal fortress, this palace of the Tatrix of Tharna, justice could be done.

The guardsman motioned to the door, and stepped behind me. I was facing the door, first in the narrow passage.

"We do not enter," said the guardsman. "Only you and Ost."

I turned to regard them, and three spears dropped level with my chest.

There was a sound of sliding bolts and the iron door swung open, revealing nothing but darkness within.

"Enter," commanded the guardsman.

I glanced once more at the spears, smiled grimly at the guardsman, turned and, lowering my head, entered the small door.

Suddenly I cried out in alarm, pawing at nothing, hurtling downward. I heard Ost scream with surprise and terror as he was shoved through the door behind me.

Some twenty feet below the level of the door, in the absolute darkness, with brutal impact, I struck bottom, a stone floor covered with wet straw. Ost's body struck mine almost at the same time. I fought for breath. My vision seemed ringed with gold and purple specks. I was dimly conscious of being seized by the mouth of some large animal and being tugged through a round tunnel-like opening. I tried to struggle, but it was useless. My breath had been driven from me, the tunnel allowed me no room to move. I smelled the wet fur of the animal, a rodent of some kind, the smells of its den, the soiled straw. I was aware, far off, of Ost's hysterical screams.

For some time the animal, moving backwards, its prey seized in its jaws, scrambled through the tunnel. It dragged me in a series of quick, vicious jerks through the tunnel, scraping me on its stone walls, lacerating me, ripping my tunic.

At last it dragged me into a round, globelike space, lit by two torches in iron racks, which were set into the fitted stone walls. I heard a voice of command, loud, harsh. The animal squealed in displeasure. I heard the crack of a whip and the same command, more forcibly uttered. Reluctantly the animal released its grip and backed away, crouching down, watching me with its long, oblique blazing eyes, like slits of molten gold in the torchlight.

It was a giant urt, fat, sleek and white; it bared its three rows of needlelike white teeth at me and squealed in anger; two horns, tusks like flat crescents curved from its jaw; another two horns, similar to the first, modifications of the bony tissue forming the upper ridge of the eye socket, protruded over those gleaming eyes that seemed to feast themselves upon me, as if waiting the permission of the keeper to hurl itself on its feeding trough. Its fat body trembled with anticipation.

The whip cracked again, and another command was uttered, and the animal, its long hairless tail lashing in frustration, slunk into another tunnel. An iron gate, consisting of bars, fell behind it.

Several pairs of strong hands seized me, and I caught a glimpse of a heavy, curved, silverish object. I tried to rise but was pressed down, my face to the stone. A heavy object, thick as a hinged beam, was thrust beneath and over my throat. My wrists were held in position, and the device closed on my throat and wrists. With a sinking sensation I heard the snap of a heavy lock.

"He's yoked," said a voice.

"Rise, Slave," said another.

I tried to rise to my feet, but the weight was too much. I heard the hiss of a whip and gritted my teeth as the leather coil bit at my flesh. Again and again it struck downward like lightning bolts of leather fire. I managed to get my knees under me, and then, painfully, heaved the yoke upward, struggling unsteadily to my feet.

"Well done, Slave," said a voice.

Amidst the burning of the lash wounds I felt the cold air of the dungeon on my back. The whip had opened my tunic, I would be bleeding. I turned to look at the man who had spoken. It was he who held the whip. I noted grimly that its leather was wet with my blood.

"I am not a slave," I said.

The man was stripped to the waist, a brawny fellow wearing buckled leather wrist straps, his hair bound back on his head with a band of gray cloth.

"In Tharna," said he, "a man such as you can be nothing else."

I looked about the room, which curved to a dome some twenty-five feet above the floor. There were several exits, most of them rather small, barred apertures. From some I heard groaning. From some others I heard the shuffling and squealing of animals, perhaps more of the giant urts. By one wall there was a large bowl of burning coals, from which protruded the handles of several irons. A rack of some sort was placed near the bowl of coals. It was large enough to accommodate a human being. In certain of the walls chains were fixed, and here and there, other chains dangled from the ceiling. On the walls, as though in some workshop, there hung instruments of various sorts, which I shall not describe, other than to say that they were ingeniously designed for the torment of human beings.

It was an ugly place.

"Here," said the man proudly, "peace is kept in Tharna."

"I demand," I said, "to be taken to the Tatrix."

"Of course," said the man. He laughed unpleasantly. "I shall take you to the Tatrix myself."

I heard the winding of a chain on a windlass, and saw one of the barred gates leading from the chamber slowly lifting. The man gestured with his whip. I understood I was to go through the opening.

"The Tatrix of Tharna is expecting you," he said.

11

LARA, TATRIX OF THARNA

I PASSED THROUGH THE OPENING, and painfully
began to climb a small, circular passage, staggering with
each step under the weight of the heavy metal yoke. The
man with the whip, cursing, urged me to greater speed. He
poked me savagely with the whip, the narrowness of the
passage not allowing him to use it as he wished.

Already my legs and shoulders ached from the strain of
the yoke.

We emerged in a broad, but dim hall. Several doors led
from this hall. With his whip, prodding me scornfully, the
man in wrist straps directed me through one of these
doors. This door led again into a corridor, from which
again several doors led, and so it continued. It was like
being driven through a maze or sewer. The halls were lit
occasionally by tharlarion oil lamps set in iron fixtures
mounted in the walls. The interior of the palace seemed to
me to be deserted. It was innocent of color, of adornment.
I staggered on, smarting from the whip wounds, almost
crushed by the burden of the yoke. I doubted if I could,
unaided, find my way from this sinister labyrinth.

At last I found myself in a large, vaulted room, lit by
torches set in the walls. In spite of its loftiness, it too was
plain, like the other rooms and passageways I had seen,
somber, oppressive. Only one adornment relieved the walls
of their melancholy aspect, the image of a gigantic golden
mask, carved in the likeness of a beautiful woman.

Beneath this mask, there was, on a high dais, a monumental throne of gold.

On the broad steps leading to the throne, there were curule chairs, on which sat, I supposed, members of the High Council of Tharna. Their glittering silver masks, each carved in the image of the same beautiful woman, regarded me expressionlessly.

About the room, here and there, stood stern warriors of Tharna, grim in their blue helmets, each with a tiny silver mask on the temple—members of the palace guard. One such helmeted warrior stood near the foot of the throne. There seemed to be something familiar about him.

On the throne itself there sat a woman, proud, lofty in haughty dignity, garbed regally in majestic robes of golden cloth, wearing a mask not of silver but of pure gold, carved like the others in the image of a beautiful woman. The eyes behind the glittering mask of gold regarded me. No one need tell me that I stood in the presence of Lara, Tatrix of Tharna.

The warrior at the foot of the throne removed his helmet. It was Thorn, Captain of Tharna, whom I had met in the fields far from the city. His narrow eyes, like those of an urt, looked upon me contemptuously.

He strode to face me.

"Kneel," he commanded. "You stand before Lara, Tatrix of Tharna."

I would not kneel.

Thorn kicked my feet from under me, and, under the weight of the yoke, I crashed to the floor, helpless.

"The whip," said Thorn, extending his hand. The burly man in wrist straps placed it in his hand. Thorn lifted the instrument to lay my back open with its harsh stroke.

"Do not strike him," said an imperious voice, and the whip arm of Thorn dropped as though the muscles had been cut. The voice came from the woman behind the golden mask, Lara herself. I was grateful.

Hot with sweat, each fiber in my body screaming in agony, I managed to gain my knees. Thorn's hand would allow me to rise no further. I knelt, yoked, before the Tatrix of Tharna.

The eyes behind the yellow mask regarded me, curiously.

"Is it thus, Stranger," she asked, her tones cold, "that you expected to carry from the city the wealth of Tharna?"

I was puzzled, my body was racked with pain, my vision was blurred with sweat.

"The yoke is of silver," said she, "from the mines of Tharna."

I was stunned, for if the yoke was truly of silver, the metal on my shoulders might have ransomed a Ubar.

"We of Tharna," said the Tatrix, "think so little of riches that we use them to yoke slaves."

My angry glare told her that I did not consider myself a slave.

From the curule chair beside the throne rose another woman, wearing an intricately wrought silver mask and magnificent robes of rich silver cloth. She stood haughtily beside the Tatrix, the expressionless silver mask gleaming down at me, hideous in the torchlight it reflected. Speaking to the Tatrix, but not turning the mask from me, she said, "Destroy the animal." It was a cold, ringing voice, clear, decisive, authoritative.

"Does the law of Tharna not give it the right to speak, Dorna the Proud, Second in Tharna?" asked the Tatrix, whose voice, too, was imperious and cold, yet pleased me more than the tones of she who wore the silver mask.

"Does the law recognize beasts?" asked the woman whose name was Dorna the Proud. It was almost as if she challenged her Tatrix, and I wondered if Dorna the Proud was content to be Second in Tharna. The sarcasm in her voice had been ill concealed.

The Tatrix did not choose to respond to Dorna the Proud.

"Has he still his tongue?" asked the Tatrix of the man with the wrist straps, who stood behind me.

"Yes, Tatrix," said the man.

I thought that the woman in the silver mask, who had been spoken of as Second in Tharna, seemed to stiffen with apprehension at this revelation. The silver mask turned upon the man in wrist straps. His voice stammered, and I wondered if, behind me, his burly frame trembled. "It was the wish of the Tatrix that the slave be yoked and brought to the Chamber of the Golden Mask as soon as possible, and unharmed."

I smiled to myself, thinking of the teeth of the urt and the whip, both of which had found my flesh.

"Why did you not kneel, Stranger?" asked the Tatrix of Tharna.

"I am a warrior," I responded.

"You are a slave!" hissed Dorna the Proud from behind that expressionless mask. Then she turned to the Tatrix. "Remove his tongue!" she said.

"Do you give orders to she who is First in Tharna?" asked the Tatrix.

"No, Beloved Tatrix," said Dorna the Proud.

"Slave," said the Tatrix.

I did not acknowledge the salutation.

"Warrior," she said.

Beneath the yoke I raised my eyes to her mask. In her hand, covered with a glove of gold, she held a small, dark leather sack, half filled with coins. I assumed they were the coins of Ost and wondered where the conspirator might be. "Confess that you stole these coins from Ost of Tharna," said the Tatrix.

"I stole nothing," I said. "Release me."

Thorn laughed unpleasantly from behind me.

"I advise you," said the Tatrix, "to confess."

I gathered that, for some reason, she was eager that I plead guilty to the crime, but as I was innocent, I refused.

"I did not steal the coins," I said.

"Then, Stranger," said the Tatrix, "I am sorry for you."

I could not understand her remark, and my back felt ready to snap under the weight of the yoke. My neck ached under its weight. The sweat poured down my body and my back still stung from the lash.

"Bring in Ost!" ordered the Tatrix.

I thought Dorna the Proud stirred uneasily in the curule chair. She smoothed the silver folds of her robes with a nervous hand, gloved in silver.

There was a whimpering and a scuffling from behind me, and, to my astonishment, one of the guardsman of the palace, the tiny silver mask blazed across the left temple of his helmet, flung Ost, the conspirator, yoked and sniveling, to the foot of the throne. Ost's yoke was much lighter than mine but, as he was a smaller man, the weight might have been as much for him.

"Kneel to the Tatrix," commanded Thorn, who still retained the whip.

Ost, squealing with fear, tried to rise, but could not lift the yoke.

Thorn's whip hand was raised.

I expected the Tatrix to intervene on his behalf, as she had on mine, but, instead, she said nothing. She seemed to be watching me. I wondered what thoughts glittered behind that placid mask of gold.

"Do not strike him," I said.

Without taking her eyes from me, Lara spoke to Thorn. "Prepare to strike," she said.

The yellowish, purple-marked face split into a grin and Thorn's fist tightened on the whip. He did not take his eyes from the Tatrix, wanting to strike at the first instant she permitted the blow.

"Rise," said the Tatrix to Ost, "or you will die on your belly like the serpent you are."

"I can't," wept Ost. "I can't."

The Tatrix coldly lifted her gloved hand. When it fell so too would the whip.

"No," I said.

Slowly, every muscle straining to keep my balance, the cords in my legs and back like tortured cables, I reached out my hand to Ost's and, struggling in agony to keep my balance, added the weight of his yoke to mine as I drew him to his knees.

There was a gasp from the silver-masked women in the room. One or two of the warriors, heedless of the proprieties of Tharna, acknowledged my deed by smiting their shields with the bronze heads of their spears.

Thorn, in irritation, hurled the whip back into the hands of the man with wrist straps.

"You are strong," said the Tatrix of Tharna.

"Strength is the attribute of beasts," said Dorna the Proud.

"True," said the Tatrix.

"Yet he is a fine beast, is he not?" asked one of the silver-masked women.

"Let him be used in the Amusements of Tharna," urged another.

Lara held up her gloved hand for silence.

"How is it," I asked, "that you spare a warrior the whip and would use it on so miserable a wretch as Ost?"

"I had hoped you guiltless, Stranger," said she. "The guilt of Ost I know."

"I am guiltless," I said.

"Yet," said she, "you admit you did not steal the coins."

My brain reeled. "That is true," I said, "I did not steal the coins."

"Then you are guilty," said the voice of Lara, I thought sadly.

"Of what?" I asked to know.

"Of conspiracy against the throne of Tharna," said the Tatrix.

I was dumbfounded.

"Ost," said the Tatrix, her voice like ice, "you are guilty of treason against Tharna. It is known you conspire against the throne."

One of the guards, the fellow who had brought Ost in, spoke. "It is as your spies reported, Tatrix. In his quarters were found seditious documents, letters of instruction pertaining to the seizure of the throne, sacks of gold to be used in obtaining accomplices."

"Has he confessed these things as well?" asked Lara.

Ost blubbered helplessly for mercy, his thin neck wiggling in the yoke.

The guardsman laughed. "One sight of the white urt and he admitted all."

"Who, Serpent," asked the Tatrix, "supplied the gold? From whom came the letters of instruction?"

"I do not know, Beloved Tatrix," whined Ost. "The letters and the gold were delivered by a helmeted warrior."

"To the urt with him!" sneered Dorna the Proud.

Ost writhed, squealing for mercy. Thorn kicked him to silence him.

"What more do you know of this plot against the throne?" asked Lara of the sniveling Ost.

"Nothing, Beloved Tatrix," he whimpered.

"Very well," said Lara, and turned the glittering mask to the guardsman who had hurled the yoked Ost to her feet, "take him to the Chamber of the Urts."

"No, no, no!" whimpered Ost. "I know more, more!"

The silver-masked women leaned forward in their chairs. Only the Tatrix herself and Dorna the Proud sat straight. Although the room was cool I noted that Thorn, Captain of Tharna, was sweating. His hands clenched and unclenched.

"What more do you know?" demanded the Tatrix.

Ost looked about himself as well as he could, his eyes bulging with terror.

"Do you know the warrior who brought you the letters and gold?" she demanded.

"Him I do not know," said Ost.

"Let me," begged Thorn, "bloody the yoke." He drew his sword. "Let me end this wretch here!"

"No," said Lara. "What more then do you know, Serpent?" she asked the miserable conspirator.

"I know," said Ost, "that the leader of the conspiracy is

a high person in Tharna—one who wears the silver mask, a woman."

"Unthinkable!" cried Lara, rising to her feet. "None who wear the silver mask could be disloyal to Tharna!"

"Yet it is so," sniveled Ost.

"Who is the traitress?" demanded Lara.

"I do not know her name," said Ost.

Thorn laughed.

"But," said Ost, hopefully, "I once spoke with her and I might recognize her voice if I were but allowed to live."

Thorn laughed again. "It is a trick to buy his life."

"What think you, Dorna the Proud?" asked Lara of she who was Second in Tharna.

But instead of answering, Dorna the Proud seemed strangely silent. She extended her silver-gloved hand, palm facing her body and chopped brutally down with it, as though it might have been a blade.

"Mercy, Great Dorna!" screamed Ost.

Dorna repeated the gesture, slowly, cruelly.

But the hands of Lara were extended, palms up, and she lifted them slightly; it was a gracious gesture that spoke of mercy.

"Thank you, Beloved Tatrix," whimpered Ost, his eyes bursting with tears, "Thank you!"

"Tell me, Serpent," said Lara, "did the warrior steal the coins from you?"

"No, no," blubbered Ost.

"Did you give them to him?" she demanded.

"I did," he said. "I did."

"And did he accept them?" she asked.

"He did," said Ost.

"You pressed the coins upon me and ran," I said. "I had no choice."

"He accepted the coins," muttered Ost, looking at me malevolently, determined apparently that I would share whatever fate lay in store for him.

"I had no choice," I said calmly.

Ost shot a venomous look in my direction.

"If I were a conspirator," I said, "if I were in league with this man, why would he have charged me with the theft of the coins, why would he have had me arrested?"

Ost blanched. His tiny, rodentlike mind scurried from thought to thought, but his mouth only moved uncontrollably, silently.

Thorn spoke. "Ost knew himself to be suspected of plotting against the throne."

Ost looked puzzled.

"Thus," said Thorn, "to make it seem he had not given the money to this warrior, or assassin as the case may be, he pretended it had been stolen from him. In that way he might at one time appear free from guilt and destroy the man who knew of his complicity."

"That is true," exclaimed Ost gratefully, eager to take his cue from so powerful a figure as Thorn.

"How is it that Ost gave you the coins, Warrior?" asked the Tatrix.

"Ost gave them to me," I said, ". . . as a gift."

Thorn threw back his head and laughed.

"Ost never gave anything away in his life," roared Thorn, wiping his mouth, struggling to regain his composure.

There was even a slight sound of amusement from the silver-masked figures who sat upon the steps to the throne.

Ost himself snickered.

But the mask of the Tatrix glittered upon Ost, and his snicker died in his thin throat. The Tatrix arose from her throne, and pointed her finger at the wretched conspirator. Her voice was cold as she spoke to the guardsman who had brought him to the chamber. "To the mines with him," she said.

"No, Beloved Tatrix, no!" cried Ost. Terror, like a trapped cat, seemed to scratch behind his eyes, and he began to shake in his yoke like a diseased animal. Scornfully the guardsman lifted him to his feet and dragged him stumbling and whimpering from the room. I gathered the sentence to the mines was equivalent to a sentence of death.

"You are cruel," I said to the Tatrix.

"A Tatrix must be cruel," said Dorna.

"That," I said, "I would hear from the mouth of the Tatrix herself."

Dorna stiffened at the rebuff.

After a time the Tatrix, who had resumed her throne, spoke. Her voice was quiet. "Sometimes, Stranger," she said, "it is hard to be First in Tharna."

I had not expected that answer.

I wondered what sort of woman was the Tatrix of Tharna, what lay concealed behind that mask of gold. For a moment I felt sorry for the golden creature before whose throne I knelt.

"As for you," said Lara, her mask glittering down upon me, "you admit that you did not steal the coins from Ost, and in this admission you admit that he gave them to you."

"He thrust them in my hand," I said, "and ran." I looked at the Tatrix. "I came to Tharna to obtain a tarn. I had no money. With Ost's coins I could have purchased one and continued my journey. Should I have thrown them away?"

"These coins," said Lara, holding the tiny sack in her hand, gloved in gold, "were to buy my death."

"So few coins?" I asked skeptically.

"Obviously the full sum would follow upon the accomplishment of the deed," she said.

"The coins were a gift," I said. "Or so I thought."

"I do not believe you," she said.

I was silent.

"What full sum did Ost offer you?" she asked.

"I refused to be a party to his schemes," I said.

"What full sum did Ost offer you?" repeated the Tatrix.

"He spoke," I said, "of a tarn, a thousand golden tarn disks and provisions for a long journey."

"Golden tarn disks—unlike those of silver—are scarce in Tharna," said the Tatrix. "Someone is apparently willing to pay highly for my death."

"Not your death," I said.

"Then what?" she asked.

"Your abduction," I said.

The Tatrix stiffened suddenly, her entire body trembling with fury. She rose, seemingly beside herself with rage.

"Bloody the yoke," urged Dorna.

Thorn stepped forward, his blade raised.

"No," screamed the Tatrix, and, to the astonishment of all, herself descended the broad steps of the dais.

Shaking with fury she stood before me, over me, in her golden robes and mask. "Give me the whip!" she cried. "Give it to me!" The man with the wrist straps hastily knelt before her, lifting it to her hands. She snapped it cruelly in the air, and its report was sharp and vicious.

"So," she said to me, both hands clenched on the butt of the whip, "you would have me before you on the scarlet rug bound with yellow cords, would you?"

I did not understand her meaning.

"You would have me in a camisk and collar would you?" she hissed hysterically.

The women of the silver masks recoiled, shuddering. There were exclamations of anger, of horror.

"I am a woman of Tharna," she screamed, "First in Tharna! First!"

Then, beside herself with rage, holding the whip in both hands, she lashed madly at me. "It is the kiss of the whip for you!" she screamed. Again and again she struck me, yet through it all I managed to stay on my knees, not to fall.

My senses reeled, my body, tortured by the weight of the silver yoke, now wrapped in the flames of the whip, shook with uncontrollable agony. Then, when the Tatrix had exhausted herself, by some effort I find it hard to comprehend, I managed to stand on my feet, bloody, wearing the yoke, my flesh in tatters—and look down upon her.

She turned and fled to the dais. She ran up the steps and turned only when she stood at last before her throne.

She pointed her hand imperiously at me, that hand wearing its glove of gold, now spattered with my blood, wet and dark from the sweat of her hand.

"Let him be used in the Amusements of Tharna!" she said.

12

ANDREAS OF THE
CASTE OF POETS

I HAD BEEN HOODED AND driven through the streets, stumbling under the weight of the yoke. At last I had entered a building and had descended a long, swirling ramp, through dank passages. When I was unhooded, my yoke had been chained to the wall of a dungeon.

The place was lit by a small, foul tharlarion lamp set in the wall near the ceiling. I had no idea how far below ground it might be. The floor and the walls were of black stone, quarried in giant blocks of perhaps a ton apiece. The lamp dried the stone in its vicinity, but, on the floor and most of the walls, there was a dampness and the smell of mold. Some straw was scattered on the floor. From where I was chained, I could reach a cistern of water. A food pan lay near my foot.

Exhausted, my body aching from the weight of the yoke and the sting of the lash, I lay on the stones and slept. How long I slept I don't know. When I awoke, each of my muscles ached, but now it was a dull, cold ache. I tried to move and my wounds tortured me.

In spite of the yoke I struggled to a cross-legged sitting position, and shook my head. In the food pan I saw half a loaf of coarse bread. Yoked as I was, there was no way to pick it up and get it to my mouth. I might crawl to it on my belly, and if my hunger were great enough, I knew I must, but the thought angered me. The yoke was not simply a device to secure a man, but to humiliate him, to treat him as if he were a beast.

"Let me help you," said a girl's voice.

I turned, the momentum of the yoke almost carrying me into the wall. Two small hands caught it, and struggling, managed to swing it back, keeping my balance.

I looked at the girl. Perhaps she was plain, but I found her attractive. There was a warmth in her I would not have expected to find in Tharna. Her dark eyes regarded me, filled with concern. Her hair, which was reddish brown, was bound behind her head with a coarse string.

As I gazed on her she lowered her eyes shyly. She wore only a single garment, a long, narrow rectangle of rough, brown material, perhaps eighteen inches in width, drawn over her head like a poncho, falling in front and back a bit above her knees and belted at the waist with a chain.

"Yes," she said with shame. "I wear the camisk."

"You are lovely," I said.

She looked at me, startled, yet grateful.

We faced each other in the half darkness of the dungeon, not speaking. There was no sound in that dark, cold place. The shadows of the tiny tharlarion lamp far above flickered on the walls, on the face of the girl.

Her hand reached out and touched the silver yoke I wore. "They are cruel," she said.

Then, without speaking more, she picked up the bread from the pan, and held it for me. I bit two or three voracious mouthfuls of the coarse stuff and chewed it and gulped it down.

I noted her throat was encircled by a collar of gray metal. I supposed it indicated that she was a state slave of Tharna.

She reached into the cistern, first scraping the surface of the water to clear it of the green scum that floated there, and then, in the palms of her cupped hands, carried water to my parched lips.

"Thank you," I said.

She smiled at me. "One does not thank a slave," she said.

"I thought women were free in Tharna," I said, gesturing with my head toward the gray metal collar she wore.

"I will not be kept in Tharna," she said. "I will be sent from the city, to the Great Farms, where I will carry water to Field Slaves."

"What is your crime?" I asked.

"I betrayed Tharna," she said.

"You conspired against the throne?" I asked.

"No," said the girl. "I cared for a man."

I was speechless.

"I once wore the silver mask, Warrior," said the girl. "But now I am only a Degraded Woman, for I allowed myself to love."

"That is no crime," I said.

The girl laughed merrily. I love to hear the sudden glad music of a woman's laughter, that laughter that so delights a man, that acts on his senses like Ka-la-na wine.

Suddenly it seemed I no longer felt the weight of the yoke.

"Tell me about him," I said, "but first tell me your name."

"I am Linna of Tharna," she said. "What is your name?"

"Tarl," I said.

"Of what city?"

"Of no city."

"Ah!" said the girl, smiling, and inquired no further. She would have concluded that she shared her cell with an outlaw. She sat back on her heels, her eyes happy. "He was," she said, "not even of this city."

I whistled. That would be a serious matter in Gorean eyes.

"And worse than that," she laughed, clapping her hands, "he was of the Caste of Singers."

It could have beeen worse, I thought. After all, though the Caste of Singers, or Poets, was not a high caste, it had more prestige than, for example, the Caste of Pot-Makers or Saddle-Makers, with which it was sometimes compared. On Gor, the singer, or poet, is regarded as a craftsman who makes strong sayings, much like a pot-maker makes a good pot or a saddle-maker makes a

worthy saddle. He has his role to play in the social struc-
ture, celebrating battles and histories, singing of heroes and
cities, but also he is expected to sing of living, and of love
and joy, not merely of arms and glory; and, too, it is his
function to remind the Goreans from time to time of
loneliness and death, lest they should forget that they are
men.

The singer was thought to have an unusual skill, but so,
too, were the tarn-keeper and the woodsman. Poets on
Gor, as in my native world, were regarded with some
skepticism and thought to be a little foolish, but it had not
occurred to anyone that they might suffer from divine
madness or be the periodic recipients of the inspiration of
the gods. The Priest-Kings of Gor, who served as the
divinities of this rude planet, inspired little but awe, and
occasionally fear. Men lived in a truce with the Priest-
Kings, keeping their laws and festivals, making the required sacrifices and libations, but, on the whole, forget-
ting about them as much as possible. Had it been suggested to a poet that he had been inspired by a Priest-King
the fellow would have been scandalized. "I, So-and-So of
Such-and-Such a City, made this song," he would say,
"not a Priest-King."

In spite of some reservations the Poet, or Singer, was
loved on Gor. It had not occurred to him that he owed
misery and torment to his profession, and, on the whole,
the Caste of Poets was thought to be a most happy band
of men. "A handful of bread for a song," was a common
Gorean invitation extended to members of the caste, and
it might occur on the lips of a peasant or a Ubar, and the
poet took great pride that he would sing the same song in
both the hut of the peasant and the halls of the Ubar,
though it won for him only a crust of bread in one place
and a cap of gold in the other, gold often squandered on a
beautiful woman who might leave him nothing but his
songs.

Poets, on the whole, did not live well on Gor, but they
never starved, were never forced to burn the robes of their
caste. Some had even sung their way from city to city,

their poverty protecting them from outlaws, and their luck from the predatory beasts of Gor. Nine cities, long after his death, claimed the man who, centuries ago, had called Ko-ro-ba the Towers of the Morning.

"The Caste of Poets is not so bad," I said to Linna.

"Of course not," she said, "but they are outlawed in Tharna."

"Oh," I said.

"Nonetheless," she said, her eyes happy, "this man, Andreas, of the Desert City of Tor, crept into the city—looking for a song, he said." She laughed. "But I think he really wanted to look behind the silver masks of our women." She clapped her hands with delight. "It was I," she continued, "who apprehended and challenged him, I who saw the lyre beneath his gray robes and knew him for a singer. In my silver mask I followed him, and determined that he had been within the city for more than ten hours."

"What is the significance of that?" I asked, for I had heard something of the sort before.

"It means one is made welcome in Tharna," said the girl, "and this means one is sent to the Great Farms to be a Field Slave, to cultivate the soil of Tharna in chains until one dies."

"Why are strangers not warned of this," I asked, "when they enter the gates?"

"That would be foolish indeed, would it not?" laughed the girl. "For how then would the ranks of Field Slaves be replenished?"

"I see," I said, now understanding for the first time something of the motivation behind the hospitality of Tharna.

"As one who wore the silver mask," continued the girl, "it was my duty to report this man to the authorities. Yet I was curious for I had never known a man not from Tharna. I followed him, until we were alone, and then I challenged him, informing him of the fate that lay before him."

"Then what did he do?" I asked.

She dropped her head shyly. "He pulled away my silver mask and kissed me," she said, "so that I could not even cry for help."

I smiled at her.

"I had never been in the arms of a man before," she said, "for the men of Tharna may not touch women."

I must have looked puzzled.

"The Caste of Physicians," she said, "under the direction of the High Council of Tharna, arranges these matters."

"I see," I said.

"Yet," she said, "though I had worn the silver mask, and counted myself a woman of Tharna, when he took me in his arms, I did not find the sensation unpleasant." She looked at me, a little sadly. "I knew then that I was no better than he, no better than a beast, worthy only to be a slave."

"You do not believe that?" I demanded.

"Yes," she said, "but I do not care, for I would rather wear the camisk and have felt his kiss, than live forever behind my silver mask." Her shoulders shook. I wished that I could have taken her in my arms, and comforted her. "I am a degraded creature," she said, "shamed, a traitress to all that is highest in Tharna."

"What happened to the man?" I asked.

"I sheltered him," she said, "and managed to smuggle him from the city." She sighed. "He made me promise to follow him, but I knew I could not."

"What did you do?" I asked.

"When he was safe," she said, "I did my duty, giving myself to the High Council of Tharna and confessing all. It was decreed that I must lose my silver mask, don the camisk and be collared, and be sent to the Great Farms to carry water to Field Slaves."

She began to weep.

"You should not have given yourself to the High Council," I said.

"Why?" she asked. "Was I not guilty?"

"You were not guilty," I said.

"Is love not a crime?" she asked.

"Only in Tharna," I said.

She laughed. "You are strange, too," she said, "like Andreas of Tor."

"What of Andreas?" I asked. "When you do not join him, will he not come searching for you, re-enter the city?"

"No," she said. "He will think I no longer love him." She lowered her head. "He will go away, and find himself another woman, one more lovely than a girl of Tharna."

"Do you believe that?" I asked.

"Yes," said she. "And," she added, "he will not enter the city. He knows he would be caught and, considering his crime, he might be sent to the mines." She shuddered. "Perhaps even be used in the Amusements of Tharna."

"So you think he will fear to enter the city?" I asked.

"Yes," said she, "he will not enter the city. He is not a fool."

"What," cried a merry young voice, insolent and good natured, "could a wench like you know of fools, of the Caste of Singers, of Poets?"

Linna sprang to her feet.

Through the door of the dungeon a yoked figure was thrust by the butt ends of two spears. He stumbled through the entire room before he struck the wall with the yoke. He managed to turn the yoke and slide down the wall to a seated position.

He was an unkempt, strong-looking lad, with cheerful blue eyes and a mop of hair like the mane of a black larl. He sat on the straw, and smiled at us, a jolly, impish, shamefaced smile. He stretched his neck in the yoke and moved his fingers.

"Well, Linna," he said. "I have come to carry you off."

"Andreas," she cried, rushing to him.

13

THE AMUSEMENTS OF THARNA

THE SUN HURT MY EYES. The white sand, perfumed, sprinkled with mica and red lead, burned my feet. I blinked again and again, trying to lessen the torture of the glare. Already I could feel the heat of the sun soaking into the silver yoke I wore.

My back felt the jab of spears as I was prodded ahead and stumbled forward, unsteady under the weight of the yoke, my feet sinking to their ankles in the hot sand. On both sides of me were other wretched fellows, similarly yoked, some whining, some cursing, as they, too, were driven forward like beasts. One, silent, to my left, I knew to be Andreas of the Desert City of Tor. At last I no longer felt the spear point in my back.

"Kneel to the Tatrix of Tharna," commanded an imperious voice, speaking through some type of trumpet.

I heard the voice of Andreas next to me. "Strange," said he, "usually the Tatrix does not attend the Amusements of Tharna."

I wondered if I might be the reason that the Tatrix herself was present.

"Kneel to the Tatrix of Tharna," repeated the imperious voice.

Our fellow prisoners knelt. Only Andreas and I remained standing.

"Why do you not kneel?" I asked.

"Do you think that only warriors are brave?" he asked.

Suddenly he was struck from behind, brutally in the

back by the butt of a spear, and, with a groan he sank downwards. The spear struck me, too, again and again, in the back and across the shoulders, but I stood, somehow strong in the yoke, like an ox. Then with a harsh crack a lash suddenly struck my legs and curled about them like a fiery snake. My legs were jerked from beneath me and I fell heavily in the sand.

I looked about myself.

As I had expected I and my fellow prisoners knelt in the sands of an arena.

It was an oval enclosure, perhaps a hundred yards in diameter on its longest axis, and enclosed by walls about twelve feet high. The walls were divided into sections, which were brightly colored, with golds, purples, reds, oranges, yellows and blues.

The surface of the area, white sand, perfumed and sparkling with mica and red lead, added to the colorful mien of the place. Hanging over favored portions of the stands, which ascended on all sides, were giant striped awnings of billowing red and yellow silk.

It seemed that all the glorious colors of Gor which had been denied the buildings of Tharna were lavished on this place of its amusements.

In the stands, shaded by the awnings, I saw hundreds of silver masks, the lofty women of Tharna, reclining on benches softened with cushions of colored silk—come to view the Amusements.

I also noted the gray of men in the stands. Several were armed warriors, perhaps stationed there to keep the peace, but many must have been common citizens of Tharna. Some seemed to be conversing among themselves, perhaps laying wagers of one sort or another, but most sat still on the stone benches, glum and silent in their gray robes, their thoughts not easily read. Linna, in the dungeon, had told Andreas and me that a man of Tharna must attend the Amusements of Tharna at least four times a year, and that, failing that, he must take part in them himself.

There were cries of impatience from the stands, shrill, female voices oddly contrasting with the placidity of the silver masks. All eyes seemed turned to one section of the stands, that before which we knelt, a section that gleamed with gold.

I looked above the wall and saw, vested in her robes of gold, regal on a golden throne, she who alone might wear a golden mask, she who was First in Tharna—Lara, the Tatrix herself.

The Tatrix arose and lifted her hand. Pure in its glove of gold it held a golden scarf.

The stands fell silent.

Then, to my astonishment, the men of Tharna who were yoked in the arena, kneeling, rejected by their city, condemned, chanted a strange paean. Andreas and I, not being of Tharna, were alone silent, and I would guess he was as surprised as I.

> Though we are abject beasts
> Fit only to live for your comfort
> Fit only to die for your pleasure
> Yet we glorify the Masks of Tharna.
> Hail to the Masks of Tharna.
> Hail to the Tatrix of our City.

The golden scarf fluttered to the sands of the arena and the Tatrix resumed her throne, reclining upon its cushions.

The voice speaking through the trumpet said, "Let the Amusements of Tharna begin."

Squeals of anticipation greeted this announcement but I had little time to listen for I was jerked roughly to my feet.

"First," said the voice, "there will be the Contests of Oxen."

There were perhaps forty yoked wretches in the arena. In a few moments the guards had divided us into teams of four, harnessing our yokes together with chains. Then, with their whips, they drove us to a set of large blocks of quarried granite, weighing perhaps a ton apiece, from the sides of which protruded heavy iron rings. More chains fixed each team to its own block.

The course was indicated to us. The race would begin and end before the golden wall behind which, in lofty splendor, sat the Tatrix of Tharna. Each team would have its driver, who would bear a whip and ride upon the block. We painfully dragged the heavy blocks to the golden wall. The silver yoke, hot from the sun, burned my neck and shoulders.

As we stood before the wall I heard the laughter of the Tatrix and my vision blackened with rage.

Our driver was the man in wrist straps, he from the Chamber of Urts, who had first brought me into the presence of the Tatrix. He approached us, individually, checking the harness chains. As he examined my yoke and chain, he said, "Dorna the Proud has wagered a hundred golden tarn disks on this block. See that it does not lose."

"What if it does?" I asked.

"She will have you all boiled alive in tharlarion oil," he said, laughing.

The hand of the Tatrix lifted slightly, almost languorously, from the arm of her throne, and the race began.

Our block did not lose.

Savagely, our backs breaking, stinging under the frenzied lashing of our driver, cursing the colorful sands of the arena that mounted before the block as we dragged it foot by foot about the course, we managed to come first within the zone of the golden wall. When we were unchained we discovered we had been dragging one man who had died in the chains.

Shamelessly we fell in the sand.

"The Battles of Oxen," cried one of the silver masks, and her cry was taken up by ten and then a hundred others. Soon the stands themselves seemed to ring with the cry. "The Battles of Oxen," cried the women of Tharna. "Let them begin!"

We were thrown on our feet again, and, to my horror,

our yokes were fitted with steel horns, eighteen inches in length and pointed like nails.

Andreas, as his yoke was similarly garnished with the deadly projections, spoke to me. "This may be farewell, Warrior," said he. "I hope only that we are not matched."

"I would not kill you," I said.

He looked at me strangely. "Nor would I kill you," he said, after a time. "But," he said, "if we are matched and we do not fight, we will both be slain."

"Then so be it," I said.

Andreas smiled at me. "So be it, Warrior," he agreed.

Though yoked, we faced one another, men, each knowing that he had found a friend on the sands of the arena of Tharna.

My opponent was not Andreas, but a squat, powerful man with short-clipped yellow hair, Kron of Tharna, of the Caste of Metal Workers. His eyes were blue like steel. One ear had been torn from his head.

"I have survived the Amusements of Tharna three times," he said as he faced me.

I observed him carefully. He would be a dangerous opponent.

The man with wrist straps circled us with the whip, his eye on the throne of the Tatrix. When the glove of gold once more lifted, the dread conflict would begin.

"Let us be men," I said to my opponent, "and refuse to slay one another for the sport of those in silver masks."

The yellow, short-cropped head glared at me, almost without comprehension. Then it seemed as though what I had said struck, deep within him, some responsive chord. The pale blue eyes glimmered briefly; then they clouded. "We would both be slain," he said.

"Yes," I said.

"Stranger," said he, "I intend to survive the Amusements of Tharna at least once more."

"Very well," I said, and squared off against him.

The hand of the Tatrix must have lifted. I did not see it for I did not care to take my eyes from my opponent. "Begin," said the man in wrist straps.

And so Kron and I began to circle one another, slightly bent so that the projections on the yoke might be used to best advantage.

One, twice, he charged, but pulled up short, seeing if he could bring me forward, off balance to meet the charge. We moved cautiously, occasionally feinting with the terrible yokes. The stands grew restless. The man in wrist straps cracked his whip. "Let there be blood," he said.

Suddenly the foot of Kron swept through the white perfumed sand, bright with mica and red lead, and kicked a broad sheet of particles toward my eyes. It came like a silver and crimson storm, taking me by surprise, blinding me.

I fell on my knees almost instantly, and the charging horns of Kron passed over me. I reared up under his body, heaving it on my shoulder, backwards, over on the sand. I heard it hit heavily behind me, and heard Kron's grunt of anger, and fear. I couldn't turn and drive the spikes through him because I could not risk missing.

I shook my head wildly; my hands, yoked helplessly, tried vainly to reach my eyes, to tear the blinding particles from my vision. In the sweat and blindness, unsteady under the violently swinging yoke, I heard the squeals of the frenzied crowd.

Blinded I heard Kron regain his feet, lifting the heavy yoke that bound him. I heard his harsh breathing, like the snorting of an animal. I heard his short, quick, running steps in the sand, thudding toward me in a bull-like charge.

I turned my yoke obliquely, slipping between the horns, blocking the blow. It sounded like anvils hurled together. My hands sought his, but he kept his fists clenched and withdrawn as far as he could in the bracelet of the yoke. My hand clutched his withdrawn fist and slipped off, unable to keep its grip from the sweat, his and mine.

Once, twice more he charged, and each time I managed to block the blow, withstanding the shock of the crashing yokes, escaping the thrust of the murderous horns. Once I was not so fortunate and a steel horn furrowed my side, leaving a channel of blood. The crowd screamed in delight.

Suddenly I managed to get my hands under his yoke.

It was hot, like mine in the sun, and my hands burned on the metal. Kron was a heavy, but short man, and I lifted his yoke, and mine, to the astonishment of the stands, which had fallen silent.

Kron cursed as he felt his feet leave the sand. Painfully, as he writhed, hung in the yoke, I carried him to the golden wall, and hurled him against it. The shock to Kron, bound in the yoke, might have killed a lesser man, breaking his neck.

Kron, still a captive of the yoke, now unconscious, slid down the wall, the weight of the yoke tumbling his inert body sideways in the sand. My sweat and the tears from the burning irritation of the sand had now cleared my vision.

I looked up into the glittering mask of the Tatrix. Beside her I saw the silver mask of Dorna the Proud.

"Slay him," said Dorna the Proud, gesturing to the unconscious Kron.

I looked about the stands.

Everywhere I saw the silver masks, and heard the shrill command, "Slay him!" On every side I saw the merciless gesture, the extended right hand, palm turned inwards, the cruel, downward chopping motion. Those who wore the silver masks had risen to their feet, and the force of their cries pressed in on me like knives, the air itself seemed filled with the bedlam of their command, "Slay him!"

I turned and walked slowly to the center of the arena.

I stood there, ankle deep in the sand, covered with sweat and sand, my back open from the lash of the race, my side torn from the driving horn of Kron's yoke. I stood unmoving.

The fury of the stands was uncontrolled.

As I stood there in the center of the arena, alone, silent, aloof, not seeming to hear them, those hundreds, rather thousands, who wore the silver masks understood that their will had been spurned, that this creature alone on the sand beneath them had thwarted their pleasure. Standing, screaming, shaking their silver-gloved fists at me, they hurled their frustration, their invective and abuse on my head. The shrill rage of these masked creatures seemed to know no bounds, to verge on hysteria, on madness.

Calmly I waited in the center of the arena for the warriors.

The first man to reach me was the man in wrist straps, his face livid with rage. He savagely struck me across the face with his coiled whip. "Sleen," cried he, "you have spoiled the Amusements of Tharna!" Two warriors hastily unbolted the horns from the yoke and dragged me to the golden wall.

Once more I stood beneath the golden mask of the Tatrix.

I wondered if my death would be quick.

The stands fell silent. There was a tenseness in the air, as all waited for the words of the Tatrix. Her golden mask and robes glittered above me. Her words were clear, unmistakable.

"Remove his yoke," she said.

I could not believe my ears.

Had I won my freedom? Was it thus in the Amusements of Tharna? Or had the fierce, proud Tatrix now recognized the cruelty of the Amusements? Had that heart hidden in those cold, glistening robes of unfeeling gold at last relented, shown itself to be susceptible of compassion? Or had the call of justice at last triumphed in her bosom, that my innocence might be acknowledged, my cause vindicated, that I might now be sped honorably on my way from gray Tharna?

One emotion leapt in my heart, gratitude. "Thank you, Tatrix," I said.

She laughed. "—that he may be fed to the tarn," she added.

14

THE BLACK TARN

I WAS UNYOKED.

The other prisoners, still yoked, had been whipped from the arena, to the dungeons below, to be used yet again in the Amusements of Tharna, or perhaps sent to the mines. Andreas of Tor tried to remain at my side, to share my fate, but he was beaten and dragged senseless from the arena.

The crowd seemed eager to observe what would happen next. It stirred impatiently beneath the billowing silk of the awnings, rearranged its silken cushions, partook distractedly of candies and sweetmeats distributed by gray-robed figures. Mingled with calls for the tarn, occasional taunts and jibes carried across the sand.

Perhaps the Amusements of Tharna were not spoiled at all; perhaps the best was yet to come? Surely my death beneath the beak and talons of a tarn would provide a gratifying spectacle for the insatiable masks of Tharna, adequate compensation for the disappointments of the afternoon, for the disregard of their will, for the defiance they had witnessed?

Though I sensed I was to die, I was not ill pleased at the manner. Hideous though the death might seem to the silver masks of Tharna, they did not know that I was a tarnsman, and knew these birds, their power, their ferocity; that in my way I loved them; and that as a warrior I would not find a death by tarn ignoble.

Grimly I smiled to myself.

Like most members of my Caste, more than the monstrous tarns, those carnivorous hawklike giants of Gor, I dreaded such creatures as the tiny ost, that diminutive, venomous reptile, orange, scarcely more than a few inches in length, that might lurk at one's very sandal and then, without provocation or warning, strike, its tiny fangs the prelude to excruciating torment, concluding only with sure death. Among warriors, the bite of an ost is thought to be one of the most cruel of all gates to the Cities of Dust; far preferable to them are the rending beak, the terrible talons of a tarn.

I was not bound.

I was free to wander on the sand, enclosed only by the walls. I rejoiced in this new freedom, in the absence of the yoke, though I knew it was given to me only in order to improve the spectacle. That I might run, that I might scream and grovel, that I might try to cover myself in the sand would surely delight the silver masks of Tharna.

I moved my hands and shoulders, my back. My tunic had long since been torn to my waist and now I ripped it away to my belt, angry at the tattered cloth. The muscles rolled exuberantly under my flesh, delighting in their liberty.

I walked slowly to the foot of the golden wall, where lay the golden scarf of the Tatrix, that scarf whose fluttering signal had initiated the Amusements.

I picked it up.

"Keep it as a gift," rang a haughty voice from above me.

I looked up into the glittering, golden mask of the Tatrix.

"As something by which to remember the Tatrix of Tharna," said the voice behind the golden mask, amused.

I grinned up at the golden mask, and taking the scarf slowly wiped the sand and sweat from my face.

Above me the Tatrix cried out in rage.

I looped the scarf about my shoulders and went to the center of the arena.

No sooner had I reached the center than one of the

sections of the wall rolled back, revealing a portal almost as high as the wall and perhaps thirty feet in width. Through this portal, in two long lines, lashed by overseers, yoked slaves harnessed in chains drew a great wooden platform mounted on heavy wooden wheels. I waited for the platform to emerge into the sunlight.

There were cries of awe and wonder, of pleasure, from the thrilled silver masks of Tharna.

Slowly as the creaking platform rolled out onto the sand, drawn by its struggling slaves, yoked like oxen, I saw the tarn revealed, a black giant, hooded, its beak belted together, a great bar of silver chained to one of its legs. It would not be able to fly, but it could move about, dragging the bar of silver. It, too, in Tharna, wore its yoke.

The platform drew closer, and to the wonder of the crowd I went to meet it.

My heart was beating wildly.

I scrutinized the tarn.

Its lineaments were not unfamiliar. I examined the glistening, sable plumage; the monstrous yellow beak now cruelly belted together. I saw the great wings snap, smiting the air, the hurricane from their blow spilling slaves into the sand, tangling chains, as the great beast, lifting its head and smelling the open air, struck it with his wings.

It would not attempt to fly while hooded; indeed, I doubted that the bird would attempt to fly while it dragged its bar of silver. If it was the bird I thought it to be it would not futilely contest the weight of the degrading hobble, would not provide a spectacle of its helplessness for its captors. I know this sounds strange, but I believe some animals have pride, and if any did, I knew that this monster was one of them.

"Stand back," cried one of the men with a whip.

I jerked the whip from his hand, and with my arm struck him aside. He flew tumbling into the sand. I threw the whip scornfully after him.

I stood near the platform now. I wanted to see the ankle ring the bird wore. I noted with satisfaction that its talons were shod with steel. It was a War Tarn, bred for courage, for endurance, for combat in the skies of Gor. My nostrils drank in the wild, strong odor of the tarn, so offensive to some, yet an ambrosia to the nostrils of the tarnsman. It recalled the tarn cots of Ko-ro-ba and Ar, the Compound of Mintar in Pa-Kur's City of Tents on the Vosk, the outlaw encampment of Marlenus among the crags of the Voltai Range.

As I stood beside the bird, I felt happy, though I knew it was intended to be my executioner. It was perhaps the foolish affection which a tarnsman feels for these danger- ous, fierce mounts, almost as much a threat to him as to anyone else. Yet it was perhaps more, for as I stood by the bird, I felt almost as though I had come home to Ko-ro-ba, as though I stood here now with something in this gray, hostile city that knew me and mine, that had looked upon the Towers of the Morning, and had spread its wings above the glistening cylinders of Glorious Ar, that had carried me in battle and had borne Talena, my love, and me back from the siege of Ar to the Feast of our Free Companionship at Ko-ro-ba. I seized the ankle ring, and noted as I had expected that the name of its city had been filed away.

"This bird," I said to one of the yoked slaves, "is from Ko-ro-ba."

The slave shook in his yoke at the mention of this name. He turned away, eager to be unchained and led like a beast to the safety of the dungeons.

Though to most of those who observed it would seem that the tarn was unusually quiet, I sensed that it was trembling, like myself, with excitement. It seemed uncer- tain. Its head was high, alert in the leather darkness of its hood. Almost inaudibly it sucked in air through the slits in its beak. I wondered if it had caught my scent. Then the great yellow beak, hooked for rending prey, now belted shut, turned curiously, slowly, toward me.

The man in wrist straps, the burly fellow who had so delighted in striking me, he with the band of gray cloth

wound about his forehead, approached me, his whip
lifted.

"Get away from there," he cried.

I turned to face him. "I am not now a yoked slave," I
said. "You confront a warrior."

His hand tightened on the whip.

I laughed in his face. "Strike me now," I said, "and I
will kill you."

"I am not afraid of you," he said, his face white,
backing away. His arm with the whip lowered. It trembled.

I laughed again.

"You will be dead soon enough," he said, stammering
on the words. "A hundred tarnsmen have tried to mount
this beast, and one hundred tarnsmen have died. The
Tatrix decreed it is only to be used in the Amusements, to
feed on sleen like you."

"Unhood it," I commanded. "Free it!"

The man looked at me as though I might have been
insane. To be sure, my exuberance astonished even me.
Warriors with spears rushed forward, forcing me back,
away from the tarn. I stood in the sand, away from the
platform, and watched the ticklish business of unhooding
the tarn.

No sound came from the stands.

I wondered what thoughts passed behind the golden
mask of Lara, Tatrix of the city of Tharna.

I wondered if the bird would recognize me.

A nimble slave, wasting no time, and held on the
shoulders of a fellow slave, loosened the belts that held the
beak of the tarn and the hood that bound its head. He did
not remove them but only loosened them, and as soon as
he had, he and his fellow scurried for the safety of the
open section of wall, which then slid noiselessly shut.

The tarn opened its beak and the belts that bound it
loosely flew asunder. It shook its head, as if to throw
water from its feathers and the leather hood was thrown
far into the air and behind the bird. Now it spread its
wings and smote the air, and lifted its beak and uttered

the terrifying challenge scream of its kind. Its black crest, now unconfined by the hood, sprang erect with a sound like fire, and the wind seemed to lift and preen each feather.

I found him beautiful.

I knew that I gazed upon one of the great and terrible predators of Gor.

But I found him beautiful.

The bright round eyes, the pupils like black stars, gleamed at me.

"Ho! Ubar of the Skies!" I cried, holding my arms extended. My eyes glistened with tears. "Do you not know me? I am Tarl! Tarl of Ko-ro-ba!" I cried. I know not what effect this cry may have had on the stands of the arena, for I had forgotten them. I addressed myself to the giant tarn, as though he had been a warrior, a member of my caste. "You at least," I said, "do not fear the accents of my city."

Regardless of the danger I ran to the bird. I leaped to the heavy wooden platform on which it stood. I flung my arms around its neck, weeping. The great beak questioningly touched me. There could be no emotion, of course, in such a beast. Yet as its great round eyes regarded me I wondered what thoughts might course through its avian brain. I wondered if it too recalled the thunder of the wind, the clash of arms as tarnsmen dueled in flight, the sight of Gor's tarn cavalries wheeling in formation to the beat of the tarn drums, or the long, steady, lonely soaring flights we had known together over the green fields of Gor. Could it remember the Vosk, like a silver ribbon beneath its wings; could it recall fighting the blasts and upwinds of the rugged Voltai Range; could it recall Thentis, famed for its tarn flocks, Ko-ro-ba's gleaming towers, or the lights of Ar as they had blazed that night of the Planting Feast of Sa-Tarna, when we two had dared to strike for the Home Stone of the greatest city of all known Gor? No, I suppose that none of these memories, so dear to me, could find their place in the simple brain of this plumed giant. Gently the great bird thrust its beak beneath my arm.

I knew that the warriors of Tharna would have to kill two of us, for the tarn would defend me to the death.

It lifted its huge, terrible head, scrutinizing the stands. It shook the leg which was chained to the great silver bar. It would be able to move, dragging that weight, but it could not fly.

I knelt to examine the hobble. It had not been forged in place inasmuch as it would be removed in the confines of the tarn cot, to allow the bird its perch, its exercise. Luckily it had not been locked in place. It had, however, been bolted, fastened with a heavy, square-headed bolt, much like an oversized machine bolt, the shaft of which was perhaps an inch and a half in diameter.

My hands tried the bolt. It was tight. It had been affixed with a wrench. My hands locked on it, trying to twist it open. It held. I struggled with it. I cursed it. Inwardly I screamed for it to open. It would not.

I was now aware of cries from the stands. They were not simply cries of impatience but of consternation. The silver masks of Tharna were not simply cheated of a spectacle, but dumbfounded, confused. It did not take long for them to understand that the tarn, for whatever strange reason, was not going to attack me, and, whatever they considered my chances, it took only a moment longer to determine that it was my intention to free the bird.

The voice of the Tatrix drifted across the sands. "Kill him," she cried. I heard, too, the voice of Dorna the Proud urging the warriors to their task. Soon the spearmen of Tharna would be upon us. Already one or two had leapt over the wall from the stands and were approaching. The great door through which the tarn had been drawn was also opening, and a line of warriors was hurrying through the opening.

My hands clenched even more tightly on the pieces of the bolt. It was now stained with my blood. I could feel the muscles of my arm and back pitting their strength against the obdurate metal. A spear sank into the wood of

the platform. Sweat burst out from every pore on my
body. Another spear struck the wood, closer than the first.
It seemed the metal would tear the flesh from my hands,
break the bones of my fingers. Another spear struck the
wood, creasing my leg. The tarn thrust its head over me
and uttered a piercing, fierce scream, a terrible cry of rage
that must have shaken the hearts of all within the confines
of the arena. The spearmen seemed frozen, and dropped
back, as if the great bird could have freely attacked them.

"Fools!" cried the voice of the man with wrist straps.
"The bird is chained! Attack! Kill them both!"

In that instant the bolt gave, and the nut spun from the
shaft!

The tarn, as if it understood it was free, shook the
hated metal from its leg and lifted its beak to the skies and
uttered such a cry as must have been heard by all in
Tharna, a cry seldom heard except in the mountains of
Thentis or among the crags of the Voltai, the cry of the
wild tarn, victorious, who claims for his territory the earth
and all that lies within it.

For an instant, perhaps an unworthy instant, I feared
the bird would immediately take to the skies, but though
the metal was shaken from its leg, though it was free,
though the spearmen advanced, it did not move.

I leapt to its back and fastened my hands in the stout
quills of its neck. What I would have given for a tarn
saddle and the broad purple strap that fastens the warrior
in the saddle!

As soon as it felt my weight the tarn cried again and
with an explosion of its broad wings sprang into the air,
climbing in dizzy circles. Some spears fell in lazy loops
below us, short by far, falling back again into the gala-
colored sand of the arena. There were cries of rage that
drifted up from below as the silver masks of Tharna began
to understand that they had been cheated of their prey,
that the Amusements had turned out badly.

I had no way to guide the tarn proficiently. Normally
the tarn is guided by a harness. There is a throat strap to
which, customarily, six reins are attached in a clockwise

fashion. These pass from the throat strap to the main
saddle ring, which is fixed on the saddle. By exerting
pressure on these reins, one directs the bird. But I lacked
both saddle and harness. Indeed, I did not even have a
tarn-goad, without which most tarnsmen would not even
approach their fierce mounts.

I did not fear much on this score, however, as I had
seldom used the goad on this bird. In the beginning I had
refrained from using it often because I feared that the
effect of the cruel stimulus might be diminished through
overfrequent application, but eventually I had abandoned
its use altogether, retaining it only to protect myself in
case the bird, particularly when hungry, should turn on
me. In several cases tarns have devoured their own masters, and it is not unusual for them, when loosed for
feeding, to attack a human being with the same predatory
zest they bestow on the yellow antelope, the tabuk,
their favorite kill, or the ill-tempered, cumbersome bosk, a
shaggy, long-haired wild ox of the Gorean plains. I found
that the goad, with this monster at least, did not improve,
but rather impaired his performance. He seemed to resent
the goad, to fight it, to behave erratically when it was
used; when struck with it he might even slow his flight, or
deliberately disobey the commands of the tarn straps.
Accordingly the goad had seldom left its sheath on the
right side of the saddle.

I wondered sometimes if that bird, my Ubar of the
Skies, that tarn of tarns, of a race of birds spoken of by
Goreans as Brothers of the Wind, might have considered
himself as above the goad, resented its shocks and sparks,
resented that that puny human device would pretend to
teach him, he, a tarn of tarns, how to fly, how swiftly and
how far. But I dismissed such thoughts as absurd. The
tarn was but another of the beasts of Gor. The feelings I
was tempted to ascribe to it would lie beyond the ken of
so simple a creature.

I saw the towers of Tharna, and the glittering oval of its
arena, that cruel amphitheater, dropping away beneath the
wings of the tarn. Something of the same exhilaration

which I had felt in my first wild flight on a tarn, this very giant, now thrilled in me again. Beyond Tharna and its gloomy soil, continually broken by its stony outcroppings, I could see the green fields of Gor, glades of yellow Ka-la-na trees, the shimmering suface of a placid lake and the bright blue sky, open and beckoning.

"I am free!" I cried.

But I knew even as I cried out that I was not free, and I burned with shame that I had so bespoke myself, for how could I be free when others in that gray city were bound?

There was the girl, warm-eyed Linna, who had been kind to me, whose auburn hair was knotted with coarse string, who wore the gray collar of a state slave of Tharna. There was Andreas of Tor, of the Caste of Singers, young, valiant, irrepressible, his hair wild like the mane of a black larl, who would rather die than try to kill me, condemned to the Amusements or the mines of Tharna. And there were how many more, yoked and unyoked, bound and free, in the mines, on the Great Farms, in the city itself who suffered the misery of Tharna and her laws, who were subject to the crushing weight of her traditions, and knew at best nothing better in life than a bowl of cheap Kal-da at the end of a day's arduous, inglorious labor?

"Tabuk!" I cried to the plumed giant. "Tabuk!"

The tabuk is the most common Gorean antelope, a small graceful animal, one-horned and yellow, that haunts the Ka-la-na thickets of the planet and occasionally ventures daintily into its meadows in search of berries and salt. It is also one of the favorite kills of a tarn.

The cry of "Tabuk!" is used by the tarnsman on long flights when time is precious, and he does not wish to dismount and free the bird to find prey. When he spots a tabuk in the fields below, or, indeed, any animal in the prey range of the tarn, he may cry "Tabuk!" and this is the signal that the tarn may hunt. It makes its kill, devours it, and the flight resumes, the tarnsman never leaving the saddle. This was the first time I had called "Tabuk!" but the bird would have been conditioned to the call by the tarn-keepers of Ko-ro-ba years ago, and might still respond. I myself had always freed the bird to feed. I thought it well to rest the bird, unsaddle it, and, also, frankly I did not find myself eager to be present at the feeding of a tarn.

The great sable tarn, upon hearing the cry of "Tabuk!", to my joy, began to describe its long, soaring hunting circles, almost as if it might have received its training yesterday. It was truly a tarn of tarns, my Ubar of the Skies!

It was a desperate plan I had seized upon, no more than one chance in a million, unless the great tarn could tip the scales in my favor. Its wicked eyes gleamed, scanning the ground, its head and beak thrust forward, its wings still, gliding silently in great sweeps, lower and lower, over the gray towers of Tharna.

Now we passed over the arena of Tharna, still boiling with its throbbing, angry multitudes. The awnings had been struck, but the stands were still filled, as the thousands of silver masks of Tharna waited for the golden Tatrix herself to be the first to leave that scene of the macabre amusements of the gray city.

Far below in the midst of the crowd I caught sight of the golden robes of the Tatrix.

"Tabuk!" I cried. "Tabuk!"

The great predator wheeled in the sky, turning as smoothly as a knife on wire. It hovered, the sun at its back. Its talons, shod with steel, dropped like great hooks; it seemed to tremble almost motionless in the air; and then its wings, parallel, lifted, almost enfolding me, and were still.

The descent was as smooth and silent as the falling of a rock, the opening of a hand. I clung fiercely to the bird. My stomach leaped to my throat. The stands of the arena, filled with its robes and masks, seemed to fly upward.

There were shrill screams of terror from below. On every hand, robes and regalia flying, the silver masks of Tharna which had so insolently screamed but moments before for blood fled now for their lives in panic-stricken rout, trampling one another, scratching and tearing at one another, scrambling over the benches, thrusting one another even over the wall into the sands below.

In one instant that must have been the most terrifying in her life the Tatrix stood alone, looking up, deserted by all, on the steps before her golden throne in the midst of tumbled cushions and trays of candies and sweetmeats. A wild scream issued from behind that placid, expressionless golden mask. The golden arms of her robe, the hands gloved in gold, were flung across her face. The eyes behind the mask, which I saw in that split second, were hysterical with fear.

The tarn struck.

Its steel-shod pinioning talons closed like great hooks on the body of the screaming Tatrix. And so for an instant stood the tarn, its head and beak extended, its wings snapping, its prey locked in its grasp, and uttered the terrifying capture scream of the tarn, at once a scream of victory, and of challenge.

In those titanic, merciless talons the body of the Tatrix was helpless. It trembled in terror, quivering uncontrollably like that of a graceful, captured tabuk, waiting to be borne to the nest. The Tatrix could no longer even scream.

With a storm of wings the tarn smote the air and rose, in the sight of all, above the stands, above the arena, above the towers and walls of Tharna, and sped toward the horizon, the golden-robed body of the Tatrix clutched in its talons.

15

A BARGAIN IS STRUCK

THE TABUK-CRY IS THE only word to which a tarn
is trained to react. Beyond this it is all a matter of the
tarn-straps and the tarn goad. I bitterly criticized myself
for not having conditioned the bird to respond to voice
commands. Now, of all times, without a harness and
saddle, such a training would have been invaluable.

A wild thought occurred to me. When I had borne
Talena home from Ar to Ko-ro-ba I had tried to teach her
the reins of the tarn-harness and help her, at least with me
at hand, to learn to master the brute.

In the whistling wind, as the need arose, I had called
the straps to her, "One-strap!", "Six-strap!" and so on, and
she would draw the strap. That was the only association
between the voice of man and the arrangements of the
strap harness which the tarn had known. The bird, of
course, could not have been conditioned in so short a
time, nor for that matter had it even been my intention to
condition the bird—for I had spoken only for the benefit
of Talena. Moreover, even if it had been the case that the
bird had been inadvertently conditioned in that short a
time, it was not possible that it would still retain the
memory of that casual imprinting, which had taken place
more than six years ago.

"Six-strap!" I cried.

The great bird veered to the left and began to climb
slightly.

"Two-strap!" I called, and the bird now veered to the right, still climbing at the same angle.

"Four-strap!" I called, and the bird began to drop toward the earth, preparing to land.

"One-strap!" I laughed, delighted, bursting with pleasure, and the plumed giant, that titan of Gor, began to climb steeply.

I said no more and the bird leveled off, its wings striking the air in great rhythmical beats, alternating occasionally with a long, soaring, shallow glide. I watched the pasangs flow by below, and saw Tharna disappear in the distance.

Spontaneously, without thinking, I threw my arms around the neck of the great creature and hugged it. Its wings smote on, unresponsive, paying me no attention. I laughed, and slapped it twice on the neck. It was, of course, only another of the beasts of Gor, but I cared for it.

Forgive me if I say that I was happy, as I should not have been in the circumstances, but my feelings are those that a tarnsman would understand. I know of few sensations so splendid, so godlike, as sharing the flight of a tarn.

I was one of those men, a tarnsman, who would prefer the saddle of one of those fierce, predatory titans to the throne of a Ubar.

Once one has been a tarnsman, it is said, one must return again and again to the giant, savage birds. I think that this is a true saying. One knows that one must master them or be devoured. One knows that they are not dependable, that they are vicious. A tarnsman knows that they may turn upon him without warning. Yet the tarnsman chooses no other life. He continues to mount the birds, to climb to their saddle with a heart filled with joy, to draw upon the one-strap and, with a cry of exultation, to urge the monster aloft. More than the gold of a hundred merchants, more than the countless cylinders of Ar, he treasures those sublime, lonely moments, high over the earth, cut by the wind, he and the bird as one creature, alone, lofty, swift, free. Let it be said simply I was pleased, for I was on tarnback again.

From beneath the bird there came a long, shivering moan, a helpless, uncontrolled sound from the golden prey seized in its talons.

I cursed myself for a thoughtless fool, for in the exhilaration of the flight, incomprehensible though it seems to me now, I had forgotten the Tatrix. How frightful for her must have been those minutes of flight, grasped in the talons, hundreds of feet above the plains of Tharna, not knowing if she might be dropped at any instant, or carried to some ledge to be ripped to pieces by that monstrous beak, those hideous steel-shod talons.

I looked behind me to see if there was pursuit. It would surely come, on foot and on tarnback. Tharna did not maintain large cavalries of tarns, but it would surely be able to launch at least some squadrons of tarnsmen to rescue and avenge its Tatrix. The man of Tharna, taught from birth to regard himself as an unworthy, ignoble and inferior creature, at best a dull-witted beast of burden, did not, on the whole, make a good tarnsman. Yet I knew there would be tarnsmen in Tharna, and good ones, for her name was respected among the martial, hostile cities of Gor. Her tarnsmen might be mercenaries, or perhaps men like Thorn, Captain of Tharna, who in spite of their city thought well of themselves and maintained at least the shreds of caste pride.

Though I scrutinized the sky behind me, looking for those tiny specks that would be distant tarns in flight, I saw nothing. It was blue and empty. By now every tarnsman in Tharna should be flying. Yet I saw nothing.

Another moan escaped the golden captive.

In the distance, perhaps some forty pasangs away, I saw a set of ridges, lofty and steep, rearing out of a broad, yellow meadow of talenders, a delicate, yellow-petaled flower, often woven into garlands by Gorean maidens. In their own quarters, unveiled Gorean women, with their family or lovers, might fix talenders in their hair. A crown of talender was often worn by the girl at the feast celebrating her Free Companionship.

In perhaps ten minutes the ridges were almost below us.

"Four-strap!" I shouted.

The great bird paused in flight, braking with its wings, and then smoothly descended to a high ledge on one of the ridges, a ledge commanding the countryside for pasangs around, a ledge accessible only on tarnback.

I leaped from the back of the monster and rushed to the Tatrix, to protect her in case the tarn should begin to feed. I pulled the locked talons from her body, calling to the tarn, shoving its legs back. The bird seemed puzzled. Had I not cried "Tabuk!"? Was this thing it had seized not now to be devoured? Was it not prey?

I shoved the tarn back and away from the girl, and gathered her in my arms. I set her down gently against the far wall of the cliff, as far from the edge as I could. The rocky shelf on which we found ourselves was perhaps twenty feet wide and twenty feet deep, about the size that a tarn chooses for nesting.

Standing between the Tatrix and the winged carnivore, I cried "Tabuk!" It began to stalk toward the girl, who rose to her knees, her back pressed against the unyielding wall of the cliff, and screamed.

"Tabuk!" I cried again, taking the great beak in my hands and turning it toward the open fields below.

The bird seemed to hesitate, and then, with a motion almost tender, it thrust its beak against my body. "Tabuk," I said quietly, once more turning it toward the open fields.

With one last look at the Tatrix the bird turned and stalked to the brink of that awesome ledge and, with a single snap of its great wings, leaped into space, its soaring shadow a message of terror to any game below.

I turned to face the Tatrix.

"Are you hurt?" I asked.

Sometimes when the tarn strikes a tabuk, the animal's back is broken. It was a risk which I had decided to take.

I did not feel I had much choice. With the Tatrix in hand, I might be in a position to bargain with Tharna. I did not think I would be able to work any reform in her harsh ways, but I did hope to sue for the freedom of Linna and Andreas, and perhaps for that of the poor wretches whom I had met in the arena. It would surely be a small enough price for the return of the golden Tatrix herself.

The Tatrix struggled to her feet.

It was customary on Gor for a female captive to kneel in the presence of her captor, but she was, after all, a Tatrix, and I did not wish to enforce the point. Her hands, still in their gloves of gold, went to the golden mask, as if she feared most that it might not be in place. Only then did her hands try to arrange and smooth her torn robes. I smiled. They had been ripped by the talons, tattered by the raging winds. Haughtily she drew them about herself, covering herself as best she could. Aside from the mask, metallic, cold, glittering as always, I decided the Tatrix might be beautiful.

"No," she said proudly, "I am unhurt."

It was the answer I had expected, though undoubtedly her body was almost broken, her flesh bruised to the bone.

"You are in pain," I said, "but mostly, now, you are cold and numb from the loss of circulation." I regarded her. "Later," I said, "it will be even more painful."

The expressionless mask gazed upon me.

"I, too," I said, "was once in the talons of a tarn."

"Why did the tarn not kill you in the arena?" she asked.

"It is my tarn," I said simply. What more could I tell her? That it had not killed me, knowing the nature of tarns, seemed almost as incredible to me as it did to her. Had I not known more of tarns, I might have guessed that it held me in some sort of affection.

The Tatrix looked about, examining the sky. "When will it return?" she asked. Her voice had been a whisper. I knew that if there was anything that struck terror into the heart of the Tatrix, it was the tarn.

"Soon," I said. "Let us hope it finds something to eat in the fields below."

The Tatrix trembled slightly.

"If it doesn't find game," she said, "it will return angry and hungry."

"Surely," I agreed.

"It may try to feed on us—" she said.

"Perhaps," I said.

At last the words came out, slowly, carefully formed. "If it doesn't find game," she asked, "are you going to give me to the tarn?"

"Yes," I said.

With a cry of fear the Tatrix fell on her knees before me, her hands extended, pleading. Lara, Tatrix of Tharna, was at my feet, a supplicant.

"Unless you behave yourself," I added.

Angrily the Tatrix scrambled to her feet. "You tricked me!" she cried. "You tricked me into assuming the posture of the captive female!"

I smiled.

Her gloved fists struck at me. I caught her wrists and held her fast. I noted that her eyes behind the mask were blue. I allowed her to twist free. She ran to the wall, and stood, her back to me.

"Do I amuse you?" she asked.

"I'm sorry," I said.

"I am your prisoner, am I not?" she asked, insolently.

"Yes," I said.

"What are you going to do with me?" she asked, her face to the wall, not deigning to look upon me.

"Sell you for a saddle and weapons," I said. I thought it well to alarm the Tatrix, the better to improve my bargaining position.

Her frame shook with fear, and fury. She spun about to face me, her gloved fists clenched. "Never!" she cried.

"I shall if it pleases me," I said.

The Tatrix, trembling with rage, regarded me. I could scarcely conjecture the hatred that seethed behind that placid golden mask. At last she spoke. Her words were like drops of acid.

"You are joking," she said.

"Remove the mask," I suggested, "in order that I may better judge what you will bring on the Street of Brands."

"No!" she cried, her hands flying to the golden mask.

"I think the mask alone," I said, "might bring the price of a good shield and spear."

The Tatrix laughed bitterly. "It would buy a tarn," she said.

I could tell that she was not certain that I was serious, that she did not really believe I could mean what I said. It was important to my plans to convince her that she stood in jeopardy, that I would dare to put her in a camisk and collar.

She laughed, testing me, holding the tattered hem of her robe towards me. "You see," she said, in mock despair, "I will not bring much in this poor garment."

"That is true," I said.

She laughed.

"You will bring more without it," I added.

She seemed shaken by this matter of fact answer. I could tell she was no longer confident of where she stood. She decided to play her trump card. She squared off against me, regal, haughty, insolent. Her voice was cold, each word a crystal of ice. "You would not dare," she said, "to sell me."

"Why not?" I asked.

"Because," she said, drawing herself to her full height, gathering the golden tattered robes about her, "I am Tatrix of Tharna."

I picked up a small rock and threw it from the ledge, watching it sail toward the fields below. I watched the clouds scudding across the darkening sky, listened to the wind whistling among those lonely ridges. I turned to the Tatrix.

"That will improve your price," I said.

The Tatrix seemed stunned. Her haughty manner deserted her.

"Would you truly," she asked, her voice faltering, "put me up for sale?"

I looked at her without answering.

Her hands went to the mask. "Would it be taken from me?"

"And your robes," I said.

She shrank back.

"You will be simply another slave girl among slave girls," I said, "neither more nor less."

The words came hard to her. "Would I be—exhibited?"

"Of course," I said.

"—unclothed?"

"Perhaps you will be permitted to wear slave bracelets," I snapped in irritation.

She looked as though she might swoon.

"Only a fool," I said, "would buy a woman clothed."

"No—no," she said.

"It is the custom," I said simply.

She had backed away from me, and now her back touched the obdurate granite of the cliff wall. Her head was shaking. Although that placid mask showed no emotion, I could read the despair in the body of the Tatrix.

"You would do this to me?" she asked, her voice a frightened whisper.

"Within two nights," I said, "you will stand stripped on the block at Ar and be sold to the highest bidder."

"No, no, no," she whimpered, and her tortured body refused to sustain her any longer. She crumpled piteously against the wall, weeping.

This was more than I had counted on, and I had to resist an urge to comfort her, to tell her that I would not hurt her, that she was safe, but, mindful of Linna and Andreas, and the poor wretches in the Amusements, I restrained my compassion. Indeed, as I thought of the cruel Tatrix, of what she had done, I wondered if, in fact, I should not take her to Ar and dispose of her on the Street of Brands. Surely she would be more harmless in

the Pleasure Gardens of a tarnsman than on the throne of
Tharna.

"Warrior," she said, her head lifting piteously, "must
you exact so terrible a vengeance on me?"

I smiled to myself. It sounded now as though the Tatrix
might bargain. "You have wronged me mightily," I said
sternly.

"But you are only a man," she said. "Only a beast."

"I, too, am human," I told her.

"Give me my freedom," she begged.

"You put me in a yoke," I said. "You lashed me. You
condemned me to the Arena. You would have fed me to
the tarn." I laughed. "And you ask for your freedom!"

"I will pay you a thousand times what I would bring on
the block at Ar," she pleaded.

"A thousand times what you would bring on the block
at Ar," I said harshly, "would not satisfy my vengeance—
only you on the block at Ar."

She moaned.

Now, I thought, is the time. "And," I said, "not only
have you injured me, but you have enslaved my friends."

The Tatrix rose to her knees. "I will free them!" she
cried.

"Can you change the laws of Tharna?" I demanded.

"Alas," she cried, "not even I can do that, but I can
free your friends! I will free them! My freedom for
theirs!"

I appeared to think the matter over.

She sprang to her feet. "Think, Warrior," she cried, "of
your honor." Her voice was triumphant. "Would you
satisfy your vengeance at the price of slavery for your
friends?"

"No," I cried angrily, inwardly delighted, "for I am a
warrior!"

Her voice was exultant. "Then, Warrior, you must bargain with me!"

"Not with you!" I cried, attempting to sound dismayed.

"Yes," she laughed, "my freedom for theirs!"

"It is not enough," I growled.

"Then what?" she cried.

"Free all those used in the Amusements of Tharna!"

The Tatrix seemed taken aback.

"All," I cried, "—or the block at Ar!"

Her head dropped. "Very well, Warrior," she said. "I will free them all."

"Can I trust you?" I asked.

"Yes," she said, not meeting my gaze, "you have the word of the Tatrix of Tharna."

I wondered if I could trust her word. I realized I had little choice.

"My friends," I said, "are Linna of Tharna and Andreas of Tor."

The Tatrix looked up at me. "But," she said, unbelievingly, "they have cared for one another."

"Nonetheless," I said, "free them."

"She is a Degraded Woman," said the Tatrix, "and he a member of a caste outlawed in Tharna."

"Free them," I said.

"Very well," said the Tatrix humbly. "I shall."

"And I will need weapons and a saddle," I said.

"You shall have them," she said.

In that moment the shadow of the tarn covered the ledge and, with a great beating of wings, the monster rejoined us. In its talons it held a great piece of meat, bloody and raw, which had been torn from some kill, perhaps a bosk more than twenty pasangs away. It dropped the great piece of meat before me.

I did not move.

I had no wish to contest this prize with the great bird. But the tarn did not attack the meat. I gathered that it had already fed somewhere on the plains below. An examination of its beak confirmed this guess. And there was no nest on the ledge, no female tarn, no screeching brood of tarnlings. The great beak nudged the meat against my legs.

It was a gift.

I slapped the bird affectionately. "Thank you, Ubar of the Skies," I said.

I bent down, and with my hands and teeth, tore a chunk free. I saw the Tatrix shudder as I attacked the raw flesh, but I was famished, and the niceties of the low tables, for what they were, were abandoned. I offered a piece to the Tatrix, but her body swayed as though she were ill and I would not insist.

While I fed on the tarn's gift, the Tatrix stood near the edge of the rocky shelf, gazing out on the meadow of talenders. They were beautiful, and their delicate fragrance was wafted even to the harsh ledge. She held her robes about her and watched the flowers, like a yellow sea, roll and ripple in the wind. I thought she seemed a lonely figure, rather forlorn and sad.

"Talenders," she said to herself.

I was squatting beside the meat, my mouth chewing, filled with raw flesh. "What does a woman of Tharna know of talenders?" I taunted her.

She turned away, not answering.

When I had eaten, she said, "Take me now to the Pillar of Exchanges."

"What is that?" I asked.

"A pillar on the borders of Tharna," she said, "where Tharna and her enemies effect the exchange of prisoners. I will guide you." She added, "You will be met there by men of Tharna, who are waiting for you."

"Waiting?" I asked.

"Of course," she said, "have you not wondered why there was no pursuit?" She laughed ruefully. "Who would be fool enough to carry away the Tatrix of Tharna when she might be ransomed for the gold of a dozen Ubars?"

I looked at her.

"I was afraid," she said, her eyes downcast, "that you were such a fool." There seemed to be an emotion in her voice that I could not understand.

"No," I laughed, "it is back to Tharna with you!"

I still wore the golden scarf about my neck, from the arena, that scarf which had initiated the games, and which I had picked up from the sand to wipe away the sand and sweat. I took it from my neck.

"Turn around," I said to the Tatrix, "and place your hands behind your back."

Her head in the air, the Tatrix did as she was told. I pulled the gloves of gold from her hands and thrust them in my belt. Then, with the scarf, using the simple capture knots of Gor, I lashed her wrists together.

I threw the Tatrix lightly to the back of the tarn and leaped up beside her. Then, holding her in one arm, and fastening one hand deep in the quills of the Tarn's neck, I called "One-strap!" and the beast sprang from the ledge and began climbing.

16

THE PILLAR OF EXCHANGES

GUIDED BY THE TATRIX, IN perhaps no more than thirty minutes, we saw, gleaming in the distance, the Pillar of Exchanges. It lay about one hundred pasangs northwest of the city, and was a lonely white column of solid marble, perhaps four hundred feet in height and a hundred feet in diameter. It was accessible only on tarnback.

It was not a bad place for the exchange of prisoners, and offered an almost ideal situation from the point of view of avoiding ambush. The solid pillar would not allow entrance to men on the ground, and approaching tarns would be easily visible for miles before they could reach it.

I examined the countryside carefully. It seemed bare. On the pillar itself there were three tarns, and as many warriors, and one woman, who wore the silver mask of Tharna. As I passed over the pillar, a warrior removed his helmet, and signaled for me to bring the tarn down. I saw that it was Thorn, Captain of Tharna. I noted that he and his fellows were armed.

"Is it customary," I asked the Tatrix, "for warriors to carry weapons to the Pillar of Exchanges?"

"There will be no treachery," said the Tatrix.

I considered turning the tarn and abandoning the venture.

"You can trust me," she said.

"How do I know that?" I challenged.

"Because I am Tatrix of Tharna," she said proudly.

"Four-strap!" I cried to the bird, to bring it down on the pillar. The bird seemed not to understand. "Four-strap!" I repeated, more severely. For some reason the bird seemed unwilling to land. "Four-strap!" I shouted, commanding it harshly to obey.

The great giant landed on the marble pillar, its steel-shod talons ringing on the stone.

I did not dismount, but held the Tatrix more firmly.

The tarn seemed nervous. I tried to calm the bird. I spoke to it in low tones, patted it roughly on the neck.

The woman in the silver mask approached. "Hail to our Beloved Tatrix!" she cried. It was Dorna the Proud.

"Do not approach more closely," I ordered.

Dorna stopped, about five yards in advance of Thorn and the two warriors, who had not moved at all.

The Tatrix acknowledged the salutation of Dorna the Proud with merely a regal nod of her head.

"All Tharna is yours, Warrior," cried Dorna the Proud, "if you but relinquish our noble Tatrix! The city weeps for her return! I fear there will be no more joy in Tharna until she sits again upon her golden throne!"

I laughed.

Dorna the Proud stiffened. "What are your terms, Warrior?" she demanded.

"A saddle and weapons," I answered, "and the freedom of Linna of Tharna, Andreas of Tor, and those who fought this afternoon in the Amusements of Tharna."

There was a silence.

"Is that all?" asked Dorna the Proud, puzzled.

"Yes," I said.

Behind her, Thorn laughed.

Dorna glanced at the Tatrix. "I shall add," she said, "the weight of five tarns in gold, a room of silver, helmets filled with jewels!"

"You truly love your Tatrix," I said.

"Indeed, Warrior," said Dorna.

"And you are excessively generous," I added.

The Tatrix squirmed in my arms.

"Less," said Dorna the Proud, "would insult our Beloved Tatrix."

I was pleased, for though I would have little use for such riches in the Sardar Mountains, Linna and Andreas, and the poor wretches of the arena, might well profit from them.

Lara, the Tatrix, straightened in my arms. "I do not find the terms satisfactory," she said. "Give him in addition to what he asks, the weight of ten tarns in gold, two rooms of silver and a hundred helmets filled with jewels."

Dorna the Proud bowed in gracious acquiescence. "Indeed, Warrior," said she, "for our Tatrix we would give you even the stones of our walls."

"Are my terms satisfactory to you?" asked the Tatrix, rather condescendingly I thought.

"Yes," I said, sensing the affront that had been offered to Dorna the Proud.

"Release me," she commanded.

"Very well," I said.

I slid down from the back of the tarn, the Tatrix in my arms. I set her on her feet, on the top of that windy pillar on the borders of Tharna, and bent to remove the golden scarf which restrained her.

As soon as her wrists were free she was once again every inch the royal Tatrix of Tharna.

I wondered if this could be the girl who had had the harrowing adventure, whose garments were tattered, whose body must still be wretched with pain from its sojourn in the claws of my tarn.

Imperiously, not deigning to speak to me, she gestured to the gloves of gold which I had placed in my belt. I returned them to her. She drew them on, slowly, deliberately, facing me all the while.

Something in her mien made me uneasy.

She turned and walked majestically to Dorna and the warriors.

When she had reached their side she turned and with a sudden swirl of those golden robes pointed an imperious finger at me. "Seize him," she said.

Thorn and the warriors leaped forward, and I found myself ringed with their weapons.

"Traitress!" I cried.

The voice of the Tatrix was merry. "Fool!" she laughed, "do you not know by now that one does not make pacts with an animal, that one does not bargain with a beast?"

"You gave me your word!" I shouted.

The Tatrix drew her robes about her. "You are only a man," she said.

"Let us kill him," said Thorn.

"No," said the Tatrix, imperiously, "that would not be enough." The mask glittered on me, reflecting the light of the descending sun. It seemed, more than ever before, to possess a ferocity, to be hideous, molten. "Shackle him," she said, "and send him to the mines of Tharna."

Behind me the tarn suddenly screamed with rage and its wings smote the air.

Thorn and the warriors were startled, and in this instant I leapt between their weapons, seized Thorn and a warrior, dashed them together, and threw them both, weapons clattering, to the marble flooring of the pillar. The Tatrix and Dorna the Proud screamed.

The other warrior lunged at me with his sword and I side-stepped the stroke and seized the wrist of his sword arm. I twisted it and thrust it up and high over my left arm, and with a sudden downward wrench snapped it at the elbow. He collapsed whimpering.

Thorn had regained his feet and leaped on me from behind, and the other warrior a moment later. I grappled with them, fiercely. Then, slowly, as they cursed helplessly, I drew them inch by inch over my shoulders, and threw them suddenly to the marble at my feet. In that moment both the Tatrix and Dorna the Proud plunged sharp instruments, pins of some sort, into my back and arm.

I laughed at the absurdity of this, and then, my vision blackening, the pillar whirling, I fell at their feet. My muscles no longer obeyed my will.

"Shackle him," said the Tatrix.

As the world slowly turned under me I felt my legs and arms, limp, as weak as fog, thrown roughly together. I heard the rattle of a chain and felt my limbs clasped in shackles.

The merry victorious laugh of the Tatrix rang in my ears.

I heard Dorna the Proud say, "Kill the tarn."

"It's gone," said the uninjured warrior.

Slowly, though no strength returned to my body, my vision cleared, first in the center, and then gradually toward the edges, until I could once again see the pillar, the sky beyond and my foes.

In the distance I saw a flying speck, which would be the tarn. When it had seen me fall it had apparently taken flight. Now, I thought, it would be free, escaping at last to some rude habitat where it might, without saddle and harness, without a silver hobble, reign as the Ubar of the Skies that it was. Its departure saddened me, but I was glad that it had escaped. Better that than to die under the spear of one of the warriors.

Thorn seized me by the wrist shackles and dragged me across the top of the pillar to one of the three tarns that waited. I was helpless. My legs and arms could not have been more useless if every nerve in them had been cut by a knife.

I was chained to the ankle ring of one of the tarns.

The Tatrix had apparently lost interst in me, for she turned to Dorna the Proud and Thorn, Captain of Tharna.

The warrior whose arm had been broken knelt on the marble flooring of the pillar, bent over, rocking back and forth, the injured arm held against his body. His fellow stood near me, among the tarns, perhaps to watch me, perhaps to steady and soothe the excitable giants.

Haughtily the Tatrix addressed Dorna and Thorn. "Why," she asked them, "are there so few of my soldiers here?"

"We are enough," said Thorn.

The Tatrix looked out over the plains, in the direction of the city. "By now," she said, "lines of rejoicing citizens will be setting out from the city."

Neither Dorna the Proud, nor Thorn, Captain of Tharna, answered her.

The Tatrix walked across the pillar, regal in those tattered robes, and stood over me. She pointed across the plains, toward Tharna. "Warrior," said she, "if you were to remain long enough on this pillar you would see processions come to welcome me back to Tharna."

The voice of Dorna the Proud drifted across the pillar. "I think not, Beloved Tatrix," she said.

The Tatrix turned, puzzled. "Why not?" she asked.

"Because," said Dorna the Proud, and I could tell that behind that silver mask, she smiled, "you are not going back to Tharna."

The Tatrix stood as if stunned, not understanding.

The uninjured warrior had now climbed to the saddle of the tarn, to whose ankle ring I lay helplessly chained. He hauled on the one-strap and the monster took flight. Painfully I was wrenched into the air and, cruelly hanging by my shackled wrists, I saw the white column dropping away beneath me, and the figures upon it, two warriors, a woman in a silver mask, and the golden Tatrix of Tharna.

17

THE MINES OF THARNA

THE ROOM WAS LONG, LOW, narrow, perhaps four feet by four feet, and a hundred feet long. A small, foul tharlarion lamp burned at each end. How many such rooms lay beneath the earth of Tharna, in her many mines, I did not know. The long line of slaves, shackled together, stooped and crawled the length of the room. When it was filled with its wretched occupants, an iron door, containing a sliding iron observation panel, closed. I heard four bolts being shoved into place.

It was a dank room. There were pools of water here and there on the floor; the walls were damp; water in certain places dripped from the ceiling. It was ventilated inadequately by a set of tiny circular apertures, about an inch in diameter, placed every twenty feet. One larger aperture, a circular hole perhaps two feet in diameter, was visible in the center of the long room.

Andreas of Tor, who was shackled at my side, pointed to it. "That hole," he said, "floods the room."

I nodded, and leaned back against the damp, solid stone that formed the sides of the chamber. I wondered how many times, under the soil of Tharna, such a chamber had been flooded, how many chained wretches had been drowned in such dismal, sewerlike traps. I was no longer puzzled that the discipline in the mines of Tharna was as good as it was. I had learned that only a month before, in a mine not five hundred yards from this one, there had been a disturbance created by a single prisoner.

"Drown them all," had been the decision of the Administrator of the Mines. I was not surprised then that the prisoners themselves looked with horror upon the very thought of resistance. They would strangle one of their fellows who thought of rebellion, rather than risk the flooding of the chamber. Indeed, the entire mine itself could, in an emergency, be flooded. Once, I was told, it had happened, to quell an uprising. To pump out the water and clear the shafts of bodies had taken weeks.

Andreas said to me, "For those who are not fond of life, this place has many conveniences."

"To be sure," I agreed.

He thrust an onion and a crust of bread into my hands. "Take this," he said.

"Thanks," I said. I took them and began to chew on them.

"You will learn," he said, "to scramble with the rest of us."

Before we had been ushered into the cell, outside, in a broad, rectangular chamber, two of the mine attendants had poured a tub of bread and vegetables into the feed trough fixed in the wall, and the slaves had rushed upon it, like animals, screaming, cursing, pushing, jostling, trying to thrust their hands into the trough and carry away as much as they could before it was gone. Revolted, I had not joined in this wretched contest, though by my chains I had been dragged to the very edge of the trough. Yet I knew, as Andreas had said, I would learn to go to the trough, for I had no wish to die, and I would not continue to live on his charity.

I smiled, wondering why it was that I, and my fellow prisoners, seemed so determined to live. Why was it that we chose to live? Perhaps the question is foolish, but it did not seem so in the mines of Tharna.

"We must think of escape," I said to Andreas.

"Be quiet, you fool!" hissed a thin, terrified voice from perhaps a dozen feet away.

It was Ost of Tharna, who, like Andreas and myself, had been condemned to the mines.

He hated me, blaming me somehow for the fact that he found himself in this dire predicament. Today, more than once, he had scattered the ore which, on my hands and knees, I had chipped from the narrow shafts of the mine. And twice he had stolen the pile of ore I had accumulated, poking it into the canvas sack we slaves wore about our necks in the mines. I had been beaten by the Whip Slave for not contributing my share to the day's quota of ore required of the chain of which I was a member.

If the quota was not met, the slaves were not fed that night. If the quota was not met three days in a row, the slaves would be whipped into the long cell, the door bolted, and the cell flooded. Many of the slaves looked upon me with disfavor. Perhaps it was because the quota had been increased the day that I was added to their chain. I myself guessed this was more than a coincidence.

"I shall inform against you," hissed Ost, "for plotting an escape."

In the half light, from the small tharlarion lamps set in each end of the room, I saw the heavy, squat figure beside Ost loop his wrist chain silently about the creature's thin throat. The circle of chain tightened, and Ost scratched helplessly at it with his fingers, his eyes bulging. "You will inform against no one," said a voice, which I recognized as that of the bull-like Kron of Tharna, of the Caste of Metal Workers, he whose life I had spared in the arena during the Battles of Oxen. The chain tightened. Ost shuddered like a convulsive monkey.

"Do not kill him," I said to Kron.

"As you wish, Warrior," said Kron, and dropped the frightened Ost, roughly disengaging his chain from the creature's throat. Ost lay on the damp floor, his hands on his throat, gasping for breath.

"It seems you have a friend," said Andreas of Tor.

With a rattle of chain and a roll of his great shoulders, Kron stretched himself out as well as he could in the cramped quarters. Within a minute his heavy breathing told me he was asleep.

"Where is Linna?" I asked Andreas.

For once his voice was sad. "On one of the Great Farms," he said. "I failed her."

"We have all failed," I said.

There was not much conversation in the cell, for the men perhaps had little to say, and their bodies were worn with the cruel labors of the day. I sat with my back against the damp wall, listening to the sounds of their sleep.

I was far from the Sardar Mountains, far from the Priest-Kings of Gor. I had failed my city, my beloved Talena, my father, my friends. There would not be a stone set upon another stone. The riddle of the Priest-Kings, of their cruel, incomprehensible will, would not be solved. Their secret would be kept, and I would die, sooner or later, whipped and starved, in the kennels that were the mines of Tharna.

Tharna has perhaps a hundred or more mines, each maintained by its own chain of slaves. These mines are torturous networks of tunnels worming themselves inch by inch irregularly through the rich ores that are the foundation of the wealth of the city. Most of the shaft tunnels do not allow a man to stand upright in them. Many are inadequately braced. As the slave works the tunnel, he crawls on his hands and knees, which bleed at first but gradually develop calluses of thick, scabrous tissue. About his neck hangs a canvas bag in which pieces of ore are carried back to the scales. The ore itself is freed from the sides of the mine by a small pick. Light is supplied by tiny lamps, no more than small cups of tharlarion oil with fiber wicks.

The working day is fifteen Gorean hours (Ahns), which, allowing for the slight difference in the period of the planet's rotation, would be approximately eighteen Earth hours. The slaves are never brought to the surface, and once plunged into the cold darkness of the mines never again see the sun. The only relief in their existence comes once a year, on the birthday of the Tatrix, when they are served a small cake, made with honey and sesame seeds, and a small pot of poor Kal-da. One fellow on my

chain, little more than a toothless skeleton, boasted that he
had drunk Kal-da three times in the mines. Most are not
so fortunate. The life expectancy of the mine slave, given
the labor and food, if he does not die under the whips of
the overseers, is usually from six months to one year.

I found myself gazing at the large circular hole in the
ceiling of the narrow cell.

In the morning, though I knew it was morning only by
the curses of the Whip Slaves, the cracking of the whips,
the cries of the slaves and the rattle of chains, I and my
fellow prisoners crawled from our cell, emerging again
into the broad, rectangular room which lay directly beyond.

Already the feed trough had been filled.

The slaves edged toward the trough, but were whipped
back. The word had not yet been given which would allow
them to fall upon it.

The Whip Slave, another of the slaves of Tharna, but
one in charge of the chain, was pleased with his task.
Though he might never see the light of the sun, yet it was
he who held the whip, he who was Ubar in this macabre
dungeon.

The slaves tensed, their eyes fixed on the trough. The
whip lifted. When it fell, that would be the signal that they
might rush to the trough.

There was pleasure in the eyes of the Whip Slave as he
enjoyed the tormenting moment of suspense which his
uplifted whip inflicted on the ragged, hungry slaves.

The whip cracked. "Feed!" he shouted.

The slaves lunged forward.

"No!" I cried, my voice checking them.

Some of them stumbled and fell, sprawling with a rattle
of chains on the floor, dragging others down. But most
managed to stand upright, catching their balance, and,
almost as one man, that wretched degraded huddle of
slaves turned its frightened, empty eyes upon me.

'Feed!" cried the Whip Slave, cracking the whip again.

"No," I said.

The huddle of men wavered.

Ost tried to pull toward the trough, but he was chained to Kron, who refused to move. Ost might as well have been chained to a tree.

The Whip Slave approached me. Seven times the whip struck me, and I did not flinch.

Then I said, "Do not strike me again."

He backed away, the whip arm falling. He had understood me, and he knew that his life was in danger. What consolation would it be to him if the entire mine were flooded, if he had first perished with my chain about his throat?

I turned to the men. "You are not animals," I said. "You are men."

Then, gesturing them forward, I led them to the trough.

"Ost," I said, "will distribute the food."

Ost thrust his hands into the trough, and crammed a fistful of bread into his mouth.

Kron's wrist chains struck him across the cheek and ear, and the bread flew from his mouth.

"Distribute the food," said Kron.

"We chose you," said Andreas of Tor, "because you are known for your honesty."

And amazing to say, those chained wretches laughed.

Sullenly, while the Whip Slave stood by and watched, angry, fearful, Ost distributed the poor fare that lay in the trough.

The last piece of bread I broke in two, taking half and giving the other half to Ost. "Eat," I said.

In fury, his eyes darting back and forth like those of an urt, he bit into the bread and gulped it down. "The chamber will be flooded for this," he said.

Andreas of Tor said, "I, for one, would be honored to die in the company of Ost."

And again the men laughed, and I thought that even Ost smiled.

The Whip Slave watched while we filed up the long incline to the shafts, his whip arm limp. Wondering, he watched us, for one of the men, of the Caste of Peasants, had begun to hum a plowing song, and, one by one, the others joined him.

The quota was well met that day, and the day following.

18

WE ARE OF THE SAME CHAIN

OCCASIONALLY A BIT OF NEWS filtered down into the mines, brought by the slaves who filled the feeding trough. These slaves were fortunate for they had access to the central shaft. Each of the hundred mines of Tharna, at one level or another, opened on this shaft. It is to be distinguished from the much smaller ore shafts, which are individual to each mine. The ore shafts are like narrow wells sunk in the stone and their platforms can scarcely accommodate a slave's sack of ore.

It is through the central shaft that the mines of Tharna are supplied. Down that shaft comes not only food but, when needed, canvas, tools and chains. Drinking water, of course, is supplied by the natural sumps in each mine. I myself, and my fellow slaves, had descended the central shaft. Only dead slaves made the ascent.

Beginning with the slaves who worked the pulleys that controlled the supply platform in the central shaft, the news had spread, from one mine to another, until at last it had reached even ours, which was the deepest on the shaft.

There was a new Tatrix in Tharna.

"Who is the new Tatrix?" I asked.

"Dorna the Proud," said the slave, who tumbled onions, turnips, radishes, potatoes and bread into the feed trough.

"What happened to Lara?" I asked.

He laughed. "You are ignorant!" he exclaimed.

"News does not travel fast in the mines," I said.

"She was carried off," he said.

"What?" I cried.

"Yes," said he, "by a tarnsman, as it turned out."

"What is his name?" I asked.

"Tarl," said he, and his voice fell to a whisper, "—of Ko-ro-ba."

I was dumbfounded.

"He is the outlaw," said the man, "who survived the Amusements of Tharna."

"I know," I said.

"There was a tarn, wearing the silver hobble, that was to kill him, but he freed the tarn, leaped on its back and made good his escape." The slave put down the tub of vegetables and bread. His eyes were wet with amusement and he slapped his thigh. "He returned only long enough to tarnstrike the Tatrix herself," he said. "The tarn carried her off like a tabuk!" His laughter, which spread to the other slaves in the room, those chained to me, was uproarious, and I understood better than I had understood before the affection with which the Tatrix of Tharna was held in the mines.

But I alone did not laugh.

"What of the Pillar of Exchanges?" I asked. "Was the Tatrix not returned at the Pillar, and freed?"

"Everyone thought she would be," said the slave, "but the tarnsman apparently wanted her more than the riches of Tharna."

"What a man!" cried one of the slaves.

"Perhaps she was very beautiful," said another.

"She was not exchanged?" I asked the slave with the food tub.

"No," he said. "Two of those who are highest in Tharna, Dorna the Proud, and Thorn, a Captain, went to the Pillar of Exchanges, but the Tatrix was never returned. Pursuit was launched, the hills and fields combed without success. Only her tattered robes and the mask of gold were found, by Dorna the Proud and Thorn, Captain of Tharna." The slave sat down on the tub. "Now," said he, "Dorna wears the mask."

"What," I asked, "do you surmise to be the fate of Lara, who was Tatrix?"

The slave laughed, and so, too, did some of the others.

"Well," said he, "we know she no longer wears her golden robes."

"Doubtless," said one of the slaves, "some more suitable raiment has replaced them."

The slave laughed. "Yes," he roared, slapping his thigh. "Pleasure silk!" He rocked on the tub. "Can you imagine!" he laughed, "Lara, the Tatrix of Tharna, in pleasure silk!"

The chain of slaves laughed, all except myself, and Andreas of Tor, who regarded me questioningly. I smiled at him, and shrugged. I did not have the answer to his question.

Little by little, I tried to restore the self-respect of my fellow slaves. It began simply enough at the feeding trough. Then I began to encourage them to speak to one another, and to call one another by their names, and their cities, and though there were men of different cities there, they shared the same chain and trough, and they accepted one another.

When one man was ill, others saw that his ore sack was filled. When one man was beaten, others would pass water from hand to hand that his wounds might be bathed, that he might drink though the chain did not allow him to the water. And in time, each of us knew the others who shared his chain. We were no longer dark, anonymous shapes to one another, huddling in the dampness of the mines of Tharna. In time only Ost remained frightened by this change, for he continually feared the flooding of the chamber.

My chain of men worked well, and the quota was filled day after day, and when it was raised, it was filled again. Sometimes even, the men would hum as they worked, the strong sound resonant in the tunnels of the mine. The Whip Slaves wondered, and began to fear us.

News of the distribution of food at the feeding trough had spread, by means of the slaves who carried the tubs of food, from mine to mine. And, too, they told of the strange, new things that happened in the mine at the bottom of the central shaft, how men helped one another, and could find the time and will to remember a tune.

And as time passed I learned from the food slaves that this revolution, as unannounced and silent as the foot of a larl, had begun to spread from mine to mine. Soon I noticed that the food slaves spoke no more, and gathered that they had been warned to silence. Yet from their faces I knew that the contagion of self-respect, of nobility, flamed in the mines beneath Tharna. Here, underground, in the mines, home of that which was lowest and most degraded in Tharna, men came to look upon one another, and themselves, with satisfaction.

I decided it was time.

That night, when we were herded into the long cell, and the bolts were shoved in place, I spoke to the men.

"Who among you," I asked, "would be free?"

"I," said Andreas of Tor.

"And I," growled Kron of Tharna.

"And I!" cried other voices.

Only Ost demurred. "It is sedition to speak thus," he whimpered.

"I have a plan," I said, "but it will require great courage, and you may all die."

"There is no escape from the mines," whimpered Ost.

"Lead us, Warrior," said Andreas.

"First," I said, "we must have the chamber flooded."

Ost shrieked with terror, and Kron's great fist shut on his windpipe, silencing him. Ost squirmed, scuffling in the dark, helpless. "Be quiet, Serpent," said the bull-like Kron. He dropped Ost, and the conspirator crawled to the length of his chain and huddled against the wall, trembling with fear.

Ost's shriek had told me what I wanted to know. I now knew how we could arrange to have the chamber flooded.

"Tomorrow night," I said simply, looking in Ost's direction, "we will make our break for freedom."

The next day, as I had expected, an accident befell Ost. He seemed to injure his foot with the pick, and he pleaded so earnestly with the Whip Slave that the fellow removed him from the chain and, putting a collar on his throat, led him limping away. This would have been unusual solicitation on the part of a Whip Slave but it was obvious to him as to the rest of us that Ost wished to speak with him alone, to communicate information of extreme importance.

"You should have killed him," said Kron of Tharna.

"No," I said.

The bull-like man of Tharna looked at me questioningly and shrugged.

That night the slaves who brought the tub of food were accompanied by a dozen warriors.

That night Ost was not returned to the chain. "His foot requires care," said the Whip Slave, gesturing us toward the long cell.

When the iron door was shut and the bolts shot into place, I heard the Whip Slave laugh.

The men were despondent.

"Tonight," said Andreas of Tor, "you know the chamber will be flooded."

"Yes," I said, and he looked at me in disbelief.

I called to the man at the far end of the chamber. "Pass the lamp," I said.

I took the lamp and went, some of my fellow prisoners perforce accompanying me, and held it to the circular shaft, about two feet in diameter, down which the water would hurtle. There was an iron grating set in the stone, about eight feet high in the shaft. From somewhere above we heard the movement of a valve.

"Lift me!" I cried, and on the shoulders of Andreas and the slave shackled beside me, I was lifted into the shaft. Its sides were smooth and slimy. My hands slipped on them.

Chained as I was I could not get to the grating.

I cursed.

Then it seemed that Andreas and the slave grew beneath my feet. Other slaves knelt beneath them, giving their backs that the two might rise higher. Standing side by side they lifted me higher into the shaft.

My shackled wrists seized the grating.

"I have it," I cried. "Drag me down!"

Then Andreas and the slave fell in the shaft and I felt the chains that fastened my wrists and ankles to theirs tearing at my limbs. "Pull!" I cried, and the hundred slaves in the long room began to draw on the chains. My hands bled on the grating, the blood falling back in my upturned face, but I would not release the bars. "Pull!" I cried.

A trickle of water from above moved down the sides of the stones.

The valve was opening.

"Pull!" I cried again.

Suddenly the grating sprang free and I and it fell clattering with a rattle of chains and metal to the floor.

Now there was a stream of water flowing down the shaft.

"First on the chain!" I called.

With a rattle of chains a small man with a wisp of straw-colored hair across his forehead snaked past the others and stood before me.

"You must climb," I said.

"How?" he asked, bewildered.

"Brace your back against the wall of the shaft," I said. "Use your feet!"

"I can't," he said.

"You will," I said.

I and his fellow took him and thrust him bodily through the opening.

We heard him in the shaft, grunting, gasping, the

sounds of chains scraping on stones as he began the torturous inch by inch ascent.

"I'm slipping!" he cried, and rattled down the shaft and fell to the cell floor weeping.

"Again!" I said.

"I can't," he cried hysterically.

I seized him by the shoulders and shook him. "You are of Tharna," I said. "Show us what a man of Tharna can do!"

It was a challenge which had been put to few men of Tharna.

We lifted him again into the shaft.

I set the second on the chain beneath him, and the third on the chain beneath the second.

The water was sloshing through the aperture now, in a stream about as wide as my fist. In the tunnel it rose to our ankles.

Then the first man on the chain supported his own weight, and the second, chains rattling, began to ascend the vertical tunnel, supported by he who was third, who now stood on the back of the fourth man, and so it continued.

Once the second man slipped, dragging the first down with him, and causing the third to lose his grip, but by now there was a solid chain of men in the tunnel, and the fourth and the fifth men held. The first began his torturous ascent once more, followed by the second and third.

The water was perhaps two feet high in the cell, pressing upward toward the low ceiling, when I followed Andreas into the tunnel. Kron was the fourth man behind me.

Andreas, Kron and I were in the tunnel, but what of the poor wretches on the chain behind us?

I looked up the long shaft, at the line of slaves moving upward, inch by inch.

"Hurry!" I cried.

The stream of water now seemed to press us down, to impede our progress. It was like a small waterfall.

"Hurry! Hurry!" cried the voice of a man still below, a hoarse, terrified cry.

The first man on the chain had now ascended the tunnel to the very source of the water, another tunnel. We heard a sudden, loud swift rushing of water. He cried out in fear, "It's coming, all of it!"

"Brace yourselves!" I shouted to those above and below me. "Drag the last men into the tunnel!" I yelled. "Get them out of the cell!"

But my last words were drowned in a hurtling plunging cataract of water that shattered on my body like a great fist, knocking my breath out. It roared down the shaft, pounding on the men. Some lost their footing, and bodies were wedged in the shaft. It was impossible to breathe, to move, to see.

Then as suddenly as it had begun, the cataract ceased. Above, whoever worked the valve must have grown impatient and thrown it open completely, or perhaps the sudden torrent of water had been intended as a gesture of mercy to drown any survivors quickly.

As soon as I had caught my breath, I shook the sopping hair from my eyes. I peered up into the sodden blackness, crowded with chained bodies.

"Keep climbing!" I said.

In perhaps another two or three minutes I had reached the horizontal tunnel down which the tumult of the water had been fed into the vertical tunnel. I found those ahead of me on the chain. Like myself they were soaked to the skin and shivering, but alive. I clutched the first man by the shoulders.

"Well done!" I said to him.

"I am of Tharna," he said proudly.

At last each man of the chain was within the horizontal tunnel, though the last four men had of necessity been dragged to its level, for they hung limp in their chains. How long they had been under water was hard to say.

We worked on them, bending over them in the darkness, I and three men from Port Kar, who understood what must be done. The other slaves on the chain waited patiently, not one complaining, not one urging us to greater speed. At last, one by one, the inert bodies stirred, their lungs opening to draw in the damp, cold air of the mine.

The man whom I had saved reached up and touched me.

"We are of the same chain," I said.

It was a saying we had developed in the mines.

"Come!" I said to the men.

Leading them in two lines, shackled behind me, we crawled down the horizontal tunnel.

19

REVOLT IN THE MINES

"NO, NO!" OST HAD SCREAMED.

We had found him at the valve which emptied the reservoir of water into the slave dungeon more than two hundred feet below. He now wore the habiliments of the Whip Slave, a reward for his treachery. He threw down the whip and tried to run, scurrying like an urt, but everywhere he turned, the chain of haggard, violent men confined him, and as the chain closed, Ost fell quivering to his knees.

"Do not harm him," I said.

But the bull-like Kron of Tharna's hand was on the neck of the conspirator.

"This is a matter for the men of Tharna," said he. Those blue eyes like steel looked about the unyielding faces of the chained slaves.

And the eyes of Ost, too, like those of a terrified urt, looked from face to face, pleading, but Ost found no pity in those eyes that looked upon him as though they might have been composed of stone.

"Is Ost of the chain?" asked Kron.

"No," cried a dozen voices. "He is not of the chain."

"Yes," cried Ost. "I am of the chain." He peered like a rodent into the faces of his captors. "Take me with you. Free me!"

"It is sedition to speak thus," said one of the men.

Ost trembled.

"Tie him and leave him here," I said.

"Yes," begged Ost hysterically, groveling at the feet of Kron. "Do that, Masters!"

Andreas of Tor spoke up. "Do as Tarl of Ko-ro-ba asks," he said. "Do not stain your chains with the blood of this serpent."

"Very well," said Kron, unnaturally calm. "Let us not stain our chains."

"Thank you, Masters," said Ost, sniveling with relief, his face once more resuming that pinched, sly look I knew so well.

But Kron looked down into the face of Ost, and Ost turned white.

"You will have a better chance than you gave us," said the bull-like man from Tharna.

Ost shrieked with terror.

I tried to press forward, but the men of the chain held firm. I could not come to the conspirator's assistance.

He tried to crawl toward me, his hands extended. I put out my hands, but Kron had seized him and pulled him back.

Bodily the small conspirator was thrown from slave to slave down the length of the chain until the last man hurled him, headfirst, screaming for mercy, down that dark narrow channel which we had ascended. We heard his body hit the sides a dozen times, and his frightened scream fading, only to be silenced by the distant, hollow splash in the water far below.

It was a night like no other in the mines of Tharna.

Leading the chain of slaves in two lines behind me, we swept through the shafts like an eruption from the molten core of the earth. Armed only with ore and the picks that chip the ore from the walls we stormed into the quarters of Whip Slaves and guardsmen, who had scarcely time to seize their weapons. Those not killed in the savage fighting, much of it in the darkness of the shafts, were locked into leg shackles and herded into storage chambers, and the men of the chain did not treat their former oppressors gently.

We had soon come on the hammers that would strike our chains from us and, one by one, we filed past the great anvil where Kron of Tharna, of the Caste of Metal Workers, with expert blows, struck them from our wrists and ankles.

"To the Central Shaft!" I cried, holding a sword that had been taken from a guardsman now chained in the shafts behind.

A slave who had carried tubs of food to the troughs below was only too pleased to guide us.

At last we stood by the Central Shaft.

Our mine opened on it perhaps a thousand feet below the surface. We could see the great chains dangling down the shaft, outlined by the small lamps in the openings of other mines above us, and, very high above, by the white reflection of moonlight. The men crowded out onto the floor of the shaft, which lay only a foot below the opening of our mine, for our mine was the lowest of all.

They stared upward.

The man who had boasted that he had drunk Kal-da three times in the mines of Tharna wept as he gazed upward and caught sight of one of the three hurtling moons of Gor.

I sent several men climbing to the top of the chains, so high above.

"You must protect the chains," I said. "They must not be cut."

Determined dark shapes, agile with the fury of hope, began to climb the chain toward the moons above.

To my pride none of the men suggested that we follow them, none begged that we might steal our freedom before the general alarm could be given.

No! We climbed to the second mine!

How terrible those moments for the guards and Whip Slaves, to suddenly see, unchained and irresistible, the avalanche of wrath and vengeance that broke in upon them! Dice and cards and game boards and drinking goblets scattered to the rocky floors of the guard chambers as Whip Slaves and guardsmen looked up to find at their throats the blades of desperate and condemned men, now drunk with the taste of freedom and determined to free their fellows.

Cell after cell was emptied of its wretched chained occupants, only to be refilled with shackled guardsmen and Whip Slaves, men who knew that the least sign of resistance would bring only a swift and bloody death.

Mine after mine was freed, and as each mine was freed, its slaves, forsaking their own best chance of safety, poured into the mines above to liberate their fellows. This was done as if by plan and yet I knew that it was the spontaneous action of men who had come to respect themselves, the men of the mines of Tharna.

I was the last of the slaves to leave the mines. I climbed one of the great chains to the huge windlass set above the shaft and found myself among hundreds of cheering men, their chains struck off, their hands boasting weapons even if only a piece of jagged rock or a pair of shackles. The dark cheering shapes, many of them crooked and wasted with their labors, saluted me in the light of the three rushing moons of Gor. They shouted my name, and without fear, that of my city. I stood upon the brink of the great shaft and felt the wind of the cold night upon me.

I was happy.

And I was proud.

I saw the great valve which I knew would flood the mines of Tharna, and saw that it remained closed.

I was proud when I saw that my slaves had defended the valve, for about it lay the bodies of soldiers who had tried to reach it; but I was most proud when I realized that the slaves had not now opened the valve, when they knew that below, in the confines of those dismal shafts and cells, chained and helpless, were their oppressors and mortal enemies. I could imagine the terror of those poor creatures cringing in those traps beneath the ground waiting to hear the distant rush of water through the tunnels. Yet it would not come.

I wondered if they would understand that such an action was beneath the hand of a truly free man, and that the men who fought them—who had conquered on this windy and cold night, who had fought like larls in the darkness of the tunnels below, who had not sought their own safety but the liberation of their fellows—were such men.

I leaped to the windlass and raised my arms, the darkness of the central shaft looming beneath me.

There was silence.

"Men of Tharna," I cried, "and of the Cities of Gor, you are free!"

There was a great cheer.

"Word of our deeds even now hurries to the Palace of the Tatrix," I cried.

"Let her tremble!" cried Kron of Tharna in a terrible voice.

"Think, Kron of Tharna," I cried, "soon tarnsmen will fly from the walls of Tharna and the infantry will move against us."

There was a mutter of apprehension from the masses of freed slaves.

"Speak, Tarl of Ko-ro-ba," said Kron, using the name of my city as easily as he might have said the name of any other.

"We do not have the weapons or the training or the beasts we would need to stand against the soldiers of Tharna," I said. "We would be destroyed, trampled like urts underfoot." I paused. "Therefore we must scatter to the forests and the mountains, taking cover where we can. We must live off the land. We will be sought by all the soldiers and guardsmen Tharna can set upon our trail. We will be pursued and ridden down by the lancers who ride the high tharlarions! We will be hunted and slain from the air by the bolts of tarnsmen!"

"But we will die free!" cried Andreas of Tor, and his cry was echoed by hundreds of voices.

"And so must others!" I cried. "You must hide by day and move by night. You must elude your pursuers. You must carry your freedom to others!"

"Are you asking us to become warriors?" cried a voice.

"Yes!" I cried, and such words had never before been spoken on Gor. "In this cause," I said, "whether you are of the Caste of Peasants, or Poets, or Metal Workers, or Saddle-Makers, you must be warriors!"

"We shall," said Kron of Tharna, his fist holding the great hammer with which he had struck off our shackles.

"Is this the will of the Priest-Kings?" asked a voice.

"If it is the will of the Priest-Kings," I said, "let it be done." And then I raised my hands again and standing on the windlass over the shaft, blown by the wind, with the moons of Gor above me, I cried. "And if it be not the will of the Priest-Kings—still let it be done!"

"Let it be done," said the heavy voice of Kron.

"Let it be done," said the men, first one and then another, until there was a sober chorus of assent, quiet but powerful, and I knew that never before in this harsh world had men spoken thus. And it seemed strange to me that this rebellion, this willingness to pursue the right as they saw it, independently of the will of the Priest-Kings, had come not first from the proud Warriors of Gor, nor the Scribes, nor the Builders nor Physicians, nor any of the high castes of the many cities of Gor, but had come from the most degraded and despised of men, wretched slaves from the mines of Tharna.

I stood there and watched the slaves depart, silently now, like shadows, forsaking the precincts of the mines to seek their outlaw fortunes, their destinies beyond the laws and traditions of their cities.

The Gorean phrase of farewell came silently to my lips. "I wish you well."

Kron stopped by the shaft.

I walked across the bar of the windlass and dropped to his side.

The squat giant of the Caste of Metal Workers stood with his feet planted wide. He held that great hammer in his massive fists like a lance across his body. I saw that the once close-cropped hair was now a shaggy yellow. I saw that those eyes, usually like blue steel, seemed softer than I remembered them.

"I wish you well, Tarl of Ko-ro-ba," he said.

"I wish you well, Kron of Tharna," I said.

"We are of the same chain," he said.

"Yes," I said.

Then he turned away, abruptly I thought, and moved rapidly into the shadows.

Now only Andreas of Tor remained at my side.

He mopped back that mane of black hair like a larl's and grinned at me. "Well," said he, "I have tried the Mines of Tharna, and now I think I shall try the Great Farms."

"Good luck," I said.

I fervently hoped that he would find the auburn-haired girl in the camisk, gentle Linna of Tharna.

"And where are you off to?" asked Andreas lightly.

"I have business with the Priest-Kings," I said.

"Ah!" said Andreas, and was silent.

We faced one another under the three moons. He seemed sad, one of the few times I had seen him so.

"I'm coming with you," he said.

I smiled. Andreas knew as well as I that men did not return from the Sardar Mountains.

"No," I said. "I think you would find few songs in the mountains."

"A poet," said he, "will look for songs anywhere."

"I am sorry," I said, "but I cannot allow you to accompany me."

Andreas clapped his hands on my shoulders. "Hear, dull-witted scion of the Caste of Warriors," he said, "my friends are more important to me than even my songs."

I tried to be light. I feigned skepticism. "Are you truly of the Caste of Poets?"

"Never more truly than now," said Andreas, "for how could my songs be more important than the things they celebrate?"

I marveled that he had said this, for I knew that the young Andreas of Tor might have given his arm or years of his life for what might be a true song, one worthy of what he had seen and felt and cared for.

"Linna needs you," I said. "Seek her out."

Andreas of the Caste of Poets stood in torment before me, agony in his eyes.

"I wish you well," I said, "—Poet."

He nodded. "I wish you well," he said, "—Warrior."

Perhaps both of us wondered that friendship should exist between members of such different castes, but perhaps both of us knew, though we did not say so, that in the hearts of men arms and song are never far distant.

Andreas had turned to go, but he hesitated, and faced me once more. "The Priest-Kings," he said, "will be expecting you."

"Of course," I said.

Andreas lifted his arm. "Tal," he said, sadly. I wondered why he had said this, for it is a word of greeting.

"Tal," I said, returning the salute.

I think perhaps he had wanted to greet me once more, that he did not believe he would ever again have the opportunity.

Andreas had turned and was gone.

I must begin my journey to the Sardar Mountains.

As Andreas had said, I would be expected. I knew that little passed on Gor that was not somehow known in the Sardar Mountains. The power and knowledge of the Priest-Kings is perhaps beyond the comprehension of mortal men, or, as it is said on Gor, of the Men Below the Mountains.

It is said that as we are to the amoeba and the paramecium so are the Priest-Kings to us, that the highest and most lyric flights of our intellect are, when compared to the thought of the Priest-Kings, but the chemical tropisms of the unicellular organism. I thought of such an organism, blindly extending its pseudopodia to encircle a particle of food, an organism complacent in its world—perhaps only an agar plate on the desk of some higher being.

I had seen the power of the Priest-Kings at work—in the mountains of New Hampshire years ago when it was so delicately exercised as to affect the needle of a compass, in the Valley of Ko-ro-ba where I had found a city devastated as casually as one might crush a hill of ants.

Yes, I knew that the power of the Priest-Kings—rumored even to extend to the control of gravity—could lay waste cities, scatter populations, separate friends, tear lovers from one another's arms, bring hideous death to whomsoever it might choose. As all men of Gor I knew that their power inspired terror throughout a world and that it could not be withstood.

The words of the man of Ar, he who had worn the robes of the Initiates, he who had brought me the message of the Priest-Kings on the road to Ko-ro-ba that violent night months before, rang in my ears, "Throw yourself upon your sword, Tarl of Ko-ro-ba!"

But I knew then that I would not throw myself upon my sword, and that I would not now. I knew then as I knew now that I would go instead to the Sardar Mountains, that I would enter them and seek the Priest-Kings themselves.

I would find them.

Somewhere in the midst of those icy escarpments inaccessible even to the wild tarn, they waited for me, those fit gods of this harsh world.

20

THE INVISIBLE BARRIER

IN MY HAND I HELD a sword, taken from one of the guardsmen in the mines. It was the only weapon I carried. Before starting for the mountains, it seemed wise to improve my equipment. Most of the soldiers who had fought the slaves at the top of the shaft had been killed or fled. Those who had been killed had been stripped of clothing and weapons, both of which the ill-clad, unarmed slaves required desperately.

I knew that I didn't have a great deal of time, for the avenging tarnsmen of Tharna would soon be visible against the three moons.

I examined the low, wooden buildings which dotted the ugly landscape in the vicinity of the mines. Almost all of them had been broken into by the slaves, and whatever they held had been taken or scattered. Not a piece of steel remained in the arms shed; not a crust of bread remained in the tubs in the commissary huts.

In the office of the Administrator of the Mines, he who once had given the command, "Drown them all," I found a stripped body, slashed almost beyond recognition. Yet I had seen it once before, when I had been turned over by the soldier to his gentle care. It was the Administrator of the Mines himself. The corpulent, cruel body was now rent in a hundred places.

On the wall there was an empty scabbard. I hoped that he had had time to seize its blade before the slaves rushed in and fell upon him. Though I found it easy to hate him I did not wish him to have died unarmed.

In the frenetic melee in the darkness, or in the light of the tharlarion lamp, perhaps the slaves had not noticed the scabbard, or wanted it. The sword itself, of course, was gone. I decided I could use the scabbard, and took it from the wall.

In the first streak of light, now gleaming through the dusty hut window, I saw that the scabbard was set with six stones. Emeralds. Perhaps not of great value, but worth taking.

I thrust my weapon into the empty scabbard, buckled the sword belt and, in the Gorean fashion, looped it over my left shoulder.

I left the hut, scanning the skies. There were no tarnsmen yet in sight. The three moons were faint now, like pale white disks in the brightening sky, and the sun was half risen from the throne of the horizon.

In the bleak light the ruin of the night stood revealed in stark, brutal lucidity. The ugly grounds of the compound, its lonely wooden huts, its brown soil and bare hard rocks, were deserted save by the dead. Among the litter of pillaging—papers, opened boxes, broken staves, split boards and wire—there lay, sprawled frozen in stiff, grotesque postures, the unsubtle shapes of death, the scattered, contorted, slashed bodies of naked men.

Some wisps of dust swirled past like animals sniffing about the feet of the bodies. A door on one of the sheds, its lock broken, swung loose on its hinges, banging in the wind.

I walked across the compound and picked up a helmet which lay half hidden in the litter. Its straps were broken but they could be knotted together. I wondered if it had been noticed by the slaves.

I had sought equipment, but I had found only a scabbard and a damaged helmet, and soon the tarnsmen of Tharna would arrive. Using the Warrior's Pace, a slow jog that can be prolonged for hours, I left the Compound of the Mines.

I had only reached the shelter of a line of trees when I saw, some thousand yards behind me, descending on the Compound of the Mines, like clouds of wasps, the tarnsmen of Tharna.

It was in the vicinity of the Pillar of Exchanges, three days later, that I found the tarn. I had seen its shadow and feared it was wild, and had prepared to sell my life dearly, but the great beast, my own plumed giant, who may have haunted the Pillar of Exchanges for weeks, settled on the plains no more than thirty yards from me, its great wings shaking, and stalked to my side.

It was for this reason that I had returned to the Pillar, hoping that perhaps the monster might linger in its vicinity. There was good hunting nearby, and the ridges where I had carried the Tatrix afforded shelter for its nest.

When it approached me and extended its head, I wondered if what I had dared not hope might be true, that the bird might have been waiting for me to return.

He offered no resistance, he showed no anger, when I leaped to his back and cried, as before, "One-strap!" at which signal, with a shrill cry and a mighty spring, those gigantic wings cracked like whips and beat their way aloft in the glory of flight.

As we passed over the Pillar of Exchanges I remembered that it was there I had been betrayed by she who was once Tatrix of Tharna. I wondered what had been her fate. I wondered too at her treachery, her strange hatred of me, for somehow it seemed not to fit well with the lonely girl on the ledge, who had stood quietly gazing at the field of talenders while a warrior had gorged himself on the kill of his tarn. Then, again, my memory blackened with fury at the thought of her imperious gesture, that insolent command, "Seize him!"

Whatever her fate, I insisted to myself that it would have been richly deserved. Yet I found myself hoping that perhaps she had not been destroyed. I wondered what vengeance would have satisfied the hatred borne to Lara, the Tatrix, by Dorna the Proud. I guessed unhappily that

she might have had Lara hurled into a pit of osts or
watched her boil alive in the foul oil of tharlarions. Perhaps she would have had her thrown naked into the
clutches of the insidious leech plants of Gor or have had
her fed to the giant urts in the dungeons beneath her own
palace. I knew the hatred of men is but a feeble thing
compared to the hatred of women, and I wondered how
much it would take to slake the thirst for vengeance of
such a woman as Dorna the Proud. What would have been
enough to satisfy her?

It was now the month of the vernal equinox on Gor,
called En'Kara, or The First Kara. The full expression is
En'Kara-Lar-Torvis, which means, rather literally, The
First Turning of the Central Fire. Lar-Torvis is a Gorean
expression for the sun. More commonly, though never in
the context of time, the sun is referred to as Tor-tu-Gor,
or Light Upon the Home Stone. The month of the autum-
nal equinox is called fully Se'Kara-Lar-Torvis, but usually
simply Se'Kara, The Second Kara, or The Second Turning.

As might be expected there are related expressions for
the months of the solstices, En'Var-Lar-Torvis and Se'-
Var-Lar-Torvis, or, again rather literally, The First Resting and the Second Resting of the Central Fire. These,
however, like the other expressions, usually occur in
speech only as En'Var and Se'Var, or The First Resting
and The Second Resting.

Chronology, incidentally, is the despair of scholars on
Gor, for each city keeps track of time by virtue of its own
Administrator Lists; for example, a year is referred to as
the Second Year when so-and-so was Administrator of the
city. One might think that some stability would be
provided by the Initiates who must keep a calendar of
their feasts and observances, but the Initiates of one city
do not always celebrate the same feast on the same date as
do those of another city. If the High Initiate of Ar should
ever succeed in extending his hegemony over the High
Initiates of rival cities, a hegemony which he claims he

possesses already incidentally, a unified calendar might be introduced. But so far there has been no military victory of Ar over other cities and, accordingly, free of the sword, the Initiates of each city regard themselves as supreme within their own walls.

There are, however, some factors which tend to reduce the hopelessness of the situation. One is the fairs at the Sardar Mountains, which occur four times a year and are numbered chronologically. The other is that sometimes cities are willing to add, in their records, beside their own dating, the dating of Ar, which is Gor's greatest city.

Chronology in Ar is figured, happily enough, not from its Administrator Lists, but from its mythical founding by the first man on Gor, a hero whom the Priest-Kings are said to have formed from the mud of the earth and the blood of tarns. Time is reckoned "Contasta Ar", or "from the founding of Ar." The current year, according to the calendar of Ar, if it is of interest, is 10,117. Actually I would suppose that Ar may not be a third of that age. Its Home Stone, however, which I have seen, attests to a considerable antiquity.

Some four days after I had recovered the tarn, we sighted in the distance the Sardar Mountains. Had I possessed a Gorean compass, its needle would have pointed invariably to those mountains, as though to indicate the home of the Priest-Kings. Before the mountains, in a panorama of silk and flags, I saw the pavilions of the Fair of En'Kara, or the Fair of the First Turning.

I wheeled the tarn in the sky, not wanting to approach more closely yet. I looked upon those mountains which I now saw for the first time. A chill not of the high winds which buffeted me on tarnback now crept into my body.

The mountains of the Sardar were not such a vast, magnificent range as the rugged scarlet crags of the Voltai, that almost impenetrable mountain vastness in which I had once been the prisoner of the outlaw Ubar, Marlenus of Ar, ambitious and warlike father of the fierce and beautiful Talena, she whom I loved, whom I had carried

on tarnback to Ko-ro-ba years before to be my Free
Companion. No, the Sardar Range was not the superb
natural wilderness that was the Voltai. Its peaks did not
scorn the plains below. Its heights did not taunt the sky
nor, in the cold of the night, defy the stars. In it would
not be heard the cry of tarns and the roar of larls. It was
inferior to the Voltai in both dimension and grandeur. Yet
when I looked upon it, more than the gloriously savage,
larl-haunted Voltai, I feared it.

I took the tarn closer.

The mountains before me were black, except for the
high peaks and passes, which showed white patches and
threads of cold, gleaming snow. I looked for the green of
vegetation on the lower slopes and saw none. In the
Sardar Range nothing grew.

There seemed to be a menace, an intangible fearful
effect about those angular shapes in the distance. I took
the tarn as high as I could, until his wings beat frantically
against the thin air, but could see nothing in the Sardar
Mountains that might be the habitation of Priest-Kings.

I wondered—an eerie suspicion that suddenly swept
through me—if the Sardar Mountains might actually be
empty—if there might be nothing, simply nothing but the
wind and the snow in those gloomy mountains, and if
men worshipped, unknowingly, nothing. What of the interminable prayers of the Initiates, the sacrifices, the observances, the rituals, the innumerable shrines, altars and
temples to the Priest-Kings? Could it be that the smoke of
the burning sacrifices, the fragrance of the incense, the
mumblings of the Initiates, their prostrations and grovel-
ings were all addressed to nothing but the empty peaks of
the Sardar, to the snow, and the cold and the wind that
howled among those black crags?

Suddenly the tarn screamed and shuddered in the air!

The thought of the emptiness of the Sardar Range was
banished from my mind, for here was evidence of the
Priest-Kings!

It was almost as if the bird had been seized by an
invisible fist.

I could sense nothing.

The bird's eyes, perhaps for the first time in his life, were filled with terror, blind uncomprehending terror.

I could see nothing.

Protesting, screaming, the great bird began to reel helplessly downward. Its vast wings, futilely, wildly, struck out, uncoordinated and frenetic, like the limbs of a drowning swimmer. It seemed the very air itself refused any longer to bear his weight. In drunken, dizzy circles, screaming, bewildered, helpless, the bird fell, while I, for my life, desperately clung to the thick quills of his neck.

When we had reached an altitude of perhaps a hundred yards from the ground, as suddenly as it had come, the strange effect passed. The bird regained his strength and senses, except for the fact that it remained agitated, almost unmanageable.

Then to my wonder, the valiant creature began once more to climb, determined to regain the altitude he had lost.

Again and again he tried to rise and again and again he was forced down.

Through the beast's back I could feel the straining of his muscles, sense the mad pounding of that unconquerable heart. But each time we attained a certain altitude, the eyes of the tarn would seem to lose their focus, and the unerring balance and coordination of the sable monster would be disrupted. It was no longer frightened, only angry. Once again it would attempt to climb, ever faster, ever more fiercely.

Then mercifully I called "Four-strap!"

I feared the courageous beast would kill himself before surrendering to the unseen force that blocked his path.

Unwillingly the bird alighted on the grassy plains about a league from the Fair of En'Kara. I thought those great eyes looked at me reproachfully. Why did I not leap again to his back and once more cry "One-strap!" Why did we not try once more?

I slapped his beak affectionately and, digging among his neck feathers with my fingers, scratched out some of the lice, about the size of marbles, that infest wild tarns. I slapped them on his long tongue. After a moment of impatient, feather-ruffling protest, the tarn succumbed, if reluctantly, to this delicacy, and the parasites disappeared into that curved scimitar of a beak.

What had happened would have been regarded by the untrained Gorean mind, particularly that of a low caste individual, as evidence of some supernatural force, as some magical effect of the will of the Priest-Kings. I myself did not willingly entertain such hypotheses.

The tarn had struck a field of some sort, which perhaps acted on the mechanism of his inner ear, resulting in the loss of balance and coordination. A similar device, I supposed, might prevent the entry of high tharlarions, the saddle lizards of Gor, into the mountains. In spite of myself I admired the Priest-Kings. I knew now that it was true, what I had been told, that those who entered the mountains would do so on foot.

I regretted having to leave the tarn, but he could not accompany me.

I talked to him for perhaps an hour, a foolish thing to do perhaps, and then gave his beak a hardy slap and shoved it from me. I pointed out over the fields, away from the mountains. "Tabuk!" I said.

The beast did not stir.

"Tabuk!" I repeated.

I think, though it may be absurd, that the beast felt that he might have failed me, that he had not carried me into the mountains. I think, too, though it is perhaps still more absurd, that he knew that I would not be waiting for him when he returned from his hunt.

The great head moved quizzically and dipped to the ground, rubbing against my leg.

Had it failed me? Was I now rejecting it?

"Go, Ubar of the Skies," I said. "Go."

When I had said Ubar of the Skies, the bird had lifted its head, now more than a yard above my own. I had called him that when I had recognized him in the arena of

Tharna, when we had been aloft as one creature in the sky.

The great bird stalked away from me, about fifteen yards, and then turned, looking at me again.

I gestured to the fields away from the mountains.

It shook its wings and screamed, and hurled itself against the wind. I watched it until, a tiny speck against the blue sky, it disappeared in the distance.

I felt unaccountably sad, and turned to face the mountains of the Sardar.

Before them, resting on the grassy plains beneath, was the Fair of En'Kara.

I had not walked more than a pasang when, from a cluster of trees to my right, on the other side of a thin, swift stream that flowed from the Sardar, I heard the terrified scream of a girl.

21

I BUY A GIRL

OUT FROM MY SCABBARD LEAPED the sword and I splashed across the cold stream, making for the grove of trees across the way.

Once more the terrified scream rang out.

Now I was among the trees, moving rapidly, but cautiously.

Then the smell of a cooking fire came to my nostrils. I heard the hum of unhurried conversation. Through the trees I could see tent canvas, a tharlarion wagon, the strap-masters unharnessing a brace of low tharlarions, the huge, herbivorous draft lizards of Gor. For all I could tell neither of them had heard the scream, or paid it any attention.

I slowed to a walk and entered the clearing among the tents. One or two guardsmen eyed me curiously. One arose and went to check the woods behind me, to see if I were alone. I glanced about myself. It was a peaceful scene, the cooking fires, the domed tents, the unharnessing of the animals, one I remembered from the caravan of Mintar, of the Merchant Caste. But this was a small camp, not like the pasangs of wagons that constituted the entourage of the wealthy Mintar.

I heard the scream once again.

I saw that the cover of the tharlarion wagon, which had been rolled back, was of blue and yellow silk.

It was the camp of a slaver.

I thrust my sword back in the scabbard and took off my helmet.

"Tal," I said to two guardsmen who crouched at the side of a fire, playing Stones, a guessing game in which one person must guess whether the number of stones held in the fist of another is odd or even.

"Tal," said one guardsman. The other, attempting to guess the stones, did not even look up.

I walked between the tents and saw the girl.

She was a blond girl with golden hair that fell behind her to the small of her back. Her eyes were blue. She was of dazzling beauty. She trembled like a frantic animal. She knelt, her back against a slender, white birchlike tree to which she was chained naked. Her hands were joined over her head and behind the tree by slave bracelets. Her ankles were similarly fastened by a short slave chain which encircled the tree.

Her eyes had turned to me, begging, pleading, as though I might deliver her from her predicament, but when she looked upon me, those fear-glazed eyes, if possible, seemed even more terrified. She uttered a hopeless cry. She began to shake uncontrollably and her head fell forward in despair.

I gathered she had taken me for another slaver.

There was an iron brazier near the tree, which was filled with glowing coals. I could feel its heat ten yards away. From the brazier protruded the handles of three irons.

There was a man beside the irons, stripped to the waist, wearing thick leather gloves, one of the minions of the slaver. He was a grizzled man, rather heavy, sweating, blind in one eye. He regarded me without too much interest, as he waited for the irons to heat.

I noted the thigh of the girl.

It had not yet been branded.

When an individual captures a girl for his own uses, he does not always mark her, though it is commonly done. On the other hand, the professional slaver, as a business

practice, almost always brands his chattels, and it is seldom that an unbranded girl ascends the block.

The brand is to be distinguished from the collar, though
both are a designation of slavery. The primary significance
of the collar is that it identifies the master and his city.
The collar of a given girl may be changed countless times,
but the brand continues throughout to bespeak her status.
The brand is normally concealed by the briefly skirted
slave livery of Gor but, of course, when the camisk is
worn, it is always clearly visible, reminding the girl and
others of her station.

The brand itself, in the case of girls, is a rather graceful
mark, being the initial letter of the Gorean expression for
slave in cursive script. If a male is branded, the same
initial is used, but rendered in a block letter.

Noting my interest in the girl, the man beside the irons
went to her side and, taking her by the hair, threw back
her face for my inspection. "She's a beauty, isn't she?" he
said.

I nodded agreement.

I wondered why those piteous eyes looked upon me
with such fear.

"Perhaps you want to buy her?" asked the man.

"No," I said.

The heavy-set man winked his sightless eye in my
direction. His voice lowered to a conspiratorial whisper.
"She's not trained," he said. "And she is as hard to
manage as a sleen."

I smiled.

"But," said the man, "the iron will take that out of
her."

I wondered if it would.

He withdrew one of the irons from the fire. It glowed a
fiery red.

At the sight of the glowing metal the girl uncontrollably
screamed, pulling at the slave bracelets, at the shackles
that held her to the tree.

The heavy-set man thrust the iron back into the brazier.

"She's a loud one," he said, shamefacedly. Then, with a shrug in my direction, as if to ask my pardon, he went to the girl and took a handful of her long hair. He wadded it into a small, tight ball and suddenly shoved it in her mouth. It immediately expanded, and before she could spit the hair out, he had looped more of her hair about her head and tied it, in such a way as to keep the expanded ball of hair in her mouth. The girl choked silently, trying to spit the ball of hair from her mouth, but of course she could not. It was an old slaver's trick. I knew tarnsmen sometimes silenced their captives in the same way.

"Sorry, Sweet Wench," said the grizzled man, giving the girl's head a friendly shake, "but we don't want Targo coming over here with his whip and beating the tharlarion oil out of us both, do we?"

Sobbing silently the girl's head fell down again on her breast.

The grizzled man absent-mindedly hummed a caravan tune while waiting for the irons to heat.

My emotions were mixed. I had rushed to the scene to free the girl, to protect her. Yet when I arrived I found that she was merely a slave, and that her owner, quite properly from Gor's point of view, was attending to the routine business of marking his property. Had I attempted to free her, it would have been as much an act of theft as if I had driven off the tharlarion wagon.

Moreover, these men bore the girl no animosity. To them she was just another wench on their chain, perhaps more poorly trained and less docile than most. If anything they were merely impatient with her, and thought she made too much of a fuss about things. They would not comprehend her feelings, her humiliation, her shame, her terror.

I supposed even the other girls, the other freight of the caravan, might think she made a bit too much of things. After all, did a slave not expect the iron? And the whip?

I saw the other girls some thirty yards away, in camisks, the cheapest of slave garments, laughing and talking to one another, disporting themselves as pleasurably as free maidens might have. I almost did not notice the chain that lay hidden in the grass. It passed through the ankle ring of each and, at each end, encircled a tree to which it was padlocked.

The irons would soon be hot.

The girl before me, so helpless in her chains, would soon be marked.

I have wondered upon occasion why brands are used on Gorean slaves. Surely Goreans have at their disposal means for indelibly but painlessly marking the human body. My conjecture, confirmed to some extent by the speculations of the Older Tarl, who had taught me the craft of arms in Ko-ro-ba years ago, is that the brand is used primarily, oddly enough, because of its reputed psychological effect.

In theory, if not in practice, when the girl finds herself branded like an animal, finds her fair skin marked by the iron of a master, she cannot fail, somehow, in the deepest levels of her thought, to regard herself as something which is owned, as mere property, as something belonging to the brute who has put the burning iron to her thigh.

Most simply the brand is supposed to convince the girl that she is truly owned; it is supposed to make her *feel* owned. When the iron is pulled away and she knows the pain and degradation and smells the odor of her burned flesh, she is supposed to tell herself, understanding its full and terrible import, I AM HIS.

Actually I suppose the effect of the brand depends greatly on the girl. In many girls I would suppose the brand has little effect besides contributing to their shame, their misery and humiliation. With other girls it might well increase their intractability, their hostility. On the other hand, I have known of several cases in which a proud, insolent woman, even one of great intelligence, who resisted a master to the very touch of the iron, once branded became instantly a passionate and obedient Pleasure Slave.

But all in all I do not know if the brand is used primarily for its psychological effect or not. Perhaps it is merely a device for merchants who must have some such means for tracing runaway slaves, which would otherwise constitute a costly hazard to their trade. Sometimes I think the iron is simply an anachronistic survival from a more technologically backward age.

One thing was clear. The poor creature before me did not wish the iron.

I felt sorry for her.

The minion of the slaver withdrew another iron from the fire. His one eye regarded it appraisingly. It was white hot. He was satisfied.

The girl shrank against the tree, her back against its white, rough bark. Her wrists and ankles pulled at the chains that fastened them behind the tree. Her breathing was spasmodic; she trembled. There was terror in her blue eyes. She whimpered. Any other sound she might have uttered was stifled by the gag of hair.

The slaver's minion locked his left arm about her right thigh, holding it motionless. "Don't wiggle, Sweet Wench," he said, not without kindness. "You might spoil the brand." He spoke to the girl soothingly, as if to calm her. "You want a clean, pretty brand, don't you? It will improve your price and you'll get a better master."

The iron was now poised for the sudden, firm imprint.

I noted that some of the delicate golden hair on her thigh, from the very proximity of the iron, curled and blackened.

She closed her eyes and tensed herself for the sudden, inevitable, searing flash of pain.

"Don't brand her," I said.

The man looked up, puzzled.

The terror-filled eyes of the girl opened, regarded me questioningly.

"Why not?" asked the man.

"I'll buy her," I said.

The minion of the slaver stood up and regarded me curiously. He turned to the domed tents. "Targo!" he called. Then he thrust the iron back into the brazier. The girl's body sagged in the chains. She had fainted.

From among the domed tents, wearing a swirling robe of broadly striped blue and yellow silk, with a headband of the same material, there approached a short, fat man, Targo the Slaver, he who was master of this small caravan. Targo wore purple sandals, the straps of which were set with pearls. His thick fingers were covered with rings, which glittered as he moved his hands. About his neck, in the manner of a steward, he wore a set of pierced coins threaded on a silver wire. From the lobe of each small, round ear there hung an enormous earring, a sapphire pendant on a golden stalk. His body had been recently oiled, and I gathered he may have been washed in his tent but moments ago, a pleasure of which caravan masters are fond at the end of a day's hot, dusty trek. His hair, long and black beneath the band of blue and yellow silk, was combed and glossy. It reminded me of the groomed, shining pelt of a pet urt.

"Good day, Master," smiled Targo, bowing as well as he could from the waist, hastily taking account of the unlikely stranger who stood before him. Then he turned to the man who watched the irons. His voice was now sharp and unpleasant. "What's going on here?"

The grizzled fellow pointed to me. "He doesn't want me to mark the girl," he said.

Targo looked at me, not quite understanding. "But why?" he asked.

I felt foolish. What could I tell this merchant, this specialist in the traffic of flesh, this businessman who stood well within the ancient traditions and practices of his trade? Could I tell him that I did not wish the girl to be hurt? He would have thought me a mad man. Yet what other reason was there?

Feeling stupid, I told him the truth. "I do not wish to see her hurt."

Targo and the grizzled master of the irons exchanged glances.

"But she is only a slave," said Targo.

"I know," I said.

The grizzled man spoke up. "He said he'd buy her."

"Ah!" said Targo, and his tiny eyes gleamed. "That's different." Then an expression of great sadness transformed his fat ball of a face. "But it is sad that she is so expensive."

"I have no money," I said.

Targo stared at me, uncomprehendingly. His fat small body contracted like a pudgy fist. He was angry. He turned to the grizzled man, and looked no more at me. "Brand the girl," he said.

The grizzled man knelt to pull one of the irons from the brazier.

My sword pushed a quarter of an inch into the belly of the merchant.

"Don't brand the girl," said Targo.

Obediently the man thrust the iron back into the fire. He noted that my sword was at the belly of his master, but did not seem unduly disturbed. "Shall I call the guardsmen?" he asked.

"I doubt they could arrive in time," I said evenly.

"Don't call the guardsmen," said Targo, who was now sweating.

"I have no money," I said, "but I have this scabbard."

Targo's eyes darted to the scabbard and moved from one emerald to the other. His lips moved silently. Six of them he counted.

"Perhaps," said Targo, "we can make an arrangement."

I resheathed the sword.

Targo spoke sharply to the grizzled man. "Awaken the slave."

Grumbling, the man went to fetch a leather bucket of water from the small stream near the camp. Targo and I regarded one another until the man returned, the leather bucket hung over his shoulder by its straps.

He hurled the bucket of cold water, from the melted snow in the Sardar, on the chained girl, who sputtering and shivering opened her eyes.

Targo, with his short, rolling steps, went to the girl and

placed one thumb, wearing a large ruby ring, under her chin, pushing her head up.

"A true beauty," said Targo. "And perfectly trained for months in the slave pens of Ar."

Behind Targo I could see the grizzled man shaking his head negatively.

"And," said Targo, "she is eager to please."

Behind him the man winked his sightless eye and stifled a snort.

"As gentle as a dove, as docile as a kitten," continued Targo.

I slipped the blade of my sword between the girl's cheek and the hair that was bound across her mouth. I moved it, and the hair, as lightly as though it had been air floated from the blade.

The girl fixed her eyes on Targo. "You fat, filthy urt!" she hissed.

"Quiet, She-Tharlarion!" he said.

"I don't think she's worth very much," I said.

"Oh, Master," cried Targo, swirling his robes in disbelief that I could have uttered such a thought. "I paid a hundred silver tarn disks for her myself!"

Behind Targo the grizzled man quickly held up his fingers, opening and closing them five times.

"I doubt," I said to Targo, "that she is worth more than fifty."

Targo seemed stunned. He looked at me with a new respect. Perhaps I had once been in the trade? Actually, fifty silver tarn disks was an extremely high price, and indicated the girl was probably of high caste as well as extremely beautiful. An ordinary girl, of low caste, comely but untrained, might, depending on the market, sell for as little as five or as many as thirty tarn disks.

"I will give you two of the stones from this scabbard for her," I said. Actually I had no idea of the value of the stones, and didn't know if the offer was a sensible one or not. In annoyance, looking over the rings of Targo and the sapphires which hung from his ears, I knew he would be a much better judge of their value than I.

"Preposterous!" said Targo, shaking his head vehemently.

I gathered that he was not bluffing, for how could he have known that I did not know the true value of the stones? How could he know that I had not purchased them and had them set in the scabbard myself?

"You drive a hard bargain," I said. "Four—"

"May I see the scabbard, Warrior?" he asked.

"Surely," I said, and removed it from the belt and handed it to him. The sword itself I retained, knotting the scabbard straps and thrusting the blade into them.

Targo gazed at the stones appreciatively. "Not bad," said he, "but not enough—"

I pretended to impatience. "Then show me your other girls," I said.

I could see that this did not please Targo, for apparently he wished to rid his chain of the blond girl. Perhaps she was a troublemaker, or was dangerous to retain for some other reason.

"Show him the others," said the grizzled man. "This one will not even say 'Buy Me, Master'."

Targo threw a violent look at the grizzled man, who smiling to himself knelt to supervise the irons in the brazier.

Angrily Targo led the way to the grassy clearing among the trees.

He clapped his hands sharply twice, and there was a scurrying and tumbling of bodies and the sound of the long chain slipping through the ankle rings. The girls now knelt, each in the position of the Pleasure Slave, in their camisks on the grass, in a line between the two trees to which their chain was fastened. As I passed each she boldly raised her eyes to mine and said, "Buy Me, Master."

Many of them were beauties, and I thought that the chain, though small, was a rich one, and that almost any man might find thereon a woman to his taste. They were vital, splendid creatures, many of them undoubtedly exquisitely trained to delight the senses of a master. And many of the cities of Gor were represented on that chain, sometimes spoken of as the Slaver's Necklace—there was a blond girl from lofty Thentis, a dark-skinned girl with black hair that fell to her ankles from the desert city of Tor, girls from the miserable streets of Port Kar in the delta of the Vosk, girls even from the high cylinders of Great Ar itself. I wondered how many of them were bred slaves, and how many had once been free.

And as I paused before each beauty in that chain and met her eyes and heard her words, "Buy Me, Master," I asked myself why I should not buy her, why I should not free her instead of the other girl. Were these marvelous creatures, each of whom already wore the graceful brand of the slave girl, any the less worthy than she?

"No," I said to Targo. "I will not buy any of these."

To my surprise a sigh of disappointment, even of keen frustration, coursed down the chain. Two of the girls, she from Tor and one of the girls from Ar wept, their heads buried in their hands. I wished I had not looked at them.

Upon reflection it seemed clear to me that the chain must, in the end, be a lonely place for a girl, filled with life, knowing that her brand has destined her for love, that each of them must long for a man to care enough for them to buy them, that each must long to follow a man home to his compartments, wearing his collar and chains, where they will learn his strength and his heart and will be taught the delights of submission. Better the arms of a master than the cold steel of the ankle ring.

When they had said to me, "Buy Me, Master," it had not been simply a ritual phrase. They had wanted to be sold to me—or I supposed, to any man who would take them from the hated chain of Targo.

Targo seemed relieved. Clutching me by the elbow, he guided me back to the tree where the blond girl knelt chained.

As I looked at her I asked myself why she, and why not another, or why any? What would it matter if her thigh, too, should wear that graceful brand? I supposed it was mostly the institution of slavery I objected to, and that

that institution was not altered if I should, as an act of foolish sentiment, free one girl. She could not go with me into the Sardar, of course, and when I abandoned her, she, alone and unprotected, would soon fall prey to a beast or find herself on yet another slaver's chain. Yes, I told myself, it was foolish.

"I have decided not to buy her," I said.

Then, strangely, the girl's head lifted and she looked into my eyes. She tried to smile. The words were soft, but clearly and unmistakably spoken, "Buy me, Master."

"Ai!" cried the grizzled man, and even Targo the Slaver looked baffled.

It had been the first time the girl had uttered the ritual phrase.

I looked upon her, and saw that she was indeed beautiful, but mostly I saw that her eyes pleaded with mine. As I saw that, my rational resolve to abandon her dissipated, and I yielded, as I sometimes had in the past, to an act of sentiment.

"Take the scabbard," I said to Targo. "I will buy her."

"And the helmet!" said Targo.

"Agreed," I said.

He seized the scabbard and the delight with which he clutched it told me that I had been, in his mind, sorely bested in the bargaining. Almost as an afterthought, he plucked the helmet from my grasp. Both he and I knew it was almost worthless. I smiled ruefully to myself. I was not much good in such matters, I supposed. But perhaps if I had better known the value of the stones?

The girl's eyes looked into mine, perhaps trying to read in my eyes what would be her fate, for her fate was now in my hands, for I was her master.

Strange and cruel are the ways of Gor, I thought, where six small green stones, weighing perhaps scarcely two ounces, and a damaged helmet, could purchase a human being.

Targo and the grizzled man had gone to the domed tent to fetch the keys to the girl's chains.

"What is your name?" I asked the girl.

"A slave has no name," she said. "You may give me one if you wish."

On Gor a slave, not being legally a person, does not have a name in his own right, just as, on earth, our domestic animals, not being persons before the law, do not have names. Indeed, from the Gorean's point of view, one of the most fearful things about slavery is that one loses one's name. That name which he has had from birth, by which he has called himself and knows himself, that name which is so much a part of his own conception of himself, of his own true and most intimate identity, is suddenly gone.

"I gather you are not a bred slave," I said.

She smiled and shook her head. "No," she said.

"I am content," I said, "to call you by the name you bore when you were free."

"You are kind," she said.

"What was your name when you were free?" I asked.

"Lara," she said.

"Lara?" I asked.

"Yes, Warrior," she said. "Do you not recognize me? I was Tatrix of Tharna."

22

YELLOW CORDS

WHEN THE GIRL HAD BEEN unchained I lifted her in my arms and carried her into one of the domed tents that had been indicated to me.

There we would wait until her collar had been engraved.

The floor of the tent was covered with thick, colorful rugs, and the inside was decorated with numerous silken hangings. The light was furnished by a brass tharlarion oil lamp which swung on three chains. Cushions were scattered about on the rugs. On one side of the tent there stood, with its straps, a Pleasure Rack.

I set the girl gently down.

She looked at the rack.

"First," she said, "you will use me, will you not?"

"No," I said.

Then she knelt at my feet and put her head to the rug, throwing her hair over her head, exposing her neck.

"Strike," she said.

I lifted her to her feet.

"Didn't you buy me to destroy me?" she asked, bewildered.

"No," I said. "Is that why you said to me, 'Buy Me, Master'?"

"I think so," she said. "I think I wanted you to kill me." Then she looked at me. "But I am not sure."

"Why did you want to die?" I asked.

"I who was Tatrix of Tharna," she said, her eyes downcast, "did not wish to live as a slave."

"I will not kill you," I said.

"Give me your sword, Warrior," said she, "and I will throw myself upon it."

"No," I said.

"Ah yes," she said, "a warrior is unwilling to have the blood of a woman on his sword."

"You are young," I said, "—beautiful and much alive. Put the Cities of Dust from your mind."

She laughed bitterly.

"Why did you buy me?" she asked. "Surely you wish to exact your vengeance? Have you forgotten it was I who put you in a yoke, who whipped you, who condemned you to the Amusements, who would have given you to the tarn? That it was I who betrayed you and sent you to the Mines of Tharna?"

"No," I said, my eyes hard. "I have not forgotten."

"Nor have I," she said proudly, making it clear that she would ask me for nothing, and expect nothing of me, not even her life.

She stood bravely before me, yet so helpless, so much at my mercy. She might have stood thus before a larl in the Voltai. It was important to her to die well. I admired her for this, and found her in her hopelessness and defiance very beautiful. Her lower lip trembled, ever so slightly. Almost imperceptibly she bit it to control its movement, lest I should see. I found her magnificent. There was a tiny drop of blood on her lips. I shook my head to drive away the thought that I wanted with my tongue to taste the blood on her lips, to kiss it from her mouth.

I said simply, "I do not wish to harm you."

She looked at me, not comprehending.

"Why did you buy me?" she asked.

"I bought you to free you," I said.

"You did not then know I was Tatrix of Tharna," she sneered.

"No," I said.

"Now that you know," she asked, "what will you do with me? Will it be the oil of tharlarions? Will you throw me to leech plants? Will you stake me out for your tarn, use me to bait a sleen trap?"

I laughed, and she looked at me, bewildered.

"Well?" she demanded.

"You have given me much to think about," I admitted.

"What will you do with me?" she demanded.

"I will free you," I said.

She stepped back in disbelief. Her blue eyes seemed filled with wonder, and then they glistened with tears. Her shoulders shook with sobs.

I put my arms around her slender shoulders and to my amazement she who had worn the golden mask of Tharna, she who had been Tatrix of that gray city, put her head upon my chest and wept. "No," she said, "I am worthy only of being a slave."

"That is not true," I said. "Remember once you told a man not to beat me. Remember once you said it was hard to be first in Tharna. Remember that once you looked upon a field of talenders and I was too dull and foolish to speak to you."

She stood within my arms, her tear-filled eyes lifted to mine. "Why did you return me to Tharna?" she asked.

"To barter you for the freedom of my friends," I said.

"And not for the silver and jewels of Tharna?" she asked.

"No," I said.

She stepped back. "Am I not beautiful?"

I regarded her.

"You are indeed beautiful," I said, "—so beautiful that a thousand warriors might give their lives to see your face, so beautiful that a hundred cities might come to ruin on your behalf."

"Would I not please—a beast?" she asked.

"It would be victory for a man to have you on his chain," I said.

"And yet, Warrior," she said, "you would not have

kept me—you threatened to put me on the block and sell
me to another."

I was silent.

"Why would you not keep me for your own?"

It was a bold question, strange to come from this girl,
once Tatrix of Tharna. "My love is Talena," I said,
"daughter of Marlenus who was once Ubar of Ar."

"A man may have many slave girls," she sniffed. "Surely in your Pleasure Gardens—wherever they may be—
many beautiful captives wear your collar?"

"No," I said.

"You are a strange warrior . . ."

I shrugged.

She stood boldly before me. "Do you not want me?"

"To see you is to want you," I admitted.

"Then take me," she challenged. "I am yours."

I looked down at the rug, wondering how to speak to
her.

"I don't understand," I said.

"Beasts are fools!" she exclaimed.

After this incredible outburst she went to the side of the
tent, and held one of the hangings with her fist, thrusting
her face against it.

She turned, still clutching the hanging in her fist. Her
eyes were filled with tears, but angry. "You returned me
to Tharna," she said, almost as if making an accusation.

"For the love of my friends," I said.

"And honor!" she said.

"Perhaps honor too," I admitted.

"I hate your honor!" she cried.

"Some things," I said, "are more compelling than even
the beauty of a woman."

"I hate you," she said.

"I'm sorry."

Lara laughed, a small, sad laugh, and sat down on the
rug at the side of the tent, tucking her knees under her
chin. "I don't hate you, you know," she said.

"I know."

"But I did—I did hate you. When I was Tatrix of Tharna I hated you. I hated you so."

I was silent. I knew she had spoken the truth. I had sensed those virulent feelings with which she had unaccountably, to my mind, regarded me.

"Do you know, Warrior," she asked, "why I—now only a miserable slave—hated you so?"

"No," I said.

"Because when I first saw you I knew you from a thousand forbidden dreams." Her eyes sought me out. She spoke softly. "In these dreams I had been proud in my palace surrounded by my council and warriors and then, shattering the roof like glass, a great tarn descended, bearing a helmeted warrior. He scattered my council and defeated my armies and took me and stripped me and bound me naked across the saddle of his bird and then, with a great cry, he carried me to his city, and there I, once proud Tatrix of Tharna, wore his brand and collar."

"Do not fear these dreams," I said.

"And in his city," said the girl, her eyes bright, "he put bells upon my ankles and dressed me in dancing silk. I had no choice you understand. I must do as he wished. And when I could dance no more he took me in his arms and like a beast forced me to serve his pleasure."

"It was a cruel dream," I said.

She laughed, and her face burned with shame. "No," she said, "it was not a cruel dream."

"I don't understand," I said.

"In his arms I learned what Tharna could not teach. In his arms I learned to share the flaming splendor of his passion. In his arms I learned mountains and flowers and the cry of wild tarns and the touch of a larl's claw. For the first time in my life my senses were kindled—for the first time I could feel the movements of clothing on my body, for the first time I noticed how an eye opens and what, truly, is the feel of a hand's touch—and I knew then that I was no more nor less than he or any other living creature and I loved him!"

I said nothing.

"I would not," she said, "have given up his collar fo all the gold and silver in Tharna, not for all the stones c her gray walls."

"But you were not free in this dream," I said.

"Was I free in Tharna?" she asked.

I stared down at the intricate pattern on the rug, nc speaking.

"Of course," she said, "as one who wore the mask c Tharna I put this dream from me. I hated it. It terrifie me. It suggested to me that I, even the Tatrix, might shar the unworthy nature of the beast." She smiled. "When saw you, Warrior, I thought that you might be the warric of this dream. So it was I hated you and wanted to destro you because you threatened me and all that I was, an at the same time I hated you I feared you, and I desire you."

I looked up, surprised.

"Yes," she said. "I desired you." Her head fell and he voice became almost inaudible. "Though I was Tatrix c Tharna," she said, "I wanted to lie at your feet on th scarlet rug. I wanted to be bound with yellow cords."

I recalled that she had said something of a rug an cords in the council chamber of Tharna, when she ha seemed consumed with rage, when it seemed she wante to lash the flesh from my bones.

"What is the significance of the rug and cords?" asked.

"In ancient days, in Tharna," said Lara, "things wer different than they are today."

And then, in the slaver's tent, Lara, who had bee Tatrix of Tharna, told me something of the strange histor of her city. In the beginning Tharna had been much a other cities of Gor, in which women were too little regard ed and enjoyed too few rights. In those days it had been portion of the Rites of Submission, as practiced in Thar na, to strip and bind the captive with yellow cords an place her on a scarlet rug, the yellow of the cord bein symbolic of talenders, a flower often associated with femi nine love and beauty, the scarlet of the rug being symbolic of blood, and perhaps of passion.

He who had captured the girl would place his sword to her breast and utter the ritual phrases of enslavement. They were the last words she would hear as a free woman.

> Weep, Free Maiden.
> Remember your pride and weep.
> Remember your laughter and weep.
> Remember you were my enemy and weep.
> Now you are my helpless captive.
> Remember you stood against me.
> Now you lie at my feet.
> I have bound you with yellow cords.
> I have placed you on the scarlet rug.
> Thus by the laws of Tharna do I claim you.
> Remember you were free.
> Know now you are my slave.
> Weep, Slave Girl.

At this point the captor would untie the girl's ankles and complete the rite. When she rose from the rug to follow him, she was, in his eyes and hers, a slave.

Over a period of time this cruel practice fell into disuse and the women of Tharna came to be more reasonably and humanely regarded. Indeed, through their love and tenderness, they taught their captors that they, too, were worthy of respect and affection. And, of course, as the captors came gradually to care for their slaves, the desire to subjugate them became less, for few men long desire to subjugate a creature for whom they genuinely care, unless perhaps it be they fear to lose her should she be free.

Yet as the status of these women became more ennobled and less clearly defined the subtle tensions of dominance and submission, instinctual throughout the animal world, tended to assert themselves.

The balance of mutual regard is always delicate and, statistically, it is improbable that it can long be maintained throughout an entire population. Accordingly, gradually exploiting, perhaps unconsciously, the opportunities afforded by the training of children and the affections of their men, the women of Tharna improved their position considerably over the generations, also adding to their social power the economic largesse of various funds and inheritances.

Eventually, largely via the conditioning of the young and the control of education, those superiorities which the female naturally possesses came to be enlarged on at the expense of those possessed by the male. And just as in our own world it is possible to condition entire populations to believe what is, from the standpoint of another population, incomprehensible and absurd, so in Tharna both the men and the women came eventually to believe the myths or the distortions advantageous to female dominance. Thus it was, gradually and unnoticed, that the gynocracy of Tharna came to be established, and honored with the full weight of tradition and custom, those invisible bonds heavier than chains because they are not understood to exist.

Yet this situation, socially viable though it might be for generations, is not one truly productive of human happiness. Indeed, it is not altogether clear that it is preferable to the male dominated ethos of most Gorean cities, which, too, surely has its unfortunate side. In a city such as Tharna the men, taught to regard themselves as beasts, as inferior beings, seldom develop the full respect for themselves essential to true manhood. But even more strangely the women of Tharna do not seem content under the gynocracy. Although they despise men and congratulate themselves on their more lofty status it seems to me that they, too, fail to respect themselves. Hating their men they hate themselves.

I have wondered sometimes if a man to be a man must not master a woman and if a woman to be a woman must not know herself mastered. I have wondered how long nature's laws, if laws they are, can be subverted in Tharna. I have sensed how a man in Tharna longs to take the mask from a woman, and I have suspected how much a

woman longs for her mask to be taken. Should there ever
be a revolution in the ways of Tharna I would pity her
women—at least at first—for they would be the object of
the pent-up frustrations of generations. If the pendulum
should swing in Tharna, it would swing far. Perhaps even
to the scarlet rug and yellow cords.

Outside the tent we heard Targo's voice.

To my surprise Lara dropped to her knees, placing
them in the position of a Pleasure Slave, and dropped her
head submissively.

Targo burst into the tent carrying a small bundle and
approvingly noted the girl's posture.

"Well, Master," he said, "it seems with you she learns
quickly." He beamed up at me. "I have cleared my records. She is yours." He thrust the bundle into my hands.
It was a folded camisk, and in its folds was a collar. "A
token of my appreciation of your business," said Targo.
"There will be no extra charge."

I smiled to myself. Most professional slavers would
have furnished far more. I noted that Targo did not even
furnish the customary slave livery of Gor but merely a
camisk, which had clearly been worn before.

Targo then dug into the pouch which he wore at his
side and held out two yellow cords, about eighteen inches
apiece. "I noted by the blue helmet," he said, "that you
were of Tharna."

"No," I said, "I am not of Tharna."

"Ah well," said Targo, "how is one to know?" He
tossed the cords to the rug before the girl.

"I have no more slave whips," said Targo, shrugging his
shoulders sadly, "but your sword belt will do as well."

"I'm sure it will," I said, handing back the collar and
camisk.

Targo looked puzzled.

"Bring her the clothing of a free woman," I said.

Targo's mouth dropped open.

"—of a free woman," I repeated.

Targo squinted at the Pleasure Rack at the side of

the tent, perhaps looking for perspiration stains on the straps.

"Are you sure?" he asked.

I laughed and spun the fat little fellow about and, with one hand on the collar of his robes and the other hand firmly affixed south of the collar, flung him stumbling toward the exit of the tent.

He caught his balance there and, earrings swinging, turned to regard me as though I might have lost my senses. "Perhaps Master is making a mistake?" he suggested.

"Perhaps," I admitted.

"Where," asked Targo, "in the camp of a legitimate slaver do you expect me to find clothing suitable to a free woman?"

I laughed, and Targo smiled and left.

I wondered on how many nights free women, bound captives, had been thrown to his feet to be assessed and purchased, how many free women had in his camp exchanged their rich garments for a camisk and an ankle ring on his chain.

In a few moments Targo stumbled back into the tent, his arms bulging with cloth. He threw it down on the rug, puffing. "Take your pick, Master," he said, and backed out of the tent, shaking his head.

I smiled and looked on Lara.

The girl had risen to her feet.

To my surprise she went to the tent flaps and closed them, tying them shut on the inside.

She turned to face me, breathless.

She was very beautiful under the lamp, against the rich hangings of the tent.

She picked up the two yellow cords and, holding them in her hands, knelt before me in the position of the Pleasure Slave.

"I am going to free you," I said.

Humbly she held the cords up for me to accept, her eyes bright, entreating, raised to mine.

"I am not of Tharna," I said.

"But I am," she said.

I saw that she knelt upon a scarlet rug.

"I am going to free you," I said.

"I am not yet free," she said.

I was silent.

"Please," she begged, "—Master."

And so it was that I took the cords from her hand, and in the same night Lara who had once been the proud Tatrix of Tharna became according to the ancient rites of her city my slave girl—and a free woman.

23

RETURN TO THARNA

OUTSIDE THE CAMP OF TARGO, Lara and I climbed a small hill and stood on its crest. I could see before me, some pasangs away, the pavilions of the Fair of En'Kara, and beyond those the looming ridges of the Sardar, ominous, black, sheer. Beyond the Fair and before the mountains, which rose suddenly from the plains, I could see the timber wall of black logs, sharpened at the top, which separated the Fair from the mountains.

Men seeking the mountains, men tired of life, young idealists, opportunists eager to learn the secret of immortality in its recesses, would use the gate at the end of the central avenue of the Fair, a double gate of black logs mounted on giant wooden hinges, a gate that would swing open from the center, revealing the Sardar beyond.

Even as we stood on the hill I could hear the slow ringing of a heavy, hollow tube of metal, which betokened that the black gate had opened. The sad, slow sound reached the hillock on which we stood.

Lara stood beside me, clad as a free woman but not in the Robes of Concealment. She had shortened and trimmed one of the gracious Gorean garments, cutting it to the length of her knees and cutting away the sleeves so that they fell only to her elbows. It was a bright yellow and she had belted it with a scarlet sash. Her feet wore plain sandals of red leather. About her shoulders, at my suggestion, she had wrapped a cloak of heavy wool. It was scarlet. I had thought she might require this for warmth. I think she thought she might require it to match her sash. I smiled to myself. She was free.

I was pleased that she seemed happy.

She had refused the customary Robes of Concealment. She maintained that she would be more of a hindrance to me so clad. I had not argued, for she was right. As I watched her yellow hair swept behind her in the wind and regarded the joyful lineaments of her beauty, I was glad that she had not chosen, whatever might be her reason, to clothe herself in the traditional manner.

Yet though I could not repress my admiration of this girl and the transformation which had been wrought in her from the cold Tatrix of Tharna to the humiliated slave to the glorious creature who now stood beside me my thoughts were mostly in the Sardar, for I knew that I had not yet kept my appointment with the Priest-Kings.

I listened to the slow, gloomy tolling of the hollow bar.

"Someone has entered the mountains," said Lara.

"Yes," I said.

"He will die," she said.

I nodded.

I had spoken to her of my work in the mountains, of my destiny which lay therein. She had said, simply, "I will go with you."

She knew as well as I that those who entered the mountains did not return. She knew as well as I, perhaps better, the fearful power of the Priest-Kings.

Yet she had said she would come with me.

"You are free," I had said.

"When I was your slave," she had said, "you could have ordered me to follow you. Now that I am free I will accompany you of my own accord."

I looked at the girl. How proudly and yet how marvelously she stood beside me. I saw that she had picked a talender on the hill, and that she had placed it in her hair.

I shook my head.

Though the full force of my will drove me to the mountains, though in the mountains the Priest-Kings waited for me, I could not yet go. It was unthinkable that

I should take this girl into the Sardar to be destroyed as I would be destroyed, that I should devastate this young life so recently initiated into the glories of the senses, which had just awakened into the victories of life and feeling.

What could I balance against her—my honor, my thirst for vengeance, my curiosity, my frustration, my fury?

I put my arm about her shoulder and led her down from the hillock.

She looked at me questioningly.

"The Priest-Kings must wait," I said.

"What are you going to do?" she asked.

"Return you to the throne of Tharna," I said.

She pulled away from me, her eyes clouding with tears.

I gathered her to my arms and kissed her gently.

She looked up at me, her eyes wet with tears.

"Yes," I said, "I wish it."

She put her head against my shoulder.

"Beautiful Lara," I said, "forgive me." I held her more closely. "I cannot take you to the Sardar. I cannot leave you here. You would be destroyed by beasts or returned to slavery."

"Must you return me to Tharna?" she asked. "I hate Tharna."

"I have no city to which I might take you," I said. "And I believe you can make Tharna such that you will hate it no longer."

"What must I do?" she asked.

"That you must decide yourself," I said.

I kissed her.

Holding her head in my hands I looked into her eyes.

"Yes," I said proudly, "you are fit to rule."

I wiped the tears from her eyes.

"No tears," I said, "for you are Tatrix of Tharna."

She looked up at me and smiled, a sad smile. "Of course, Warrior," she said, "there must be no tears—for I am Tatrix of Tharna and a Tatrix does not cry."

She pulled the talender from her hair.

I reached to her feet and replaced it.

"I love you," she said.

"It is hard to be first in Tharna," I said, and led her down the hillock, away from the Sardar Mountains.

The fires which had begun to burn in the Mines of Tharna had not been quenched. The revolt of the slaves had spread from the mines to the Great Farms. Shackles had been struck off and weapons seized. Angry men, armed with whatever tools of destruction they might find, prowled the land, evading the sorties of Tharna's soldiers, hunting for granaries to rob, for buildings to burn, for slaves to free. From farm to farm spread the rebellion and the shipments to the city from the farms became sporadic and then ceased. What the slaves could not use or hide, they cut down or burned.

Not more than two hours from the hillock where I had made the decision to return Lara to her native city the tarn had found us, as I had thought he would. As at the Pillar of Exchanges the bird had haunted the vicinity and now, for the second time, its patience was rewarded. It lit some fifty yards from us and we ran to its side, I first and Lara after me, she still apprehensive of the beast.

My pleasure was such that I hugged the neck of that sable monster.

Those round blazing eyes regarded me, those great wings lifted and shook, his beak was lifted to the sky and he screamed the shrill cry of the tarn.

Lara cried out in terror as the monster reached for me with his beak.

I did not move and that great terrible beak closed gently on my arm. Had the tarn wished, with a wrench of its glorious head, it might have torn the limb from my body. Yet its touch was almost tender. I slapped its beak and tossed Lara to its broad back and leaped up beside her.

Again the indescribable thrill possessed me and I think this time that even Lara shared my feelings. "One-strap!" I cried, and the tarn's monstrous frame addressed itself once more to the skies.

As we flew, many were the fields of charred Sa-Tarna we saw below us. The tarn's shadow glided over the blackened frames of buildings, over broken pens from which livestock had been driven, over orchards that were now no more than felled trees, their leaves and fruit brown and withered.

On the back of the tarn Lara wept to see the desolation that had come to her country.

"It is cruel what they have done," she said.

"It is also cruel what has been done to them," I said.

She was silent.

The army of Tharna had struck here and there, at reported hiding places of slaves, but almost invariably they had found nothing. Perhaps some broken utensils, the ashes of campfires. The slaves, forewarned of their approach by other slaves or by impoverished peasants, supplanted by the Great Farms, would have made good their departure, only to strike when ready, when unexpected and in strength.

The sorties of tarnsmen were more successful, but on the whole the slave bands, now almost regiments, moved only at night and concealed themselves during the day. In time it became dangerous for the small cavalries of Tharna to assault them, to brave the storm of missile weapons which would seem to rise almost from the very ground itself.

Often indeed ambushes were laid wherein a small band of slaves would allow itself to be trailed into the rocky passes of the ridge country about Tharna, where their pursuers would be assailed by hidden cohorts; sometimes tarnsmen would descend to capture a slave only to meet the arrows of a hundred men concealed in covered pits.

Perhaps in time, however, the undisciplined but courageous bands of slaves would have been scattered and destroyed by the units of Tharna, save that the very revolution which had begun in the mines and spread to the Great Farms now flamed in the city itself. Not only slaves of the city raised the banner of defiance but men of low caste, whose brothers or friends had been sent to the mines or used in the Amusements, now dared at last to seize the instruments of their trade and turn on guardsmen and soldiers. It was said the rebellion in the city was led by a short, powerful man with blue eyes and short-cropped hair, formerly of the Caste of Metal Workers.

Certain portions of the city had been burned to exterminate the rebellious elements and this cruel act of repression had only rallied confused and undecided men to the side of the rebels. Now it was said that entire portions of the city were in rebel hands. The silver masks of Tharna, when they were able, had escaped to the portions of the city still in the command of the soldiers. Many were reported to cower in the confines of the royal palace itself. The fate of those who had not escaped rebel hands was not clear.

It was late in the afternoon of the fifth day that we saw in the distance the gray walls of Tharna. We were not threatened nor investigated by patrols. It was true that we could see tarnsmen and their mounts here and there among the cylinders, but none came to challenge us.

At several places in the city long ropes of smoke spiraled upward and then unravelled into vague, dark strands.

The main gate of Tharna hung open on its hinges, and small isolated figures scurried in and out. There were no tharlarion wagons or lines of woodsmen or pedlars making their way to or from the city. Outside the walls several small buildings had been burned. On the wall itself over the gate in huge letters there was scrawled the legend "Sa'ng-Fori," literally "Without Chains" but perhaps better translated simply as "Freedom" or "Liberty".

We brought the tarn down on the walls near the gate. I freed the bird. There was no tarn cot at hand in which to enclose him, and moreover, even if there had been, I would not have trusted him to the tarn-keepers of Tharna. I did not know who was and who was not in rebellion. Perhaps mostly I wanted the bird to be free in case my hopes met with disaster, in case the Tatrix and I were to perish in some back street of Tharna.

On the summit of the wall we encountered the crumpled form of a fallen guardsman. It moved slightly. There was a small sound of pain. He had apparently been left for dead and was only now recovering consciousness. His gray garment with its scarlet strip of cloth on the shoulder was stained with blood. I unbuckled the helmet strap and gently removed the helmet.

One side of the helmet had been cracked open, perhaps by the blow of an ax. The helmet straps, the leather inside, and the blond hair of the soldier were soaked with his blood. He was not much more than a boy.

As he felt the wind on the walls reach his head he opened his grayish blue eyes. One hand attempted to clutch his weapon but the sheath had been emptied.

"Don't struggle," I said to him, looking at the wound. The helmet had largely absorbed the blow but the blade of the striking instrument had creased the skull, accounting for the flow of blood. Most likely the force of the blow had rendered him unconscious and the blood had suggested to his assailant that the job was finished. His assailant had apparently not been a warrior.

With a portion of Lara's cloak I bound the wound. It was clean and not deep.

"You'll be all right," I said to him.

His eyes looked from one of us to the other. "Are you for the Tatrix?" he asked.

"Yes," I said.

"I fought for her," said the boy, lying back against my arm. "I did my duty."

I gathered that he had not enjoyed the performance of his duty, and that perhaps his heart lay with the rebels, but the pride of his caste had kept him at his post. Even in his youth he had the blind loyalty of the warrior, a loyalty which I respected and which was perhaps no more blind than some I myself had felt. Such men made fearsome antagonists, even though their swords might be pledged to the most despicable of causes.

"You did not fight for your Tatrix," I said evenly.

The young warrior started in my arms. "I did," he cried.

"No," I said, "you fought for Dorna the Proud, pretender to the throne of Tharna—a usurper and traitress."

The eyes of the warrior widened as they regarded us.

"Here," I said, gesturing to the beautiful girl at my side, "is Lara, the true Tatrix of Tharna."

"Yes, brave Guardsman," said the girl, placing her hand gently on his forehead as though to soothe him, "I am Lara."

The guardsman struggled in my arms, and then fell back, shutting his eyes with pain.

"Lara," he said, through closed lids, "was carried away by the tarnsman in the Amusements."

"I am he," I said.

The grayish blue eyes slowly opened and gazed at my face for a long time, and gradually recognition transformed the features of the young guardsman. "Yes," said he, "I remember."

"The tarnsman," said Lara, speaking softly, "returned me to the Pillar of Exchanges. There I was seized by Dorna the Proud and Thorn, her accomplice, and sold into slavery. The tarnsman freed me and has now returned me to my people."

"I fought for Dorna the Proud," said the boy. His grayish blue eyes filled with tears. "Forgive me, true Tatrix of Tharna," he begged. And had it not been forbidden that he, a man of Tharna should touch her, a woman of Tharna, I think he would have reached his hand toward her.

To his wonder Lara took his hand in hers. "You did well," she said. "I am proud of you, my guardsman."

The boy closed his eyes and his body relaxed in my arms.

Lara looked at me, her eyes frightened.

"No," I said, "he is not dead. He is just young and he has lost much blood."

"Look!" cried the girl, pointing down the length of the wall.

Some six shapes, gray, carrying spears and shields were moving rapidly in our direction.

"Guardsmen," I said, drawing my sword.

Suddenly I saw the shields shift, facing us obliquely, and saw the right arms raise, spears high, with no change in the rapid pace of the men. In another dozen steps the six spears would fly hurled from that swift even pace.

Losing not a moment I thrust my sword into my belt and seized Lara by the waist. As she protested I turned and forced her to run at my side.

"Wait!" she pleaded. "I will speak to them!"

I swept her to my arms and ran.

No sooner had we reached the spiraling stone stairwell which led down from the wall than the six spears, their points describing a circle of perhaps a yard in diameter, struck the wall over our head with a splintering of rock.

Once we reached the bottom of the wall we kept close to its base so as not to afford a target for further spear play. On the other hand I did not believe the guardsmen would cast their weapons from the wall. If they missed, or if they did not, it would necessitate descending from the wall to retrieve the weapons. It was unlikely a small party like that above would freely lose the height of the wall to pursue two rebels.

We began to work our torturous way through the grim, bloodstained streets of Tharna. Some of the buildings had been destroyed. Shops had been boarded up. Litter was everywhere. Rubbish burned in the gutters. Largely the streets were deserted save that here and there lay a body, sometimes that of a warrior of Tharna, more often one of its gray-clad citizens. On many of the walls the legend "Sa'ng-Fori" could be read.

On occasion terrified eyes scrutinized us fearfully from behind the shutters of windows. I suspected there was not a door in Tharna but was not barred that day.

"Halt!" cried a voice, and we stopped.

From in front of us and behind us a group of men had seemed to materialize. Several of them held crossbows; at least four others had spears poised; some boasted swords; but many of them carried nothing more than a chain or sharpened pole.

"Rebels!" said Lara.

"Yes," I said.

We could read the sullen defiance, the resolve, the capacity to kill in those eyes, bloodshot with loss of sleep, the desperate carriage of those gray-clad bodies, hungry and vicious with the strain of street fighting. There were wolves in the streets of Tharna.

I slowly drew my sword, and thrust the girl to the side of the street against the wall.

One of the men laughed.

I too smiled for resistance was useless, yet I knew that I would resist, that I would not be disarmed until I lay dead on the stones of the street.

What of Lara?

What would be her fate at the hands of this pack of maddened, desperate men? I regarded my ragged foes, some of whom had been wounded. They were filthy, savage, exhausted, angry, perhaps starving. She would probably be slain against the wall by which she stood. It would be brutal but quick, on the whole merciful.

The spear arms drew back, the crossbows leveled. Chains were grasped more firmly; the few swords lifted toward me; even the sharpened poles inclined toward my breast.

"Tarl of Ko-ro-ba!" cried a voice, and I saw a small man, thin with a wisp of sandy hair across his forehead, press through the ragged band of rebels that confronted us.

It was he who had been first on the chain in the mines, he who had of necessity been first to climb the shaft from the slave kennel to freedom.

His face was transfigured with joy and he rushed forward and embraced me.

"This is he!" the man cried. "Tarl of Ko-ro-ba!"

At that point, to my wonder, the ragged band lifted their weapons and uttered a wild cheer. I was swept from my feet and thrown to their shoulders. I was carried through the streets and others of the rebels, appearing from doorways and windows, almost from the very stones of the street, joined what turned into a procession of triumph.

The voices of these haggard but transformed men began to sing. I recognized the tune. It was the plowing song I had first heard from the peasant in the mines. It had become the anthem of the revolution.

Lara, as mystified as I, ran along with the men, staying as close to me as the jostling crowds permitted.

Thus borne aloft, from street to street, in the midst of joyous shouting, weapons raised on all sides in salute, my ears ringing with the plowing song, once a song of the freeholds of Tharna, long since supplanted by the Great Farms, I found myself brought to that fateful Kal-da shop I remembered so well, where I had dined in Tharna and had awakened to the treachery of Ost. It had become a headquarters of the revolution, perhaps because men of Tharna recalled that it was there they had learned to sing.

There, standing before the low doorway, I looked once more upon the squat, powerful figure of Kron, of the Caste of Metal Workers. His great hammer was slung from his belt and his blue eyes glistened with happiness. The huge, scarred hands of a metal worker were held out to me.

Beside him, to my joy, I saw the impudent features of Andreas, that sweep of black hair almost obliterating his forehead. Behind Andreas, in the dress of a free woman, unveiled, her throat no longer encircled by the collar of a state slave, I saw the breathless, radiant Linna of Tharna.

Andreas bounded past the men at the door and rushed to me. He seized me by the hands and dragged me to the street, roughly grappling my shoulders and laughing with joy.

"Welcome to Tharna!" said he. "Welcome to Tharna!"

"Yes," said Kron, only a step behind him, seizing my arm. "Welcome to Tharna!"

24

THE BARRICADE

I DUCKED MY HEAD AND shoved open the heavy wooden door of the Kal-da shop. The sign KAL-DA SOLD HERE had been repainted in bright letters. Also, smeared across the letters, written with a finger, was the defiant rallying call of the rebellion—"Sa'ng-Fori."

I descended the low, wide steps to the interior. This time the shop was crowded. It was hard to see where to step. It was wild and noisy. It might have been a Paga Tavern of Ko-ro-ba or Ar, not a simple Kal-da shop of Tharna. My ears were assailed by the din, the jovial uproar of men no longer afraid to laugh or shout.

The shop itself was now hung with perhaps half a hundred lamps and the walls were bright with the caste colors of the men who drank there. Thick rugs had been thrown under the low tables and were stained in innumerable places with spilled Kal-da.

Behind the counter the thin, bald-headed proprietor, his forehead glistening, his slick black apron stained with spices, juices and wine, busily worked his long mixing paddle in a vast pot of bubbling Kal-da. My nose wrinkled. There was no mistaking the smell of brewing Kal-da.

From behind three or four of the low tables, to the left of the counter, a band of sweating musicians sat happily cross-legged on the rug, somehow producing from those unlikely pipes and strings and drums and disks and wires the ever intriguing, wild, enchanting—beautiful—barbaric melodies of Gor.

I wondered at this for the Caste of Musicians had been, like the Caste of Poets, exiled from Tharna. Theirs, like the Caste of Poets, had been a caste regarded by the sober masks of Tharna as not belonging in a city of serious and dedicated folk, for music, like Paga and song, can set men's hearts aflame and when men's hearts are aflame it is not easy to know where the flame may spread.

As I entered the room the men rose to their feet and shouted and lifted their cups in salute.

Almost as one they cried out, "Tal, Warrior!"

"Tal, Warriors!" I responded, raising my arm, addressing them all by the title of my caste, for I knew that in their common cause each was a warrior. It had been so determined at the Mines of Tharna.

Behind me down the stairs came Kron and Andreas, followed by Lara and Linna.

I wondered what impression the Kal-da shop would have on the true Tatrix of Tharna.

Kron seized my arm and guided me to a table near the center of the room. Holding Lara by the hand I followed him. Her eyes were stunned but like a child's were wide with curiosity. She had not known the men of Tharna could be like this.

From time to time as one of them regarded her too boldly she dropped her head and blushed.

At last I sat cross-legged behind the low table and Lara, in the fashion of the Gorean woman, knelt beside me, resting on her heels.

When I had entered the music had briefly stopped but now Kron clapped his hands twice and the musicians turned to their instruments.

"Free Kal-da for all!" cried Kron, and when the proprietor, who knew the codes of his caste, tried to object, Kron flung a golden tarn disk at him. Delightedly the man ducked and scrambled to pick it up from the floor.

"Gold is more common here than bread," said Andreas, sitting near us.

To be sure the food on the low tables was not plentiful and was coarse but one could not have known this from the good cheer of the men in the room. It might have been to them food from the tables of the Priest-Kings themselves. Even the foul Kal-da to them, reveling in the first intoxication of their freedom, was the rarest and most potent of beverages.

Kron clapped his hands again and to my surprise there was a sudden sound of bells and four terrified girls, obviously chosen for their beauty and grace, stood before our table clad only in the scarlet dancing silks of Gor. They threw back their heads and lifted their arms and to the barbaric cadence set by the musicians danced before us.

Lara, to my surprise, watched them with delight.

"Where in Tharna," I asked, "did you find Pleasure Slaves?" I had noted that the throats of the girls were encircled by silver collars.

Andreas, who was stuffing a piece of bread in his mouth, responded, his words a cheery mumble. "Beneath every silver mask," he averred sententiously, "there is a potential Pleasure Slave."

"Andreas!" cried Linna, and she made as if to slap him for his insolence, but he quieted her with a kiss, and she playfully began to nibble at the bread clenched between his teeth.

"Are these truly silver masks of Tharna?" I asked Kron, skeptically.

"Yes," said he. "Good, aren't they?"

"How did they learn this?" I asked.

He shrugged. "It is instinctive in a woman," he said. "But they are untrained of course."

I laughed to myself. Kron of Tharna spoke as might any man of any city of Gor—other than a man of Tharna.

"Why are they dancing for you?" asked Lara.

"They will be whipped if they do not," said Kron.

Lara's eyes dropped.

"You see the collars," said Kron, pointing to the slender

graceful bands of silver each girl wore at her throat. "W
melted the masks and used the silver for the collar."

Other girls now appeared among the tables, clad only i
a camisk and a silver collar, and sullenly, silently, bega
to serve the Kal-da which Kron had ordered. Each carrie
a heavy pot of the foul, boiling brew and, cup by cu
replenished the cups of the men.

Some of them looked enviously at Lara, others wi
hatred. Their look said to her why are you not clad as v
are, why do you not wear a collar and serve as we serve?

To my surprise Lara removed her cloak and took t
pot of Kal-da from one of the girls and began to serve t
men.

Some of the girls looked at her in gratitude for she w:
free and in doing this she showed them that she did n
regard herself as above them.

"That," I said to Kron, pointing out Lara, "is t
Tatrix of Tharna."

As Andreas looked upon her he said softly, "She
truly a Tatrix."

Linna arose and now began to help with the serving.

When Kron had tired of watching the dancers I
clapped his hands twice and with a discordant jangle
their ankle bells they fled from the room.

Kron lifted his cup of Kal-da and faced me. "Andre:
told me you intended to enter the Sardar," he said. "I s
that you did not do so."

Kron meant that if I had entered the Sardar I wou
not have returned.

"I am going to the Sardar," I said, "but I first hav
business in Tharna."

"Good!" said Kron. "We need your sword."

"I have come to place Lara once more on the throne
Tharna," I said.

Kron and Andreas looked at me in wonder.

"No," said Kron. "I do not know how she has bewitche
you but we will have no Tatrix in Tharna!"

"She is everything that we fight against," protested Ar

dreas. "If she again ascends the throne, our battle will have been lost. Tharna would once more be the same."

"Tharna," I said, "will never again be the same."

Andreas shook his head as if trying to comprehend what I might mean. "How can we expect him to make sense?" asked Andreas of Kron. "After all, he is not a poet."

Kron did not laugh.

"Or a metal worker," added Andreas hopefully.

Still Kron did not laugh.

His dour personality formed over the anvils and forges of his trade did not take lightly to the enormity of what I had said.

"You would have to kill me first," said Kron.

"Are we not still of the same chain?" I asked.

Kron was silent. Then regarding me evenly with those steel-blue eyes he said, "We are always of the same chain."

"Then let me speak," I said.

Kron nodded curtly.

Several other men had by now crowded about the table.

"You are men of Tharna," I said. "But the men you fight are also of Tharna."

One of the men spoke. "I have a brother in the guards."

"Is it right that the men of Tharna lift their weapons against one another, men within the same walls?"

"It is a sad thing," said Kron. "But it must be."

"It need not be," I protested. "The soldiers and guardsmen of Tharna are pledged to the Tatrix, but the Tatrix they defend is a traitress. The true Tatrix of Tharna, Lara herself, is within this room."

Kron watched the girl, who was unconscious of the conversation. Across the room she was serving Kal-da to the men whose cups were lifted to her.

"While she lives," said Kron, "the revolution is not safe."

"That is not true," I said.

"She must die," said Kron.

"No," I said. "She too has felt the chain and whip."

There was a murmur of astonishment from the men about the table.

"The soldiers of Tharna and her guardsmen will forsake the false Tatrix and serve the true Tatrix," I said.

"If she lives——" agreed Kron, looking at the innocent girl across the room.

"She must," I urged. "She will bring a new day to Tharna. She can unite both the rebels and the men who oppose you. She has learned how cruel and miserable are the ways of Tharna. Look at her!"

And the men watched the girl quietly pouring the Kal-da, willingly sharing the labors of the other women of Tharna. It was not what one would have expected of a Tatrix.

"She is worthy to rule," I said.

"She is what we fought against," said Kron.

"No," I said, "you fought against the cruel ways of Tharna. You fought for your pride and your freedom, not against that girl."

"We fought against the golden mask of Tharna," shouted Kron, pounding his fist on the table.

The sudden noise attracted the attention of the entire room and all eyes turned toward us. Lara, her back graceful and straight, set down the pot of Kal-da and came and stood before Kron.

"I no longer wear the golden mask," she said.

And Kron looked on the beautiful girl who stood before him with such grace and dignity, with no trace of pride or cruelty, or fear.

"My Tatrix," he whispered.

We marched through the city, the streets behind us filled like gray rivers with the rebels, each man with his own weapon, yet the sound of those rivers, converging on the palace of the Tatrix was anything but gray. It was the sound of the plowing song, as slow and irresistible as the breaking of ice in frozen rivers, a simple, melodic paean to the soil, celebrating the first breaking of the ground.

At the head of that splendid, ragged procession five marched; Kron, chief of the rebels; Andreas, a poet; his woman, Linna of Tharna, unveiled; I, a warrior of a city devastated and cursed of the Priest-Kings; and a girl with golden hair, a girl who wore no mask, who had known both the whip and love, fearless and magnificent Lara, she who was true Tatrix of Tharna.

It was clear to the defenders of the palace, which formed the major bastion of Dorna's challenged regime, that the issue would be decided that day and by the sword. Word had swept ahead as if on the wings of tarns that the rebels, abandoning their tactics of ambush and evasion, were at last marching on the palace.

I saw before us once again that broad, winding but ever narrowing avenue which led to the palace of the Tatrix. Singing, the rebels began to climb the steep avenue. The black cobblestones could be felt clearly through the leather of our sandals.

Once more I noted that the walls bordering the avenue rose as the avenue narrowed, but this time, long before we neared the small iron door, we saw a double rampart thrown across the avenue, the second wall topping the first and allowing missiles to be rained down on those who might storm the first wall. The rampart was thrown between the walls where they stood at perhaps fifty yards from each other. The first rampart was perhaps twelve feet high; the second perhaps twenty.

Behind the ramparts I could see the blaze of weaponry and the movement of blue helmets.

We were within crossbow range.

I motioned to the others to remain back and, carrying a shield and spear in addition to my sword, approached the rampart.

On the roof of the palace beyond the double rampart I could occasionally see the head of a tarn and I heard their screams. Tarns, however, would not be too effective against the rebels in the city. Many of them had cut long bows and many of them were armed with the spears and crossbows of fallen warriors. It would be risky business coming close enough to bring talons into play.

And should the warriors have attempted to use the tarns merely to fire down on the crowd, they would suddenly have found the streets deserted, until the shadow of the bird had passed and the rebels could move another hundred yards closer to the palace. Trained infantry, incidentally, might move rapidly through the streets of a city with shields locked over their heads, much in the fashion of the Roman *testudo,* but this formation requires discipline and precision, martial virtues not to be expected in high degree of the rebels of Tharna.

About a hundred yards from the rampart I put down the shield and spear, signifying a temporary truce.

A tall figure appeared on the rampart and did as I had done.

Though he wore the blue helmet of Tharna I knew that it was Thorn.

Once again I began to approach the rampart.

It seemed a long walk.

Step by step I climbed the black avenue wondering if the truce would be respected. If Dorna the Proud had ruled upon that rampart rather than Thorn, a Captain, and a member of my own caste, I was certain that a bolt from some crossbow would have pierced my body without warning.

When at last I stood unslain on the black cobblestones at the foot of the double rampart I knew that though Dorna the Proud might rule in Tharna, though it might be she who sat upon the golden throne of the city, that it was the word of a warrior that ruled on those ramparts above me.

"Tal, Warrior," said Thorn, removing his helmet.

"Tal, Warrior," I said.

Thorn's eyes were clearer now than I remembered them, and the large body which had been tending to corpulence had, in the stress of the fighting, hardened into muscular vigor. The purplish patches that marked his yellowish face seemed less pronounced now than before.

Two strands of hair still marked his chin in parallel
streaks and on the back of his head his long hair was still
bound in a Mongol knot. The now clear, oblique eyes
regarded me.

"I should have killed you on the Pillar of Exchanges,"
said Thorn.

I spoke loudly so that my voice might carry to all who
manned the double rampart.

"I come on behalf of Lara, who is true Tatrix of
Tharna. Sheathe your weapons. No more shed the blood
of men of your own city. I ask this in the name of Lara,
and of the city of Tharna and its people. And I ask it in
the name of the codes of your own caste, for your swords
are pledged to the true Tatrix—Lara—not Dorna the
Proud!"

I could sense the reaction of the men behind the rampart.

Thorn too now spoke loudly for the benefit of the
warriors. "Lara is dead. Dorna is Tatrix of Tharna."

"I live!" cried a voice behind me and I turned and to
my dismay I saw that Lara had followed me to the
rampart. If she were killed the hopes of the rebels might
well be blasted, and the city plunged interminably into
civil strife.

Thorn looked at the girl and I admired the coolness
with which he regarded her. His mind must have been in
tumult for he could not have expected that the girl pro-
duced by the rebels as the true Tatrix would actually be
Lara.

"She is not Lara," he said coldly.

"I am," she cried.

"The Tatrix of Tharna," sneered Thorn, looking on the
unconcealed features of Lara, "wears a golden mask."

"The Tatrix of Tharna," said Lara, "no longer chooses
to wear a mask of gold."

"Where did you get this camp wench, this impostor?"
asked Thorn.

"I purchased her from a slaver," I said.

Thorn laughed and his men behind the barricade laughed too.

"The slaver to whom you sold her," I added.

Thorn laughed no longer.

I called out to the men behind the barricade. "I returned this girl—your Tatrix—to the Pillar of Exchanges where I gave her into the hands of Thorn, this Captain, and Dorna the Proud. Then treacherously I was set upon and sent to the Mines of Tharna, and Dorna the Proud and Thorn, this Captain, seized Lara, your Tatrix, and sold her into slavery—sold her to the slaver Targo, whose camp is now at the Fair of En'Kara, sold her for the sum of fifty silver tarn disks!"

"What he says is false," shouted Thorn.

I heard a voice from behind the barricade, a young voice. "Dorna the Proud wears a necklace of fifty silver tarn disks!"·

"Dorna the Proud is bold indeed," I cried, "to flaunt the very coins whereby her rival—your true Tatrix—was delivered into the chains of a slave girl!"

There was a mutter of indignation, some angry shouts from the barricade.

"He lies," said Thorn.

"You heard him," I cried, "say to me that he should have killed me on the Pillar of Exchanges! You know that it was I who stole your Tatrix at the Amusements of Tharna. Why would I have gone to the Pillar of Exchanges if not to surrender her to the envoys of Tharna?"

A voice cried out from behind the barricade. "Why did you not take more men with you to the Pillar of Exchanges, Thorn of Tharna?"

Thorn turned angrily in the direction of the voice.

I responded to the question. "Is it not obvious?" I asked. "He wanted to protect the secret of his plan to abduct the Tatrix and put Dorna the Proud upon her throne."

Another man appeared at the top of the barricade. He removed his helmet. I saw that it was the young warrior whose wound Lara and I had tended on the wall of Tharna.

"I believe this warrior!" he cried, pointing down at me.

"It is a trick to divide us!" cried Thorn. "Back to your post!"

Other warriors in the blue helmets and gray tunics of Tharna had climbed to the top of the barricade, to see more clearly what befell.

"Back to your posts!" cried Thorn.

"You are warriors!" I cried. "Your swords are pledged to your city, to its walls, to your people and your Tatrix! Serve her!"

"I shall serve the true Tatrix of Tharna!" cried the young warrior.

He leaped down from the barricade and laid his sword on the stones at Lara's feet.

"Take up your sword," she said, "in the name of Lara, true Tatrix of Tharna."

"I do so," he said.

He knelt on one knee before the girl and grasped the hilt of the weapon. "I take up my sword," he said, "in the name of Lara, who is true Tatrix of Tharna."

He rose to his feet and saluted the girl with the weapon. "Who is true Tatrix of Tharna!" he cried.

"That is not Lara!" cried Thorn, pointing to the girl.

"How can you be so certain?" asked one of the warriors on the wall.

Thorn was silent, for how could he claim to know that the girl was not Lara, when presumably he had never looked upon the face of the true Tatrix?

"I am she," cried the girl. "Are there none of you here who have served in the Chamber of the Golden Mask? None of you who recognize my voice?"

"It is she!" cried one of the men. "I am sure!" He removed his helmet.

"You are Stam," she said, "first guardsman of the north gate and can cast your spear farther than any man of Tharna. You were first in the military games of En'Kara in the second year of my reign."

Another warrior removed his helmet.

"You are Tai," said she, "a tarnsman, wounded in the war with Thentis in the year before I ascended the throne of Tharna."

Yet another man took from his head the blue helmet.

"I do not know you," she said.

The men on the wall murmured.

"You could not," said the man, "for I am a mercenary of Ar who took service in Tharna only within the time of the revolt."

"She is Lara!" cried another man. He leaped down from the wall and placed his sword also on the stones at her feet.

Once again she graciously requested that the weapon be lifted in her name, and it was.

One of the blocks of the barricade tumbled into the street. The warriors were dismantling it.

Thorn had disappeared from the wall.

Slowly the rebels, waved ahead by me, approached the wall. They had cast down their weapons and, singing, they marched to the palace.

The soldiers streamed over the barricade and met them in the avenue with joy. The men of Tharna seized one another in their arms and clasped their hands in concord. Rebels and defenders mingled gladly in the street and brother sought brother among those who had minutes before been mortal foes.

My arm about Lara, I walked through the barricade, and behind us came the young warrior, others of the defenders of the barricade, and Kron, Andreas, Linna and many of the rebels.

Andreas had brought with him the shield and spear which I had put down in token of truce, and I took these weapons from him. We approached the small iron door that gave access to the palace, I in the lead.

I called for a torch.

The door was loose and I kicked it open, covering myself with the shield.

Within there was only silence and darkness.

The rebel who had been first on the chain in the mines thrust a torch in my hands.

I held this in the opening.

The floor seemed solid, but this time I knew the dangers it concealed.

A long plank from the scaffolding of the barricade was brought and we laid this from the threshhold across the floor.

The torch lifted high, I entered, careful to stay on the plank. This time the trap did not open and I found myself in a narrow unlit hallway opposite the door to the palace.

"Wait here," I commanded the others.

I did not listen to their protests but saying no more began my torchlit journey through the now darkened labyrinth of the palace corridors. My memory and sense of direction began to carry me unerringly from hall to hall, guiding me swiftly toward the Chamber of the Golden Mask.

I encountered no one.

The silence seemed uncanny and the darkness startling after the bright sunlight of the street outside. I could hear nothing but the quiet, almost noisless sound of my own sandals on the stones of the corridor.

The palace was perhaps deserted.

At last I came to the Chamber of the Golden Mask.

I leaned against the heavy doors and swung them open.

Inside there was light. The torches on the walls still burned. Behind the golden throne of the Tatrix loomed the dull gold mask, fashioned in the image of a cold and beautiful woman, the reflection of the torches set in the walls flickering hideously on its polished surface.

On the throne there sat a woman clad in the golden robes and mask of the Tatrix of Tharna. About her neck was a necklace of silver tarn disks. On the steps before the throne there stood a warrior, fully armed, who held in his hands the blue helmet of his city.

Thorn lowered his helmet slowly over his features. He

loosened the sword in its scabbard. He unslung his shield and the long, broad-headed spear from his left shoulder.

"I have been waiting for you," he said.

25

THE ROOF OF THE PALACE

THE WAR CRIES OF THARNA and Ko-ro-ba mingled
as Thorn hurled himself down the stairs toward me and I
raced toward him.

Both of us cast our spears at the same instant and the
two weapons passed one another like tawny blurs of lightning. Both of us had in casting our weapon inclined our
shields in such a way as to lessen the impact of a direct
hit. Both of us cast well and the jolt of the massive missile
thundering on my shield spun me half about.

The bronze head of the spear had cut through the brass
loops on the shield and pierced the seven hardened concentric layers of bosk hide which formed it. The shield, so
encumbered, was useless. Hardly had my shield been
penetrated when my sword had leaped from its sheath and
slashed through the shoulder straps of the shield, cutting it
from my arm.

Only an instant after myself Thorn's shield too was
flung to the stones of the chamber floor. My spear had
been driven a yard through it and the head had passed
over his left shoulder as he crouched behind it.

His sword too was free of its sheath and we rushed on
one another like larls in the Voltai, our weapons meeting
with a sharp, free clash of sound, the trembling brilliant
ring of well-tempered blades, each tone ringing in the
clear, glittering music of swordplay.

Seemingly almost impassive, the golden-robed figure on
the throne watched the two warriors moving backward
and forward before her, one clad in the blue helmet and

gray tunic of Tharna, the other in the universal scarlet of the Gorean Caste of Warriors.

Our reflections fought one another in the shimmering surface of the great golden mask behind the throne.

Our wild shadows like misformed giants locked in combat against the lofty walls of the torchlit chamber.

Then there was but one reflection and but one gigantic, grotesque shadow cast upon the walls of the Chamber of the Golden Mask.

Thorn lay at my feet.

I kicked the sword from the hand and turned over the body with my foot. Its chest shook under the stained tunic; its mouth bit at the air as if trying to catch it as it escaped its throat. The head rolled sideways on the stones.

"You fought well," I said.

"I have won," he said, the words spit out in a sort of whisper, a contorted grin on his face.

I wondered what he might mean.

I stepped back from the body and looked to the woman upon the throne.

Slowly, numbly, she descended the throne, step by step, and then to my amazement she fell to her knees beside Thorn and lowered her head to his bloody chest weeping.

I wiped the blade on my tunic and replaced it in the sheath.

"I am sorry," I said.

The figure seemed not to hear me.

I stepped back, to leave her with her grief. I could hear the sounds of approaching men in the corridors. It was the soldiers and rebels, and the halls of the palace echoed the anthem of the plowing song.

The girl lifted her head and the golden mask faced me.

I had not known that a woman such as Dorna the Proud could have cared for a man.

The voice, for the first time, spoke through the mask.

"Thorn," she said, "has defeated you."

"I think not," I said, wondering, "and you Dorna the Proud are now my prisoner."

A mirthless laugh sounded through the mask and the hands in their gloves of gold took the mask and, to my astonishment, removed it.

At the side of Thorn knelt not Dorna the Proud, but the girl Vera of Ko-ro-ba, who had been his slave.

"You see," she said, "my master has defeated you, as he knew he could, not by the sword but by the purchase of time. Dorna the Proud has made good her escape."

"Why have you done this!" I challenged.

She smiled. "Thorn was kind to me," she said.

"You are now free," I said.

Once again her head fell to the stained chest of the Captain of Tharna and her body shook with sobs.

At that moment into the room burst the soldiers and rebels, Kron and Lara in the lead.

I pointed to the girl on the floor. "Do not harm her!" I commanded. "This is not Dorna the Proud but Vera of Ko-ro-ba, who was the slave of Thorn."

"Where is Dorna?" demanded Kron.

"Escaped," I said glumly.

Lara looked at me. "But the palace is surrounded," she said.

"The roof!" I cried, remembering the tarns. "Quick!"

Lara raced ahead of me and I followed as she led the way to the roof of the palace. Through the darkened hallways she sped with the familiarity of long acquaintance. At last we reached a spiral stairwell.

"Here!" she cried.

I thrust her behind me and, my hand on the wall, climbed the dark stairs as rapidly as I could. At the top of the stairs I pressed against a trap and flung it open. Outside I could see the bright blue rectangle of the open sky. The light blinded me for a moment.

I caught the scent of a large furred animal and the odor of tarn spoor.

I emerged onto the roof, my eyes half shut against the intense light.

There were three men on the roof, two guardsmen and the man with the wrist straps, who had served as the master of the dungeons of Tharna. He held, leashed, the large, sleek white urt which I had encountered in the pit inside the palace door.

The two guardsmen were fixing a carrying basket to the harness of a large brown-plumaged tarn. The reins of the tarn were fixed to a ring in the front of the basket. Inside the basket was a woman whose carriage and figure I knew to be that of Dorna the Proud, though she now wore only a simple silver mask of Tharna.

"Stop! I cried, rushing forward.

"Kill!" cried the man in wrist straps, pointing the whip in my direction, and unleashing the urt, which charged viciously toward me.

Its ratlike scamper was incomprehensibly swift and almost before I could set myself for its charge it had crossed the cylinder roof in two or three bounds and pounced to seize me in its bared fangs.

My blade entered the roof of its mouth pushing its head up and away from my throat. The squeal must have carried to the walls of Tharna. Its neck twisted and the blade was wrenched from my grasp. My arms encircled its neck and my face was pressed into its glossy white fur. The blade was shaken from its mouth and clattered on the roof. I clung to the neck to avoid the snapping jaws, those three rows of sharp, frenzied white lacerating teeth that sought to bury themselves in my flesh.

It rolled on the roof trying to tear me from its neck; it leaped and bounded, and twisted and shook itself. The man with wrist straps had picked up the sword and with this, and his whip, circled us, waiting for an opportunity to strike.

I tried to turn the animal as well as I could to keep its scrambling body between myself and the man with wrist straps.

Blood from the animal's mouth ran down its fur and my arm. I could feel it splattered on the side of my face and in my hair.

Then I turned so that it was my body that was exposed to the blow of the sword carried by the man in wrist

raps. I heard his grunt of satisfaction as he rushed
rward. An instant before I knew the blade must fall I
leased my grip on the animal's neck and slipped under
s belly. It reached for me with a whiplike motion of its
rred neck and I felt the long sharp white teeth rake my
m but at the same time I heard another squeal of pain
nd the grunt of horror from the man in wrist straps.

I rolled from under the animal and turned to see it
cing the man with wrist straps. One ear had been slashed
way from its head and fur on its left side was soaked
ith spurting blood. It now had its eyes fixed on the man
ith the sword, he who had struck this new blow.

I heard his terrified command, the feeble cracking of
at whip held in an arm almost paralyzed with fear, his
brupt almost noiseless scream.

The urt was over him, its haunches high, its shoulders
lmost level with the roof, gnawing.

I shook the sight from my eyes and turned to the others
n the roof.

The carrying basket had been attached and the woman
tood in the basket, the reins in her hands.

The impassive silver mask was fastened on me and I
ensed that the dark eyes behind it blazed with indescriba-
le hatred.

Her voice spoke to the two guardsmen. "Destroy him."

I had no weapons.

To my surprise the men did not raise their arms against
ne. One of them responded to her.

"You choose to abandon your city," he said. "Hence-
orth you have no city, for you have chosen to forsake it."

"Insolent beast!" she screamed at him. Then she or-
ered the other warrior to slay the first.

"You no longer rule in Tharna," said the other warrior
mply.

"Beasts!" she screamed.

"Were you to stay and die at the foot of your throne we
ould follow you and die by your side," said the first
arrior.

"That is true," said the second. "Stay as a Tatrix, a:
our swords are bound in your service. Flee as a slave a:
you give up your right to command our metal."

"Fools!" she cried.

Then Dorna the Proud looked at me those yards acro
the roof.

The hatred she bore me, her cruelty, her pride, were
tangible as some physical phenomenon, like waves of h(
or the forming of ice.

"Thorn died for you," I said.

She laughed. "He too was a fool, like all beasts."

I wondered how it was that Thorn had given his life {
this woman. It did not seem it could have been a matt
of caste obligation for this obligation had been owed r
to Dorna but to Lara. He had broken the codes of l
caste to support the treachery of Dorna the Proud.

I suddenly knew the answer, that Thorn somehow h
loved this cruel woman, that his warrior's heart had be
turned to her though he had never looked upon her fac
though she had never given him a smile or the touch
her hand. And I knew then that Thorn, henchman thou
he might have been, dissolute and savage antagonist, h
yet been greater than she who had been the object of l
hopeless, tragic affection. It had been his doom to care {
a silver mask.

"Surrender," I called to Dorna the Proud.

"Never," she responded haughtily.

"Where will you go and what will you do?" I asked.

I knew that Dorna would have little chance alone
Gor. Resourceful as she was, even carrying riches as s
must be, she was still only a woman and, on Gor, ever
silver mask needs the sword of a man to protect her. S
might fall prey to beasts, perhaps even to her own tarn,
be captured by a roving tarnsman or a band of slavers.

"Stay to face the justice of Tharna," I said.

Dorna threw back her head and laughed.

"You too," she said, "are a fool."

Her hand was wrapped in the one-strap. The tarn w
moving uneasily.

I looked behind me and I could see that Lara now stood near, watching Dorna, and that behind her Kron and Andreas, followed by Linna, and rebels and soldiers, had ascended to the roof.

The silver mask of Dorna the Proud turned on Lara, who wore no mask, no veil. "Shameless animal," she sneered, "you are no better than they—beasts!"

"Yes," said Lara, "that is true."

"I sensed this in you," said Dorna. "You were never worthy to be Tatrix of Tharna. I alone was worthy to be true Tatrix of Tharna."

"The Tharna of which you speak," said Lara, "no longer exists."

Then as if with one voice soldiers, guardsmen and rebels lifted their weapons and saluted Lara as true Tatrix of Tharna.

"Hail Lara, true Tatrix of Tharna!" they cried, and as was the custom of the city, five times were those weapons brandished and five times did that glad shout ring out.

The body of Dorna the Proud recoiled as if struck by five blows.

Her silver-gloved hands clenched in fury upon the one-strap and beneath those shimmering gauntlets I knew the knuckles, drained of blood, were white with rage.

She looked once more at the rebels and soldiers and guardsmen and Lara with a loathing I could sense behind the impassive mask, and then that metal image turned once more upon me.

"Farewell, Tarl of Ko-ro-ba," she said. "Do not forget Dorna the Proud for we have an account to settle!"

The hands in their gloves of silver jerked back savagely on the one-strap and the wings of the tarn burst into flight. The carrying basket remained a moment on the roof and then, attached by its long ropes, interwoven with wire, it slid for a pace or two and lurched upward in the wake of the tarn.

I watched the basket swinging below the bird as it winged its way from the city.

Once the sun flashed upon that silver mask.

Then the bird was only a speck in the blue sky over the free city of Tharna.

Dorna the Proud, thanks to the sacrifice of Thorn, her captain, had made good her escape, though to what fate I dared not conjecture.

She had spoken of settling an account with me.

I smiled to myself, reasoning that she would have little opportunity for such matters. Indeed, if she managed to survive at all, she would be fortunate not to find herself wearing an ankle ring on some slaver's chain.

Perhaps she would find herself confined within the walls of some warrior's Pleasure Gardens, to be dressed in silk of his choosing, to have bells locked on her ankles and to know no will other than his; perhaps she would be purchased by the master of a Paga Tavern, or even of a lowly Kal-da shop, to dance for, and to serve and please his customers.

Perhaps she might be purchased for the scullery in a Gorean cylinder and discover her life to be bounded by the tile walls and the steam and soap of the cleaning tubs. She would be given a mat of damp straw and a camisk, leavings from the tables of the dining rooms above, and lashings if she should dare to leave the room or shirk her work.

Perhaps a peasant would buy her to help with the plowing. I wondered, if this happened, if she would bitterly recall the Amusements of Tharna. If this miserable fate were to be hers, the imperious Dorna the Proud, stripped and sweating, her back exposed to the ox whip, would learn in harness that a peasant is a hard master.

But I put from my mind these thoughts as to what might be the fate of Dorna the Proud.

I had other things with which to occupy my mind.

Indeed, I myself had business to attend to—an account to settle—only my affairs would lead me to the Sardar Mountains, for the business to which I must attend was with the Priest-Kings of Gor.

26

A LETTER FROM TARL CABOT

*Inscribed in the City of Tharna, the
Twenty-Third Day of En'Kara in the
Fourth Year of the Reign of Lara, Tatrix,
of Tharna, the Year 10,117 from the
Founding of Ar.*

TAL TO THE MEN OF Earth—

In these past days in Tharna I have taken the time to
write this story. Now that it is told I must begin my
journey to the Sardar Mountains.

Five days from now I shall stand before the black gate
in the palisades that ring the holy mountains.

I shall strike with my spear upon the gate and the gate
will open, and as I enter I will hear the mournful sound of
the great hollow bar that hangs by the gate, signifying that
another of the Men Below the Mountains, another mortal
man, has dared to enter the Sardar.

I shall deliver this manuscript to some member of the
Caste of Scribes whom I shall find at the Fair of En'Kara
at the base of the Sardar. From that point whether or not
it survives will depend like so many other things in this
barbaric world I have come to love—on the inscrutable
will of the Priest-Kings.

They have cursed me and my city.

They have taken from me my father and the girl I love,
and my friends, and have given me suffering and hard-
ship, and peril, and yet I feel that in some strange way in

245

spite of myself I have served them—that it was their will that I came to Tharna. They have destroyed a city, and in a sense they have restored a city.

What manner of things they are I know not, but I am determined to learn.

Many have entered the mountains and so many must have learned the secret of the Priest-Kings, though none has returned to tell it.

But let me now speak of Tharna.

Tharna is now a different city than it has ever been within the memory of living man.

Her ruler—the gracious and beautiful Lara—is surely one of the wisest and most just of rulers on this barbaric world, and hers has been the torturous task of reuniting a city disrupted by civil strife, of making peace among factions and dealing fairly with all. If she were not loved as she is by the men of Tharna her task would have been impossible.

As she ascended once more the throne no proscription notices were posted but a general amnesty was granted to all, both those who had espoused her cause and those who had fought for Dorna the Proud.

From this amnesty only the silver masks of Tharna were excepted.

Blood was high in the streets of Tharna after the revolt and angry men, both rebels and defenders, joined in the brutal hunt for silver masks. These poor creatures were hunted from cylinder to cylinder, from room to room.

When found they were dragged forth into the street, unmasked, cruelly bound together and driven to the palace at the point of weapons, their masks hanging about their necks.

Many silver masks were discovered hiding in obscure chambers in the palace itself and the dungeons below the palace were soon filled with chains of fair, lamenting prisoners. Soon the animal cages beneath the arena of the Amusements of Tharna had to be pressed into service and then the arena itself.

Some Silver Masks were discovered even in the sewers

beneath the city and these were driven by giant, leashed urts through the long tubes until they crowded the wire capture nets set at the openings of the sewers.

Other Silver Masks had taken refuge in the mountains beyond the walls and these were hunted like sleen by converging rings of irate peasants, who drove them into the center of their hunting circles, whence, unmasked and bound, they were herded to the city to meet their fate.

Most of the silver masks however, when it was understood their battle had been lost and the laws of Tharna were irrevocably shattered came of their own free will into the streets and submitted themselves in the traditional fashion of the captive Gorean female, kneeling, lowering the head, and lifting and raising the arms, wrists crossed for binding.

The pendulum in Tharna had swung.

I myself had stood at the foot of the steps to the golden throne when Lara had commanded that the giant mask of gold which hung behind it be pried by spears from the wall and cast to the floor at our feet.

No more would that cold serene visage survey the throne room of Tharna.

The men of Tharna watched almost in disbelief as the great mask loosened, bolt by bolt, from the wall, leaned forward and at last, dragged down by its own weight, broke loose and plunged clattering down the steps of the throne, breaking into a hundred pieces.

"Let it be melted," Lara had said, "and cast into the golden tarn disks of Tharna and let these be distributed to those who have suffered in our day of troubles."

"And add to the golden tarn disks," she had exclaimed, "tarn disks of silver to be formed from the masks of our women, for henceforth in Tharna no woman may wear a mask of either gold or silver, not even though she be Tatrix of Tharna herself!"

And as she had spoken, according to the customs of Tharna, her words had become the law and from that day forth no woman of Tharna might wear a mask.

In the streets of Tharna shortly after the end of the

revolt the caste colors of Gor began to appear openly in the garments of the citizens. The marvelous glazing substances of the Caste of Builders, long prohibited as frivolous and expensive, began to appear on the walls of the cylinders, even on the walls of the city itself. Graveled streets are now being paved with blocks of colored stone set in patterns to delight the eye. The wood of the great gate has been polished and its brass burnished. New paint blazes upon the bridges.

The sound of caravan bells is no longer strange in Tharna and strings of traders have found their way to her gates, to exploit this most surprising of all markets.

Here and there the mount of a tarnsman boasts a golden harness. On market day I saw a peasant, his sack of Sa-Tarna meal on his back, whose sandals were tied with silver straps.

I have seen private apartments with tapestries from the mills of Ar upon the walls; and my sandals have sometimes found underfoot richly colored, deeply woven rugs from distant Tor.

It is perhaps a small thing to see on the belt of an artisan a silver buckle of the style worn in mountainous Thentis or to note the delicacy of dried eels from Port Kar in the marketplace, but these things, small though they are, speak to me of a new Tharna.

In the streets I hear the shouting, the song and clamor that is typically Gorean. The marketplace is no longer simply some acres of tile on which business must be dourly conducted. It is a place where friends meet, arrange dinners, exchange invitations, discuss politics, the weather, strategy, philosophy and the management of slave girls.

One change that I find of interest, though I cannot heartily approve, is that the rails have been removed from the high bridges of Tharna. I had thought this pointless, and perhaps dangerous, but Kron had said simply, "Let those who fear to walk the high bridges not walk the high bridges."

One might also mention that the men of Tharna have

formed the custom of wearing in the belt of their tunic two
yellow cords, each about eighteen inches in length. By this
sign alone men of other cities can now recognize a man of
Tharna.

On the twentieth day following peace in Tharna the fate
of the silver masks was determined.

They were herded, roped throat to throat, unveiled,
wrists bound behind their backs, in long lines to the arena
of the Amusements of Tharna. There they would hear the
judgment of Lara, their Tatrix. They knelt before her—
once proud silver masks, now terrified and helpless captives—on the same sparkling sand that had so often been
stained with the blood of the men of Tharna.

Lara had thought long on these matters and had dis-
cussed them with many, including myself. In the end her
decision was her own. I do not know that my own decision would have been so harsh, but I admit that Lara
knew her city and its silver masks better than I.

I recognized that it was not possible to restore the old
order of Tharna, nor was it desirable. Too I recognized
that there was no longer any adequate provision—given
the destruction of Tharna's institutions—for the indefinite
shelter of large numbers of free women within her walls.
The family, for example, had not existed in Tharna for
generations, having been replaced by the division of the
sexes and the segregated public nurseries.

And too it must be remembered that the men of Tharna
who had tasted her women in the revolt now demanded
them as their right. No man who has seen a woman in
Pleasure Silk, or watched her dance, or heard the sound of
a belled ankle or watched a woman's hair, unbound, fall
to her waist can long live without the possession of such a
delicious creature.

Also it should be noted that it was not realistic to offer
the silver masks the alternative of exile, for that would
simply have been to condemn them to violent death or
foreign enslavement.

In its way, under the circumstances, the judgment of

Lara was merciful—though it was greeted with wails of lamentation from the roped captives.

Each silver mask would have six months in which she would be free to live within the city and be fed at the common tables, much as before the revolt. But within that six months she is expected to find a man of Tharna to whom she will propose herself as a Free Companion.

If he does not accept her as a Free Companion—and few men of Tharna will be in a mood to extend the privileges of Free Companionship to a silver mask—he may then, without further ado, simply collar her as his slave, or if he wishes he may reject her completely. If she is rejected she may propose herself similarly to yet another of the men of Tharna, and perhaps yet another and another.

After the six months, however—perhaps she has been reluctant to seek a master?—her initiative in these matters is lost and she belongs to the first man who encircles her throat with the graceful, gleaming badge of servitude. In such a case she is considered no differently, and treated no differently than if she were a girl brought in on tarnback from a distant city.

In effect, considering the temper of the men of Tharna, Lara's judgment gives the silver masks the opportunity, for a time, to choose a master, or after that time to be themselves chosen as a slave girl. Thus each silver mask will in time belong to a beast, though at first she is given some opportunity to determine whose yellow cords she will feel, on whose rug the ceremony of submission will take place.

Perhaps Lara understood, as I did not, that women such as silver masks must be taught love, and can learn it only from a master. It was not her intention to condemn her sisters of Tharna into interminable and miserable bondage but to force them to take this strange first step on the road she herself had traveled, one of the unusual roads that may lead to love. When I had questioned her, Lara had said to me that only when true love is learned is the

Free Companionship possible, and that some women can learn love only in chains. I wondered at her words.

There is little more to tell.

Kron remains in Tharna, where he stands high in the Council of the Tatrix Lara.

Andreas and Linna will leave the city, for he tells me there are many roads on Gor he has not wandered and thinks that on some of these he may find the song for which he has always searched. I hope with all my heart that he will find it.

The girl Vera of Ko-ro-ba, at least for the time, will reside in Tharna, where she will live as a free woman. Not being of the city she is exempted from the strictures imposed on the silver masks.

Whether or not she will choose to remain in the city I do not know. She, like myself, and all of Ko-ro-ba, is an exile, and exiles sometimes find it hard to call a foreign city home; sometimes they regard the risks of the wilderness as preferable to the shelter of alien walls. And, too, in Tharna would be found the memory of Thorn, a captain.

This morning I said good-bye to the Tatrix, the noble and beautiful Lara. I know that we have cared for one another, but that our destinies are not the same.

In parting we kissed.

"Rule well," I said.

"I shall try," she said.

Her head was against my shoulder.

"And should I ever again be tempted to be proud or cruel," she said, a smile in her voice, "I shall merely remind myself that I was once sold for fifty silver tarn disks—and that a warrior once purchased me for only a scabbard and a helmet."

"Six emeralds," I corrected her, smiling.

"And a helmet," she laughed.

I could feel the dampness of her tears through my tunic.

"I wish you well, Beautiful Lara," I said.

"And I wish you well, Warrior," said the girl.

She looked at me, her eyes filled with tears, yet smiling.

She laughed a little. "And if the time should come, Warrior, when you should desire a slave girl, some girl to wear your silk and your collar, your brand if you wish— remember Lara, who is Tatrix of Tharna."

"I shall," I said. "I shall."

And I kissed her and we parted.

She will rule in Tharna and rule well, and I will begin the journey to the Sardar.

What I shall find there I do not know.

For more than seven years I have wondered at the mysteries concealed in those dark recesses. I have wondered about the Priest-Kings and their power, their ships and agents, their plans for their world and mine; but most importantly I must learn why my city was destroyed and its people scattered, why it is that no stone may stand upon another stone; and I must learn the fate of my friends, my father and of Talena, my love. But I go to the Sardar for more than truth; foremost in my brain there burns, like an imperative of steel, the cry for blood-vengeance, mine by sword-right, mine by the affinities of blood and caste and city, mine for I am one pledged to avenge a vanished people, fallen walls and towers, a city frowned upon by Priest-Kings, for I am a Warrior of Ko-ro-ba! I seek more than truth in the Sardar; I seek the blood of Priest-Kings!

But how foolish it is to speak thus.

I speak as though my frail arm might avail against the power of Priest-Kings. Who am I to challenge their power? I am nothing; not even a bit of dust, raised by the wind in a tiny fist of defiance; not even a blade of grass that cuts at the ankles of trampling gods. Yet I, Tarl Cabot, shall go to the Sardar; I shall meet with Priest-Kings, and of them, though they be the gods of Gor, I shall demand an accounting.

Outside on the bridges I hear the cry of the Lighter of Lanterns. "Light your lamps," he calls. "Light the lamps of love."

I wonder sometimes if I would have gone to the Sardar had not my city been destroyed. It now seems to me that if I had simply returned to Gor, and to my city, my father, my friends and my beloved Talena, I might not have cared to enter the Sardar, that I would not have cared to relinquish the joys of life to inquire into the secrets of those dark mountains. And I have wondered sometimes, and the thought awes and frightens me, if my city might not have been destroyed only to bring me to the mountains of the Priest-Kings, for they would surely know that I would come to challenge them, that I would come to the Sardar, that I would climb to the moons of Gor itself, to demand my satisfaction.

Thus it is that I perhaps move in the patterns of Priest-Kings—that perhaps I pledge my vengeance and set out for the Sardar as they knew that I would, as they had calculated and understood and planned. But even so I tell myself that it is still I who move myself, and not Priest-Kings, even though I might move in their patterns; if it is their intention that I should demand an accounting, it is my intention as well; if it is their game, it is also mine.

But why would Priest-Kings desire Tarl Cabot to come to their mountains? He is nothing to them, nothing to any man; he is only a warrior, a man with no city to call his own, thus an outlaw. Could Priest-Kings, with their knowledge and power, have need of such a man? But Priest-Kings need nothing from men, and once more my thoughts grow foolish.

It is time to put aside the pen.

I regret only that none return from the Sardar, for I have loved life. And on this barbaric world I have seen it in all its beauty and cruelty, in all its glory and sadness. I have learned that it is splendid and fearful and priceless. I have seen it in the vanished towers of Ko-ro-ba and in the flight of a tarn, in the movements of a beautiful woman, in the gleam of weaponry, in the sound of tarn drums and the crash of thunder over green fields. I have found it at the tables of sword companions and in the clash of the metals of war, in the touch of a girl's lips and hair, in the blood of a sleen, in the sands and chains of Tharna, in the scent of talenders and the hiss of the whip. I am grateful

to the immortal elements which have so conspired that I
might once be.

I was Tarl Cabot, Warrior of Ko-ro-ba.

That not even the Priest-Kings of Gor can change.

It is toward evening now, and the lamps of love are lit
in many of the windows of the cylinders of Tharna. The
beacon fires are set upon her walls, and I can hear the cry
of distant guardsmen that all is well in Tharna.

The cylinders grow dark against the darkening sky. It
will soon be night. There will be few to note the stranger
who leaves the city, perhaps few to remember that he was
once within their walls.

My weapons and my shield and helmet are at hand.

Outside I hear the cry of the tarn.

I am satisfied.

I wish you well,

Tarl Cabot

A CONCLUDING NOTE
ON THE MANUSCRIPT

THE MANUSCRIPT BREAKS OFF WITH the letter of Tarl Cabot. There was nothing more. In the several months since the mysterious delivery of the manuscript, no message, no further word, has been received.

It is my surmise, if we may credit the narrative, and I am tempted to do so, that Cabot did indeed enter the Sardar Mountains. I will not speculate on what he may have found there. I do not think it likely we will ever learn.

J. N.

THE CHRONICLES
OF COUNTER-EARTH

John Norman

TARNSMAN OF GOR
OUTLAW OF GOR
PRIEST-KINGS OF GOR
NOMADS OF GOR
ASSASSIN OF GOR
RAIDERS OF GOR
CAPTIVE OF GOR

Here is the magnificent world of Gor, known also as Counter-Earth, a planet as strangely populated, as threatening, as beautiful as any you are likely to encounter in the great works of fiction. Here too is Tarl Cabot—the one picked out of millions to be trained and schooled and disciplined by the best teachers, swordsmen, bowmen on Gor . . . Toward what end, what mission, what purpose?

Only Gor holds the answer